MARK THOMPSON-O'CONNOR

Whistleblower

First published by MTOC 2022

Second edition

This book was professionally typeset on Reedsy.
Find out more at reedsy.com

CHAPTER ONE

"Come on Fatty!" called Eloise Sharp as she skipped effortlessly up the winding path of the hillside, glancing over her shoulder at her husband walking slowly behind. Benjamin Sharp smiled and raised two fingers at her in mock offence. She was lithe and energetic, whilst he had let the years pile the pounds on his body with too much food and too little exercise, and, no doubt, too many pints of real ale. The hill wasn't particularly steep; well, not for someone like Eloise. But for Benjamin it was a struggle. They had already walked four or five miles along the coastal pathway that hugged the rocks on one side and dropped away to the crashing waves below on the other. They had both dressed for the cold weather and the possibility of rain and now the extra layers and waterproof coat were making Benjamin hot and sweaty and uncomfortable. He wanted to stop for a rest, but Eloise was getting further away from him up the winding path that led away from the coastal edge and headed inland and back towards the small fishing town where they were holidaying for a long weekend. Towards the crest of the hill the trees closed in around the path and in a moment, she would disappear into the wood at the summit.

Benjamin pushed himself onwards. By the time he reached

the top and entered the wood he was panting for breath and feeling the discomfort of the lactic acid burn in his legs. In what appeared to be Divine mockery, the sun had appeared and began to warm him up even more through the several layers of clothing that he wore. By the time he entered the relative shade of the wood and saw Eloise leaning against a tree smiling at him, breathing easily, and displaying no external sign of exertion, Benjamin's face was beetroot red and dripping with sweat. Eloise laughed at him. Not in a cruel way. It was one of those laughs that the casual observer would know was given and received in fun, with love and affection.

"You look like you're going to pop!" she laughed.

"I think I am!" panted Benjamin in response as he leant his back against a tree and then bent over, hands on knees, gulping air. "Couldn't we have just sat in the pub and watched the sea crashing against the shore?" he asked in as whimsical a tone as he could muster.

Eloise laughed again. "It's eleven in the morning! And anyway, you need the exercise, Fatty! A walk will do you good!"

"It's not a walk," he panted, standing up straight and then leaning once more against the tree. "It's a bloody mountain climb! You promised me a relaxing weekend away."

She came forward and kissed him gently. "Get your breath and we'll carry on," she smiled. "There's bound to be a pub lunch at the end of this walk."

A few moments later they set off again. She walked briskly and confidently through the winding path as it snaked its way further up the side of the hill, whilst Benjamin trudged behind, the gap between them lengthening as he dragged his feet, occasionally tripping over tree roots, or stumbling when his foot sank into a hole in the path. From below it had looked like the path stopped climbing once it entered the wood, but that was just an optical illusion. But eventually the path turned away and began to gently slope downhill, winding in and out of the trees and disappearing from view.

"Thank God," he muttered to himself. Eloise paused ahead and turned to watch and wait for him to catch up. As he turned a bend in the path he heard and then saw a fast running brook that rushed down from the top of the hillside and under a short bridge made of what looked like railway sleepers laid flat and pushed together. The water sang to him and looked crystal clear; more appealing even, at that moment in time, than his favourite pint.

Slowly, and a little stiffly because the walk had now given him back ache, Benjamin lowered himself to one knee and then to the other. Eloise looked on with amused interest as Benjamin leant forward and, whilst resting on one hand, lowered his other into the running brook and brought the water to his mouth. It tasted wonderful. He quickly refilled his cupped hand and drank more, repeating the move several times during which Eloise retraced her steps and joined him next to the brook.

"Should you be drinking that?" she asked with a small frown on her face.

Benjamin slurped some more water and then rested back on his heels, smiling up at her.

"Honestly," he smiled. "You health freaks make me laugh! You're always harping on about what you should and shouldn't eat and what you should and shouldn't drink, but when it comes to something like water it has to come out of a plastic bottle to pass the 'healthy' test."

He used his index fingers to imitate quotation marks when

he said the word 'healthy'.

"This is fresh spring water," he continued with a smile on his face. "Straight from its natural source. You'll probably find that there's a bottling plant at the bottom of this hill where you can buy this stuff for a couple of quid! Try some," he said, taking another drink.

Eloise shook her head. "No thanks," she laughed. "It's probably full of sheep poo! Come on," she said, turning away and setting off down the path again.

Benjamin paused mid slurp at the mention of sheep poo and turned to watch Eloise walking away. He looked back at the remaining water cupped in his hand, thought about it for a moment and then slurped the rest of it up, wiping his lips with the back of his hand when he'd finished. Slowly and stiffly, he clambered to his feet and then set off after Eloise, feeling much cooler and refreshed.

The pub lunch that she had tempted him with was some time away yet. Before that happened, he had to finish the rest of what he likened to be a 'trek across the Amazon forest' and then, once clear of the wood and the hillside and back into the little town, he had to endure the visits to the shops. There were only a few, small, touristy type shops in the town, and Eloise made sure they visited them all, but there seemed to be an endless number of charity shops, which, of course, could not be bypassed.

Standing around waiting, was just as uncomfortable for Benjamin as walking any distance up narrow woodland paths. Being overweight and terribly unfit meant that he suffered dreadful back ache. Sciatica plagued him and his right foot would regularly feel numb and lifeless if he stood still for any period of time. Of course, it didn't help that he hated shopping.

He just couldn't see the point of browsing. Benjamin was of the opinion that if you went to the shop it should be with the intention of buying something specific and then leaving. To him, the advent of the charity shop on every high street in the country was an abomination. They drew people in with some mysterious charm in order that they could marvel at the second-hand tat that the original owner had deemed no longer worth keeping.

The two of them trudged from one charity shop to another. Well in fairness it was only Benjamin that trudged; Eloise was in her element. He began to notice the same people in each shop, obviously moving down the street in the same direction as them and drawn to each Aladdin's cave of dusty old crockery and chipped Capodimonte as Eloise was. He wondered what would happen if a find of immense value was suddenly made by any one of these bargain hunters and the find was observed by the others. What if two of them saw the coveted item at the same time? He was about to imagine some comical battle between old ladies over a broken teacup when Eloise nudged him.

"Come on Grumpy," she smiled. "I can tell you're having loads of fun. Let's get some lunch."

"What do you mean, Grumpy?" he chuckled. "You know I love shopping! Do we really have to go? Can't we stay just a little longer? I'm sure there's an old paperback somewhere in here that I've never read. And look, over there, are they.... Yes, tape cassettes!"

Eloise grinned. "Ok," she said. "We can stay."

"Like hell!" laughed Benjamin, taking hold of her elbow, and moving her firmly towards the door. "Come on, you. Pub!"

The other thing about those kinds of shops, as noticed by

Benjamin throughout his years of marriage to his lovely wife Eloise, was that they always had the heating up full, so that when you went back outside and the fresh air, or in this case, the sea wind, hit you, your body temperature plummeted.

"Bloody hell!" he moaned as he began to fasten his water-proof jacket again and pull the collar up and around his jawline. "It's freezing!"

Eloise pointed across the street to an inviting looking pub with small wooden framed windows and mellow lighting within.

"Come on," she said. "I fancy fish and chips."

Benjamin paused for a moment. He'd felt his heart rate suddenly increase and he had become a little lightheaded. His doctor had warned him for years about the risk of type 2 diabetes and he had occasions when his blood sugar would suddenly drop and make him feel faint. This felt like one of those moments.

Eloise looked at him with concern. "Are you okay," she asked, taking hold of his hand. It was sweaty and clammy.

"Blood sugar, I think," replied Benjamin. "Probably that sudden temperature change. I'll be ok in a minute."

He winced as he felt a stabbing pain in his lower stomach, his left hand moving to cover it instinctively."

"Ben?" said Eloise, worry clouding her face and a tremble in her voice.

The pain passed. It had only been for a moment and the light headedness began to fade. That was unusual but welcome. Normally when his blood sugar dropped, he had to find something to eat quickly, usually crisps or peanuts, or if he could get one, a chocolate bar. Then he would suffer with pouring sweat as his body tried to return to normality, after which he would become incredibly tired and usually fall asleep.

But this time it seemed to pass quickly, and he began to feel normal again. He smiled at Eloise, took her by the hand and led her over the road to the pub.

The inside of the pub was lovely and quaint. The floors were uneven and the ceiling quite low, with wooden beams crisscrossing above their heads. There were little alcoves off the main bar and the two of them found one that had a table free. They looked over the menu before Benjamin went to the bar to order and to choose from the several real ales on offer. He chose one that had a light colour and slight zest to the taste and asked for it to be served in a glass with a handle; one of the old-fashioned types with the dimples around the body. Eloise always preferred a glass of wine to beer or other drinks and Benjamin selected one for her before returning to the alcove to await the two large fish and chips he had ordered.

He returned to the bar for another pint before the food arrived and they then tucked in with gusto. Considering that she was so skinny, Eloise had a monster of an appetite and had no problem clearing her plate. Benjamin, in contrast, struggled with his fish, particularly the crispy batter and had to give up halfway through.

"You not hungry?" asked Eloise.

"Just full," smiled Benjamin, feeling some discomfort in his stomach again. "Room for more beer, though," he chuckled as he downed the rest of his pint and returned to the bar. Eloise's wine glass was still half full when he returned.

Eventually, when he'd finished his third pint, Eloise suggested that they walk it off down by the sea. He pulled a face in mock disgust but stood up anyway and shrugged on his waterproof coat.

"Let's go and get wet, then," he smiled.

They walked down the high street that led to the sea front. The tide was in and the wind had made the sea choppy. Every now and then a wave would splash over the low wall that separated the footpath from the pebbly beach, now hidden under the swell of water. They walked over to the little harbour and leant against the wall watching the boats rising and falling with the ebb and flow of the water, sometimes straining against their mooring lines as the tide attempted to pull them out to sea.

"I love it here," sighed Eloise.

Benjamin wrapped his big arm around her and smiled. "It is rather lovely," he agreed.

They turned away from the harbour and walked towards the other wall, looking out over the grey sea. A wave crashed high against the wall and spray flew into the air and doused them both with seawater. Eloise hunched over instinctively in the midst of the soaking and then burst out laughing. She looked up at Benjamin who was holding out his arms, his head bent forward and his face in feigned shock at the soaking he'd received. He too laughed.

"I think we better head back and get dry," he suggested, and Eloise chuckled and nodded her head in agreement. Benjamin went to put his arm around her again, but she pushed him away.

"Yuk!" she laughed. "You're soaking!"

Benjamin laughed again and moved towards her, arms out wide, preparing to give her a bear hug.

"Nooo!" she laughed, ducking under his arms, and running away up the street away from him and towards the hotel. Benjamin dropped his arms and followed, smiling first, and then wincing as another sharp pain stabbed him in the stomach again. He paused for a moment, his hand once again going to the spot where the pain was. It only lasted for a moment, slightly longer than last time, and then it subsided allowing him to move on again. Eloise hadn't noticed. She'd slowed her run from him to a walk and then to a halt as something in a shop window caught her eye.

When he'd caught up with her, she turned and smiled and then took his hand as they walked together the remaining short distance to the hotel. Eloise had found the place on the internet. There had been a special discounted offer available which they each thought was a bargain and worth snapping up. Neither of them had been to this part of the country before and the time of year, the autumn, was probably why the price was low, but neither of them were concerned about the British weather and were both enamoured by the photographs on the hotel website, showing the pleasant little seaside town with its tiny fishing port and surrounding pebble beach. They were also taken by the quaint hotel itself, small, only ten rooms, all en-suite, but decorated in a modern and tasteful way whilst keeping the olde worlde charm and character one might expect of the area. This was no normal seaside resort by any means. There was little here to attract the families with screaming kids in tow looking for amusement arcades and fairground rides, or the older couples looking for round the clock bingo. In fact, there was pretty much nothing to do here other than relax, walk in the clear fresh air, and enjoy the smell and sounds of the sea.

They headed straight to their room so that they could get out of their wet clothes. Benjamin used the en-suite first, telling Eloise that he needed to pee. Whilst urinating the pain returned, a sharp stabbing pain in his lower abdomen. He winced and drew in a sharp intake of breath. When he looked down into the toilet bowl, he noticed a red tinge and then realised he had been passing blood. Not a lot. But enough to make his heart leap with slight panic. The flow of urine had now reverted to a normal colour, without any blood and his panic subsided a little. Maybe it was just one of those things, he thought. Nothing to worry about. His doctor's repeated warnings about diabetes popped up in his head. Perhaps when they got back home, he would start thinking about some of those lifestyle changes that his doctor had talked about.

The pain subsided and he finished up in the bathroom before returning to the bedroom.

"About time!" laughed Eloise who had discarded all of her clothes and stood only in her underwear. "I'm taking a shower."

She pushed past him and pulled the en-suite door closed behind her. Benjamin heard the shower burst into life as he stripped out of his own wet clothes, leaving them in a pile on the floor. He caught sight of himself in the long mirror on the wall. He turned and studied himself, the huge stomach, the fat and wobbly thighs, and the slightly blotchy skin all over his torso.

"A picture of health," he muttered to himself a little sadly. Eloise was singing. He looked at the bathroom door and pictured her as she'd pushed past him, toned body, pretty face, full of energy. Then he looked back at himself in the mirror and not for the first time wondered what she saw in him.

When the pain hit him this time it was much worse than before. This time it felt like multiple stabbings all across his abdomen and then shooting upwards to his chest. His heart rate increased rapidly, and he became dizzy and breathless.

The pain stopped, but only for a second and then returned, front and back now. His kidneys felt like someone was kicking him whilst his stomach felt as though he was being impaled on a spike. He dropped to his knees and leant against the foot of the bed, doubled up in pain and waiting and wishing for it to subside.

Eloise always took an age in the shower, particularly if it was one with a powerful flow. She loved the feel of the hot water pummelling her skin, massaging the knots from her taught muscles. This shower was brilliant, much better than the one at home. She made a mental note to write down the make and model and then when they were home, she would look at how much it would cost to have one fitted.

When finally out of the shower, she dried off and then wrapped a large bath towel around her, folding it over at the front so that it stayed up independently. She towel dried her hair and then wrapped the smaller towel around her head. The mirror was completely steamed up, so she drew a love heart with her forefinger and added the initials of her and Benjamin. She smiled at her handiwork and then opened the bathroom door.

Benjamin was in a foetal position at the foot of the bed wearing only his pants. His entire body was in spasms and a gurgling noise and some sort of froth was coming from his mouth. Eloise's hand flew to her mouth in shock as she screamed his name. Then rushing forward, the towel falling from her head, she dropped to her knees and tried to hold his head. His eyes were open but glazed and there was no recognition in them.

"Ben," she wailed. "What happened? Ben! Talk to me!"

He continued to twitch on the floor. Eloise tried to move him, but he was too heavy. His skin was hot to the touch, yet his convulsions made it appear like he was shivering. She didn't know what to do. Panicking she looked around for her phone and seeing it on the bedside table where she had placed it when they entered, she jumped to her feet and retrieved it. No signal.

Eloise cried aloud, turning back to look at her husband on the floor. She spied the hotel phone on the dresser and jumped across the room to it, pressing the '0' button as she lifted the receiver. It seemed to take forever for someone to answer.

"Reception," said a disinterested voice.

"Help!" shouted Eloise. "Room three. I need an ambulance. My husband has collapsed!"

Moments later the proprietors of the hotel were in the room with her, crouching next to Benjamin making panicked utterances of comfort whilst being entirely unable to do anything to actually assist him. An ambulance had been called, but they were in such a remote location that it took almost an hour before they heard sirens outside. The ambulance crew worked as quickly as they could to get Benjamin moved, once they had realised that he was entirely uncommunicative. Someone suggested that Eloise should put some clothes on if she was going to accompany them to the hospital, which she did as the crew struggled to get Benjamin into the hotel's evacuation chair, used for assisting disabled people down the stairs in an emergency. They then transferred him to the ambulance's wheeled stretcher and secured him in place in the back of the vehicle. Eloise climbed in behind him.

Throughout the transfer Benjamin continued to twitch and convulse and make strange gurgling noises. One of the medics had checked his airways to see if there was a blockage but there was nothing obvious to be seen. He was gulping air but frothing at the mouth at the same time. Throughout the journey to the hospital Eloise sat watching Benjamin twitch, feeling entirely helpless and distraught.

Once at the hospital he was whisked into the emergency rooms whilst Eloise was directed to a waiting area. She sat alone, crying and scared and wondering what on earth had happened.

It seemed like an eternity before someone came to see her. A Ward Sister found her and told her that she could come and see Ben but warned her that she would likely find his condition upsetting. Eloise followed the Sister to the Ward where six beds were positioned against the walls, three on each side. All the beds were occupied and the one furthest away from her had the curtains pulled all the way around. That was the one that she was led to. The Sister opened the curtain enough for Eloise to pass through and see Benjamin lying in the bed. His breathing seemed normal and his eyes were open, but he gave no indication of recognition as she entered. Eloise took his hand and whispered his name, but there was no response.

Tears streaming down her cheeks she turned to the Sister and asked what was wrong with him; why wasn't he answering her.

"The Consultant will be around soon," she explained calmly. "Ben appears to have been poisoned," she continued. "We think it has somehow affected his nervous system, which is why his eyes are open, but he isn't responding to stimuli. The Consultant should be able to answer more questions when he comes to see you."

But he couldn't. When the Consultant opened the curtains and stood at the end of the bed in which Benjamin's unresponsive body lay, he couldn't tell Eloise anything more than the Ward Sister had. He asked whether Benjamin was on any medication or whether he'd eaten anything unusual. He even asked whether Benjamin used any kind of recreational drugs. Eloise was distraught that no-one had any clue as to what had happened to her husband.

"The nurse said he's been poisoned," she said to the Consultant.

He nodded. "That certainly appears to be the case. There are high levels of toxins in his blood and his nervous system appears to have been attacked. We are arranging for some of his blood samples to be sent to a Pharmacology expert and we hope that we'll get some better understanding about what has happened to Benjamin then."

Eloise shook her head. "It doesn't make sense," she sobbed. "We've both eaten the same things today. Neither of us has been exposed to anything. It just doesn't make any sense."

The Consultant assured her that she would be kept informed of any news and that, in the meantime, they would do everything they could to keep Benjamin as comfortable as possible. So, all Eloise could do was sit and wait, watching Benjamin's normal, regular breathing and feeling confused by his apparently conscious, yet catatonic state.

For the next two days Eloise sat with him. She watched the nursing staff clean and turn him, take readings, administer intravenous drips, and fill out the chart at the end of the bed. The curtains remained closed around his bed the whole time. Benjamin's state didn't change at all. He remained totally unresponsive; eyes open staring into space. On the first night Eloise had woken from a disturbed sleep in the uncomfortable chair next to the bed to see Benjamin's eyes open. For a moment she thought he was awake and then quickly realised that he wasn't. In the darkened Ward he made an eerie spectacle.

On the third day there was a sudden flurry of activity. She could hear raised voices and expressions of consternation on the Ward beyond the curtains surrounding the bed. She didn't pay much attention until, suddenly, the curtains were pulled aside and drawn all the way back on their runners, exposing Eloise and Benjamin to the whole Ward. She had been slouched in the chair, feet up on the edge of the bed when the curtains opened, and she now sat up with a start as a man appeared. He was covered head to toe in a white, seemingly padded, suit with a huge backpack. She could see his face through a clear plastic screen at the front of his head piece. He looked rather ludicrous and for a moment Eloise wanted to laugh. Then she looked to her right as another man, dressed in a similar suit approached carrying a bag. There were others, too, all dressed the same and milling around the Ward and the other patients. Eloise could see beyond the entrance of the Ward clear plastic sheeting being lifted and secured around the outer doors.

They were sealing off the Ward.

"What's going on?" she asked the first man as she stood up, fear gripping her.

"Quarantine," he replied sternly.

The second man spoke in a gentler tone. "Don't worry Mrs Sharp. These are only necessary precautions to ensure that everyone is safe. My name is Dr Meadows and I'm going to need you to take a seat whilst I take some blood samples from you." He was removing various items from his bag and placing them on the hospital bed table.

"Blood samples?" exclaimed Eloise, clearly shocked. "From me? Why?"

"We need to determine what exactly your husband has contracted and to what level, if at all, it is contagious. You've been with him since he was taken ill, so if it is contagious, the likelihood is that you will have contracted it. Alternatively, you might have a natural resistance to whatever it is, and if that is the case, your blood could be invaluable."

Eloise listened open mouthed. Contagious? How could this have happened? None of what this man in the strange white suit said made any sense. She didn't object to or question further the taking of blood samples from her, however, but just sat in stunned silence whilst Dr Meadows, with some dexterity, considering the restrictive nature of the suit that he wore, extracted blood from her arm into several small vials.

When it was over, the men in the padded, airtight suits left and the curtains at the end of the ward were sealed. One ward nurse had been left with them and when Eloise questioned her, she was equally perplexed with the situation and unable to answer any questions.

Two days later, Ben was dead.

CHAPTER TWO

Sir Julian Hebburn was the Second Permanent Secretary and Director General within the Department of Environment Food and Rural Affairs, referred to as DEFRA. He reported to the Permanent Secretary of DEFRA, the highest-ranking Civil Servant in the Department and the person who had the ear of the Minister in charge. Sir Julian had been a Civil Servant for almost all his adult life. He had graduated from Oxford with a first in Government and Politics and started work as an Administrative Assistant in the Department some twenty years previous. Diligent and hardworking he was recognised early on as a highflyer and progressed through the ranks quickly, ultimately being appointed to Director General after his predecessor had retired following a forty-year career within the Civil Service.

Sir Julian had developed a wealth of experience over his time in the Department, gained from dealing with some of the most difficult challenges that the world had gone through. His colleagues in other Departments had dealt with global problems ranging from wars to financial crashes, but whilst Sir Julian had not had to don a flak jacket, or prop up a few banks, he had instead advised, assisted and, on some occasions, led the fight against silent killers such as the foot and mouth disease in animals, BSE in cattle and those zoonoses that transferred from animals to humans causing, sometimes, millions of deaths across the world. The impact of SARS was a particularly challenging time for him and his team, yet one that they could proudly claim to have controlled and beaten. He had led the team that had investigated suspicions of poisoning of individuals, allegedly by Foreign States and he had worked closely with the scientists at Broughton Stretton in developing various remedies and antigens to many contagions.

It was during some of his visits to Broughton Stretton that he would bump into colleagues from the Ministry of Defence, who visited the place with, one might argue, more sinister intentions and less philanthropic designs. Sir Julian had never missed the irony of those occasions where he might be working with scientists investigating a contagion and endeavouring to discover a cure, whilst next door, figuratively speaking, his colleagues from the MoD were working with other scientists with the intention of developing some virus or similar that had the potential to wipe out half of the population of the earth.

He first became aware of Benjamin Sharp after a HazMat Team had visited a hospital in a seaside town and tested Mr Sharp, and his wife, along with various other hospital staff and patients, for poisoning. DEFRA had been alerted by the hospital when blood samples taken from Ben Sharp had shown traces of toxins not ordinarily seen in everyday life. The immediate fear amongst the advisers at the Department was that there had been another attack similar to that which had occurred in Salisbury in 2018 and the HazMat team had been mobilised rapidly just in case there was contagion in the area or traces of the toxins in public places or anywhere else where serious harm could be caused, should anyone come into contact with them.

Broughton Stretton, which was only a short distance away from the seaside town at which the Sharps had been staying for a short holiday, was where the blood and skin samples taken from all of those at the hospital, were sent. Even at that time, Sir Julian had only been made aware of the incident and not any greater detail, because the samples were still being analysed and the scientists at Broughton Stretton had assured the HazMat Team Leader, Dr Emery, that initial findings did not indicate any targeted poisoning and all the samples taken, with the exception of those belonging to Ben Sharp, proved negative.

When Ben Sharp died, his body was transferred immediately to Broughton Stretton, much to the confusion, and then anger, of his wife, Eloise. An autopsy was undertaken, without the knowledge of Eloise, and further tests carried out, this time on Ben's internal organs. The tests were repeated, and then repeated again, because the findings made, having carried out various analyses on his internal organs, confirmed with certainty what the scientists at Broughton Stratton had feared, but hoped to discount, when they had initially carried out the tests on Ben's blood and skin samples. The findings appeared to confirm that the toxins that had killed Benjamin Sharp had originated from Broughton Stretton itself.

That led to a full search of the complex and surrounding areas, followed by meetings at the highest level, all of them excluding Dr Emery. For his part, he was becoming more and more frustrated by the delay in providing him with the answers that he required to debrief his superiors. In addition, Eloise Sharp had instructed solicitors and correspondence had been received from them threatening Court action if the body of the deceased Mr Sharp was not returned to his grieving widow immediately, so that she could go about preparing the arrangements for laying her husband to rest.

As it transpired, it wasn't Dr Emery that eventually provided Sir Julian with the full details of what had happened to Ben Sharp. It was Sir Julian's counterpart in the MoD, the Permanent Secretary for the Ministry of Defence, Sir Nigel Beswick.

Sir Julian was reading his morning mail in his office at Whitehall when the door opened, and Sir Nigel entered with a loud "Morning Julian."

Sir Julian looked up, a little surprised by the discourteous entrance of his colleague, the usual manner being an announcement by Sir Julian's secretary over the internal telephone before anyone gained admission to his office. He placed the letter he was reading onto the green writing mat of his mahogany desk, slowly removed his reading glasses and looked up directly into the eyes of Sir Nigel.

"Nigel," he said softly. "What a pleasant surprise. To what do I owe the honour?"

Sir Nigel went to pull out the chair on the other side of the desk, but then seemed to think better of it and instead pushed it further in through the gap on the other side. Sir Julian watched him with mild amusement, one eyebrow raised in curiosity.

"Is everything alright?" he asked.

Sir Nigel was clearly struggling with how to formulate whatever it was he was going to tell his colleague. He shifted from side to side, mouth opening and closing, as he considered the best approach. Unable to make a decision as to the best way to deliver what he was going to say, his mouth took over from his brain and said it for him.

"Benjamin Sharp," he said flatly.

Sir Julian waited, presuming that there must be more to Nigel's communication than just a name. He continued to look up at Sir Nigel, his face impassive. The name had not registered with him.

"Benjamin Sharp," repeated Sir Nigel. "Rocky Head, a little coastal holiday resort on the south coast?"

That rang a bell for Sir Julian and was followed by a recognition of the name Sharp. "Toxin related death," he said, now understanding. "Yes, I know of it. I've got Dr Emery and a HazMat team down there investigating. Nothing has been reported back, yet. I presume that they are still working on it. What of it?"

"You won't hear back from Emery," said Sir Nigel. "Well, not immediately, anyway. Not until he is aware of the Party line."

Sir Julian furrowed his brow and looked sharply at his counterpart. "What....," he almost spat the last words. "Party line?"

Sir Nigel finally sat down. He pulled the chair from the gap on the other side of the mahogany desk and dropped into it. Involuntarily, his right hand massaged his right temple. It took an age before he could lift his eyes from the desk and look across it into those of Sir Julian's.

"There's been a bit of a balls up," he said, still massaging his temple.

Sir Julian waited. When it appeared that Nigel wasn't going to offer anything else, Julian asked "What balls up?"

"Broughton Stretton," sighed Sir Nigel. Julian sat up straight at the mention of the secret scientific facility. "There was a bit of an accident," continued Nigel.

Sir Julian's back became even straighter. He grew taller in

his chair, even though he remained seated. "What kind of accident?" he asked, his tone so stern that it made Nigel drop his hand from his temple and sit up straight, looking directly into Julian's eyes, and then looking away again, just as quickly.

"It would appear that there has been a bit of a leak," said Nigel.

"Jesus! Biological? Chemical? Gas? What kind of leak?" Julian's mind was racing with all the horrible possibilities. It was bad enough that the MoD had their hooks into Broughton Stretton, particularly when the conspiracy theorists spouted forth to all who would listen, enough theories, in a scatter gun fashion meaning that some of the theories were not actually theories and some of the conspiracy was as real as real can be. The reality of the darker goings on at that facility, at the behest of the MoD, in the interests of world peace.

"It was a leak into a natural water source," Sir Nigel tried to explain. "A virus seems to have somehow escaped the facility and made its way into a natural spring underground nearby. That spring comes out in a wooded area just up from the coast and runs down into the sea. It doesn't go near any households and there are no livestock grazing, so the impact is negligible, except..."

"Except?" asked Julian

"We think Benjamin Sharp drank from the spring."

"And now?" asked Julian. "Is the leak plugged?"

"Oh yes!" replied Nigel, clearly relieved that he could give some positive news. "As soon as the autopsy was completed and...."

"Autopsy?" interrupted Sir Julian. "His wife agreed to that?"

Nigel shook his head vigorously. "National Security," he blustered. "It had to be done. We had to get to the bottom of what the toxin was. The bloods and skin samples gave some indications, but we needed to see the impact on the internal organs to be sure. Anyway, once that was confirmed, it was relatively easy to find the source and plug the leak, so to speak." He sat back in his chair a little more relaxed and smiled.

Julian didn't say anything for a few moments. He sat and watched his colleague's face as it sought to arrange itself into a more comfortable and relaxed expression. The very notion that an autopsy had been required to identify the toxin when there were already blood and skin samples, caused him great concern.

"What was it?" he finally asked.

"Huh?" said Nigel, looking up again at Sir Julian.

"What was it?" repeated Julian. "From your description I would assume it was some form of virus? So, what was it?"

Sir Nigel started to look uncomfortable again. "It's an experimental viral agent, a mutation based on an established virus."

"I could probably have guessed that much," replied Sir Julian. "Given that we are talking about Broughton Stretton and the Ministry of Defence. Let me make the question easier to answer for you, Nigel. What was the original virus?"

It was very obvious to Julian that Nigel did not want to answer that question, but he wasn't going to be shrugged off, so he sat silently, staring into Nigel's eyes, leaving the question hanging in the air, until, after what felt like an eternity, Nigel almost whispered one word.

"Rinderpest".

Sir Julian's mouth dropped open in genuine shock. He stared aghast at Sir Nigel. "What?" he half whispered. "How?"

"Well, as I said," stuttered Sir Nigel. "It was a mutation of the original virus and..."

Sir Julian cut him off with a raise of his hand. "There is no Rinderpest left, Nigel," he said seriously. "We held the majority of it at Pirbright, but we destroyed it all years ago. I was present when it was destroyed. I signed the paperwork on behalf of the Government confirming that it had been destroyed. There is no Rinderpest!"

"Well, strictly speaking," stuttered Sir Nigel, "it's not Rinderpest. It is a mutation. It is known by a viral code number; V243."

Sir Julian slammed his hand down on his desk making Sir Nigel jump in his seat.

"You can't make a mutation without the original virus!" he growled. "Are you telling me that you have Rinderpest at Broughton Stretton?"

"Only a small supply," whined Sir Nigel.

"What?!" shouted Sir Julian, rising to his feet, placing both of his large hands on the green writing pad of his mahogany desk, and glowering at Sir Nigel. "I personally signed the confirmation that the last remnants of Rinderpest were destroyed at Pirbright, under my observation," his voice increased an octave as he stressed the point. "Where did you get it?"

Sir Nigel squirmed.

"Where?" repeated Sir Julian.

"We kept some back," Sir Nigel finally admitted.

Sir Julian stared at his colleague in disbelief, then, after a few moments, he sank back into his chair. His mobile phone began to vibrate on his desk. Absentmindedly he turned it over, screen upwards.

UNKNOWN NUMBER flashed across the screen for a few moments and then abruptly, the phone stopped buzzing.

Eventually he looked up again at Sir Nigel. "What does the mutation do?" he asked, suspiciously.

"Crosses the species," replied Nigel in a matter-of-fact manner. He didn't seem concerned by what he had declared.

Sir Julian's heart sank. "The effects?" he asked.

"Massive organ failure," replied Sir Nigel. "Quite effective."

Sir Julian's phone began to buzz again. UNKNOWN NUMBER splashed across the screen again. This time he picked it up, his mind still grappling with the truly awful information that Sir Nigel had just given him.

"Julian Hebburn," he said into the phone. A female voice replied, energetic, excited.

"Sir Julian. Zoe Carlson," said the voice.

It took him a moment to realise that he had actually answered the phone. He brought his mind back into focus. "I'm sorry," he said. "Who?"

"I used to be at the Times," was the reply. "Zoe Carlson. I ran a story on you after SARS."

He remembered now. She was, at the time, a youthful, excited reporter who hung on his every word when he explained the SARS crisis to her and then she wrote a two-page spread on him, his Department, and the contagion; all quite flattering as he remembered. But that was an age ago.

"Miss Carlson," he replied politely. "How did you get this number?"

"You gave it to me," she laughed. "Admittedly, it was a long time ago and I took a bit of a punt on whether or not you would have kept the same number. And you have. Lucky me."

"Indeed," he muttered. "Miss Carlson, I'm terribly sorry, but you have caught me at an unusually busy time. Perhaps we can talk another time."

"I'll be quick," said the freelance reporter. "I just wondered whether you have any comment on what happened to Benjamin Sharp?"

Sir Julian froze. "I'm sorry?" he asked.

"Ben Sharp," repeated Zoe. "Contracted something horrible whilst on holiday on the south coast that killed him. Your people were all over the area. Mr Sharp's widow informs me that his body was removed without her permission and given the circumstances and the involvement of DEFRA, not to mention all the attractive HazMat suits, I'm guessing it has something to do with Broughton Stretton. Any comment?"

Sir Julian looked across the desk at Sir Nigel who was watching his face with interest.

"No, Miss Carlson," he said eventually. "There is no comment. There is an investigation underway and there won't be any comment until that has been fully completed."

"Oh, come on Sir Julian," she chirped. "You must be able to give me something?"

"Goodbye, Miss Carlson," answered Sir Julian as he tapped his phone to disconnect the call. He looked at Sir Nigel again. "The bloody press are on it already!" he said.

Nigel stood up. "Well, we've got to brief the PM, anyway," he said. "Come on. He'll want us both there."

Sir Julian sighed and then pulled himself to his feet before following Nigel out of his office.

CHAPTER THREE

The two of them walked the ten minutes it took to get to Downing Street. The police officers on duty at the large iron gates across the street recognised them but checked their passes anyway and then waved them through. A few television cameras and news correspondents stood behind the barriers opposite Number 10 and gave disinterested glances in their direction as they walked up to the famous black door. There was no need to knock. Security on the inside of the entrance had already monitored them walking up the street and were primed to open the door as soon as they climbed the single step.

The PM was in his office with half a dozen advisers around him, all pouring over some documents and chattering collectively. He looked up as the two men entered the room.

"Well, that can't be good news," chuckled the PM. "Permanent Secretaries of the MOD and DEFRA coming to see me in unison. Who died?" he laughed.

"Prime Minister," began Sir Nigel. "We need a word".

The PM motioned them towards two chairs on their side of his desk. His entourage barely noticed their entrance and continued to pour over the documents laid out in front of him.

"We need to speak in private, sir," said Sir Nigel.

The entourage all looked up at that point.

"Very well," said the PM, then turning to his advisers he waived them away, saying "Regroup in an hour."

One man didn't move away, though. A tall, slim, stern looking individual, perched on the windowsill behind the PM, no tie, open neck shirt with sleeves rolled up and arms folded. Sir Nigel looked at him and made a coughing sound.

"Daniel stays," said the PM.

"Prime Minister," replied Sir Nigel. "We need to brief you on something extremely sensitive, sir. It's for your ears only."

"He stays," repeated the PM. "Whatever you want to say to me, you can say in front of Daniel."

Daniel Tomlinson was the Prime Minister's most trusted adviser and a personal friend. He was a controversial character who was also very private and maintained an aloof but sullen air about him. It was widely believed that he was to some extent a puppeteer who not only influenced the PM's decisions, but often directed them. He wouldn't follow the usual customs and norms of a position like his and had little time for civil servants generally, and the mainstream media at all.

Needless to say, the press hated him.

"Very well," said Sir Nigel, pulling out a chair and sitting down.

The PM looked up at Sir Julian. "Take a seat, Julian," he smiled.

"I'll stand, thank you, Prime Minister," was Sir Julian's sullen response.

"Very well," replied the PM. "So, gentlemen, what is so pressing?"

Sir Nigel began to explain. "We've had a little incident at Broughton Stretton, Prime Minister. Unfortunately, there was a small leak of a fairly serious toxin and, again, unfortunately, a member of the public came into contact with it and, well, he died."

"That's terrible," said the PM. "Just the one casualty?"

"Fortunately, sir, yes," smiled Sir Nigel. "All is now back under control."

"Good," smiled the PM. "Excellent!"

"The problem, though, sir," continued Sir Nigel. "Is that there was a bit of a drama when this chap was taken ill. He was taken to hospital and when the toxins were identified, Julian's boys were called in. So, there is a real chance that the media are going to be all over this."

"They already are," said Sir Julian.

Sir Nigel turned to look at him as the PM looked up and asked "Really?"

"The phone call I received before we came over here," said Sir Julian looking at Sir Nigel. "That was a freelance journalist. It sounds like she's already spoken with the widow, which probably means she's also spoken to the hospital staff and she's looking to me and my Department for a quote. We won't be able to keep a lid on this."

"I see," said the PM, his brow furrowed in thought. "So, what do we do?"

"Bacterial spillage." Daniel Tomlinson spoke for the first time. Everyone looked at him. "A bacterial spillage can be explained away as something relatively innocuous," he said. "The death will be reported as an unfortunate accident and the whole thing can be turned into a non-story."

Sir Julian, who had never warmed to Daniel Tomlinson, was indignant at his suggestion.

"It was Rinderpest," said Sir Julian flatly.

"Er, a variant, actually," replied Sir Nigel.

The PM shrugged his shoulders. "I don't follow," he said.

"Rinderpest!" snarled Sir Julian, staring at Sir Nigel. "We told the whole world that we had destroyed the last remaining stocks of it!" he almost shouted. "But the Ministry of Defence, for some unfathomable reason, decided to keep a bit back! And now, they've decided to mutate it so that it is transferable across species!"

The Prime Minister looked from one to the other and finally rested his gaze on Sir Nigel. "Is this true?"

"Yes, sir," answered Sir Nigel. "The boffins at Broughton Stretton had an idea that they could mutate the strain so that it would cross species. The only reason, though, was to develop an antiviral, which could be then used for other contagions."

Sir Julian harrumphed.

"That is factually correct," commented Daniel Tomlinson. The Prime Minister looked over his shoulder at his Chief of Staff and with a shrug of his shoulders accepted the statement without question. Not Sir Julian, though. He glared at Tomlinson.

"You knew?" he snarled. Tomlinson didn't react. Julian looked from him to the Prime Minister and then to Sir Nigel. "What the hell is going on?" he demanded. "Why is the MOD working with him?" he pointed at Tomlinson. Sir Nigel didn't reply.

"Prime Minister," continued Sir Julian. "This is unacceptable. If your Chief of Staff is influencing decisions which affect my Department, I should be informed and involved from the outset."

"I'm sure there were good reasons," said the PM dismissively, then, turning to Tomlinson he asked, "There were, weren't there?"

"Of course, Prime Minister," replied Tomlinson.

"There we are, then," smiled the PM, turning back to Sir Julian, who stared back at him in disbelief.

"Prime Minister," he breathed. "Did you know?"

The PM shrugged. "I can't know everything, Julian," he laughed. "That's why I have advisers."

Sir Julian couldn't believe what he was hearing. "Advisers are there to advise, sir," he growled. "They are not there to act without your knowledge or consent." The PM waved a hand and looked down at the papers on his desk. "Prime Minister," continued Sir Julian. "If the press were to find out about this, there would be an uproar."

"Why would they find out?" asked Tomlinson, quietly. "We've already determined what is going to be said. The PM will call a press conference and will explain that there was a bacterial spillage at the site which has now been cleared up. There was one tragic death, caused mainly by underlying health conditions which were exacerbated by ingesting the toxin, but fortunately, no further illnesses or incidents were reported."

Sir Julian was speechless. But, nevertheless, it happened the way Tomlinson described it. Within two hours the briefing room at number 10 was filled with journalists, a podium had been positioned just within the entrance to the room and the PM, accompanied by Daniel Tomlinson and Sir Julian went to face the press. Sir Nigel wasn't with them. Tomlinson thought it could prompt the wrong type of questions if the MOD were in the room.

The Prime Minister opened the conference with some general updates about policy matters that had been splashed across various newspapers and then launched into the story that Daniel Tomlinson had prepped him on. He explained that an unfortunate accident had occurred that had resulted in a minor spillage of what would ordinarily be a non-harmful substance, and through the misfortune of a member of the public taking a drink from a contaminated stream, and that member of the public already having underlying health conditions, including obesity and respiratory problems, a death had occurred. He went on to inform the attentive media group that all had now been remedied at the site and no further leaks were occurring and then he went on to express his sympathy for the family involved.

Many questions followed. Who was the member of the public? Was anyone else involved or injured? Can we be sure it won't happen again? The PM answered those and others of a similar nature in his usual manner, often appearing to be side-tracked onto other matters which he clearly preferred to comment upon, rather than directly answering the question put to him. The questions began to tail off and the PM picked up his papers from the podium and tapped them against the sloping top in order to tidy them into a neat stack. He was about to turn away and was just raising his hand to say goodbye when a voice called from the back.

"Sir Julian? Is DEFRA aware of any toxic substances being produced at Broughton Stretton?"

The PM turned back to the podium. "Who's that?" he called, looking around the room. A hand raised from a seated position towards the back of the room.

"Zoe Carlson, Prime Minister."

"I'm sorry, Miss Carlson, what was the question?" asked the PM.

"It was a question for Sir Julian, Prime Minister. I wonder whether he is aware of any toxic substances being produced at Broughton Stretton."

The Prime Minister turned to look at Sir Julian, who almost winced when he did so. It was a characteristic of this Prime Minister that if he could offload a question, a hospital pass, as Sir Julian's school rugby coach would have called it, he would. He wouldn't try and kill the question and move on, saving the embarrassment that some ill prepared individual might have, but rather he would stand and stare at you, as he did right now, seemingly oblivious to the difficulty that the question posed for Sir Julian in his position as Director General of DEFRA.

"No, Miss Carlson," he answered flatly.

The PM began to move again.

"Then why was the hospital that admitted Mr Sharp locked down and a team from your department in HazMat suits crawling all over it?" asked Zoe Carlson.

This time the PM didn't look at Sir Julian. "You've had your answer, thank you," he said, but only after Daniel Tomlinson had leaned in and muttered something to him, inaudible to the rest of the room. The PM and Tomlinson turned away and stepped out of the room, leaving Sir Julian still facing the media and a sudden interest from them, along with a new set of questions. Zoe Carlson raised her voice.

"Why was Benjamin Scott's body removed for autopsy without his wife's permission?" she called. The room went silent. Tomlinson and the PM were already part way down the corridor, not looking back. Sir Julian suddenly seemed to realise that he was the only official left in the room and quickly turned on his heels and walked out of the double doors, a barrage of questions being shouted at him as he went.

He followed the PM and Tomlinson back to the main office. Sir Nigel was waiting for them as they trooped in.

"Zoe Carlson," the PM was muttering. "Where do I know her from?"

"She covered SARS," answered Sir Julian as he followed them into the office and closed the door. "Prime Minister, this is a bloody mess!" he said. "She's going to be like a terrier with a slipper about this."

"She's had her answer," said Tomlinson. "There is no need to expand on that."

Sir Julian stuttered and gasped for air for a moment. "Did you not hear what she was asking? She knows that we carried out an autopsy. We had a Haz Team present. There's no way that she is going to fall for your bacterial spillage nonsense."

The Prime Minister sat behind his desk. "Daniel is right," he said. "The Press have had their answer. There is no need to speak further of it."

Sir Julian stood in silence for a moment, his eyes drifting from one to the other of his three opponents in this matter. "So, what happens with the remaining viral agent?" he asked.

Sir Nigel smiled. "Don't worry, Julian. There won't be any more leaks. All is nicely secure, now."

The PM smiled in satisfaction at the response from Sir Nigel.

"No more leaks?" asked Sir Julian. "Surely, you will be destroying all of the remaining stocks."

Sir Nigel shook his head. "Not possible, Julian. Not after all of the work that has gone into this. The antiviral that can be produced from this could be a real game changer in the world of viruses and toxins." The PM nodded his head in agreement. Tomlinson made no movement.

"You can't be serious?" asked Sir Julian. "I'm not some

halfwit, Nigel. I know that you are producing this as a weapon of sorts."

"Not at all!" argued Sir Nigel. "We have to develop the original strain in order to develop the antiviral. From that antiviral we can develop others to use against other strains and the risk of outbreaks of who knows what."

"This is utterly preposterous!" cried Sir Julian. "Prime Minister, I really must insist that you give an instruction here. We gave a commitment to the World Health Organisation, no, to the world, that we had destroyed the last stocks of Rinderpest. If any of it escaped in its original source it would be devastating to livestock, both in the UK and around the world. If this damn variant gets out, crossing the species, it could create a global pandemic!"

"Now, now," replied the PM. "Julian you are blowing things out of proportion. I have every faith that Nigel and the chaps at Broughton Stretton have got everything strapped down securely and this was just a fluke, a bit of a freak accident."

"Absolutely," agreed Sir Nigel.

"Prime Minister, I must insist!"

"Not really your place to insist, Julian," said Tomlinson.

"Indeed", laughed the PM. "Right. Time to move on. Thanks both," he said, waving a hand at Sir Julian and Sir Nigel.

Sir Nigel moved to the door and opened it. Sir Julian continued to stare, open mouthed, at the Prime Minister. Eventually, realising that he had lost any chance of persuading the PM to listen to him, he turned away and walked through the door, held open by Sir Nigel, who followed him through and then headed in a different direction.

When Sir Julian left number 10 the Press were crammed around the barriers opposite the entrance, shouting his name and demanding to know why there had been a Haz Team and why there had been an autopsy and, causing him to wince, was this a coverup?

Mercifully, they didn't follow him. Had he considered that matters would have proceeded in the way that they had, he would have ordered a car, but, as it transpired, it wasn't necessary. Until, that is, he was about halfway back to his office. Zoe Carlson appeared at his side. She had watched him leave Downing Street and then hung back, waiting to see whether the Prime Minister would appear at the door, or even better for her, that slimy Sir Nigel Beswick from the MOD. She had a nose for bullshit and her nostrils were flaring from the stench of the explanations provided by the PM in the press conference. She was convinced there was something dodgy going on at Brought Stretton and, if there was something dodgy at the, to all intents and purposes, secret scientific facility, she was certain that the MOD and slimy Sir Nigel Beswick were involved.

But neither appeared at the door of number 10, so whilst the other journalists busied themselves on phones to editors and the news correspondents spouted forth to the TV cameras they had in tow, she slipped away, and half ran down Whitehall until she caught up with Sir Julian.

"Hi," she smiled. He looked at her, at first in confusion, and then with impatience, before increasing his pace. She increased hers and kept up. "Hi," she smiled again. "Come on, Sir Julian, be civil."

"This really is not the time, Miss Carlson," he snapped.

"Why not?" she smiled walking sideways to him so that she could stare up at his face. She'd forgotten how tall he was.

"I have important matters to deal with, Miss Carlson," he answered.

"Broughton Stretton?" she replied. He didn't say anything and carried on walking. "Look, Sir Julian," she persisted. "Whatever happened there is eventually going to come out and surely you would rather it was reported by someone you can trust to give an accurate account, rather than let the redtops sensationalise it into meaningless crap?"

He still said nothing and continued walking. "Maybe I should speak with Sir Nigel Beswick?" she suggested. Sir Julian's pace faltered for the smallest of moments, before resuming his stride.

She'd noticed.

"I figured the Ministry of Defence would have something to do with this," she said. "What have they done now? Some nasty little chemical warfare experiment gone wrong and slipped into the watercourse?"

Sir Julian stopped and faced her. "Miss Carlson," he said. "That is enough. You've had your Press briefing and I have nothing more to say on the matter." Despite his words, she could tell that she had touched a nerve. She had been pushing her luck, chancing her arm, guessing, really. But had she actually hit on something?

"I'm right, aren't I?"

He began walking again. "I really have to go," he said. "Goodbye Miss Carlson."

She reached for his hand and pushed a business card into it. "For when you change your mind," she said. "You know me, Sir Julian. If I tell the story, it will be the real, the true story. You can trust me."

They had arrived at Sir Julian's office and he rushed up the stone steps to the front door. Zoe Carlson stopped at the foot of the stairs. Sir Julian didn't look back at her, but his right hand made its way into his right jacket pocket, dropping the business card in it. She smiled and turned away.

CHAPTER FOUR

On the Isle of White each November it is 'Turkey and Tinsel' time. For those who have never experienced it before it can be a little surprising and amusing to see Christmas trees in hotel windows and festive decorations and lights adorning the buildings. The hotels have Christmas menus and provide musical entertainment for the many guests who make the November trip an annual occasion.

Sir Julian was used to Turkey and Tinsel in November. The Isle of Wight had held a special place in his heart ever since he had been a young boy and he had holidayed there many times, later buying a house in Ryde as his own hideaway. It wasn't a holiday home. He held the island in greater affection than that. It was his escape. A place where, if he needed to, he could disappear and reset and recharge his batteries. Only a handful of his friends and even fewer of his colleagues knew about the small two bedroomed stone cottage half way up a hill overlooking the Solent. If Sir Julian needed a break, or time to think, or just to get away from the daily machinations of life in Whitehall, Ryde on the Isle of White was where he would come.

He wasn't much of a drinker, but there was a little bar right on the promenade about half a mile from his house, where he would nurse a cold pint of beer in the evening and then eat supper. The food was homecooked and simple and the atmosphere of the place was calming and welcoming, with friendly staff and a roaring fire. On other visits he would take a book and read, even pushing the boat out for a second pint, sometimes, but this time he simply stared out into the darkness, just able to make out the twinkling lights of Portsmouth across the water.

He'd been there for a week. During that time, he had travelled around the island, visiting various tourist attractions. He always liked to drop into the Garlic Farm when he visited the island and he would spend hours in the little café and observation point at the Needles, watching the wild waves crashing around the rocky white teeth that jutted out of the sea.

He had needed to get away from London. He needed to think. Nothing coming out of Parliament, Whitehall, or the Ministry of Defence ever really shocked him. He had been a part of the establishment for far too long for anything coming out of the place to shock him. He was regularly angry, though, and this latest incident was right up there at the top of his anger levels. Rinderpest, the name taken from the German, meaning 'cattle plague', had been devastating to many countries across the world, wiping out cattle and indigenous creatures, such as giraffes and antelopes. As well as endangering the continued existence of various species, it wiped out livestock on farms, invariably in poorer countries, causing greater poverty and in some cases famine. It was a disease that was mainly transmitted by water and had terribly high mortality rates.

Throughout the twentieth century scientists across the world had collaborated to devise a method of eradicating the disease. By the middle of 2011, the world had achieved just that, and global announcements were made by the World Health Organisation and individual Heads of State that this devastating disease had been overcome and destroyed forever. Never would it return to cause rampant destruction to wild animals and to livestock.

With the exception, of course, of laboratory stocks.

Sir Julian still marvelled at the repeated insistence of Governments across the world to keep hold of the last remnants of the deadliest contagions, just in case. Just in case of what? If the disease is eradicated, surely there cannot be any need for an antiviral or antidote to be made. It has been eradicated. And, even in the unlikely event of it somehow finding its way back into existence, we already know how to eradicate it. So, what possible need could there be to hold on to laboratory stocks?

That argument had, to his pleasant surprise at the time, finally been accepted and, eventually, the UK destroyed the final remnants of the disease held in laboratory stocks.

Or so Sir Julian, along with the rest of the world, had been led to believe. He was so angry and at the same time incredulous that the UK Government had sanctioned the retention by the Ministry of Defence of some of the virus. He was furious that he had been permitted to be the face of the international announcement that the laboratory stocks had been destroyed, when in reality they hadn't.

And yet worse to come. The MoD want to weaponize the damn thing. They want to create a strain that transfers to humans. A zoonotic virus. He did not buy Sir Nigel's bullshit that the intention was to develop a vaccine. Why would there be a need for a vaccine for a virus that did not exist. No, he didn't buy that. The development of this virus had, in his opinion, been based upon much more dastardly intentions.

So, he had needed to get away and think. He had to consider what was the right thing to do. What was the moral obligation that he must accept? He was the face of the Government that had told the world that he had overseen the destruction of the final laboratory stocks of this awful virus. The television camera crews had been present at Broughton Stretton and had filmed the incineration of the supposed final stocks. Should he now be the one to inform the world that it had all been a lie? More than that, should he be the one to tell the world that it was a ruse designed to enable elements of the Government to create a biological weapon?

Each evening, sitting in the bar and staring out over the Solent, he would take from his pocket the business card that Zoe Carlson had given him and place it on the table in front of him. The simplest way of avoiding being silenced by the likes of Daniel Tomlinson was to give the story to Zoe Carlson. If Sir Julian returned to Whitehall and sought permission for a Press conference, he would be pounced upon by Tomlinson and undoubtedly blocked by the Prime Minister under Tomlinson's direction. They would probably try and use the Official Secrets Act to silence him and then, even more probably, retire him out of the Service and replace him with a suitable 'yes man'.

If Zoe Carlson ran the story, though, and so long as she told it as it was, without embellishing it or seeking to directly politicise it, the Government would have to react. They couldn't deny the story. Sir Julian would have no intention of being an anonymous whistle-blower, so the Government, and that prick Tomlinson, would have to come clean and deal with the fallout. Certainly, Sir Julian would be out of a job, but how could he stay anyway?

And so it was that, on his final evening in his favourite bar in

Ryde on the Isle of Wight, Sir Julian took his mobile phone out of his pocket and entered a new contact in its memory, copying the details directly from the business card of Zoe Carlson. He then left the card on the table as he stood, donned his coat and scarf, and went outside into the cold night air.

He took his time walking back to the house. There was no rain, but the wind was brisk and cold, and he had to pull the collar of his coat up around his ears to defend his head from the chill. He walked past a couple of hotels that were brightly lit and he smiled to himself when he saw through the windows the residents inside wearing Christmas hats that had been pulled from Christmas crackers as they sang along with the live music entertainment.

Now that he had decided what was the right thing to do, he felt more at peace than he had done for some time. Realising that he would soon, no doubt, be out of a job, he began to consider moving to the island permanently. He would enjoy that. The only time he didn't really enjoy the island was during the annual Isle of Wight Festival, but that was only because the place became too busy. He loved Cowes Week, though, when he would watch the regatta from the beach and enjoy the firework display on the final Friday, although he failed to see the irony relating to just how busy the island was during that period.

He approached his cottage, the front of which had the tiniest of gardens, enclosed by a low stone wall. It had been halved in size to allow for the creation of a short driveway on which sat his other prized possession, a 1962 Austin Healey 3000 MK II in Colorado red. He had reversed it into the drive so that the toothy grin of the front grill greeted him when he approached it. As he opened the gate and walked up by the side of the car, and before he turned onto the narrow path that led to the front door of the cottage, he patted the shiny red bonnet and smiled.

"Good night, Oz," he said.

A cat leaped out in front of him with enough sudden movement to make him jump slightly and spin around facing the road. A man passing by paused and looked at him, before saying "Good evening," and moving on. Sir Julian acknowledged the stranger with a wave and then turned back to his front door. He would have one more day on the island before he needed to get to his pre-booked ferry at 4:30 pm.

He used the following day for a final drive around the island. He enjoyed pushing the Austin Healey to his personal comfort zone limit as he took the coastal roads that ran around the perimeter of the island. His mood was much lighter now that he had decided on his next course of action. The day was cold, but clear and he drove with the top down, enjoying the cold wind. That morning, as he had breakfasted on two boiled eggs and toast, with black coffee to complement the meal, he had made his decision that he would speak with Zoe Carlson the reporter and disclose all that he knew. He believed her when she had said that she would report the case properly and not sensationalise it. Well, she probably would sensationalise it, at least a little, but the story would still be as he recounted it and not embellished. He had telephoned her, but her number rang straight to voicemail.

"Miss Carlson," he had said when the automated message told him to start speaking. "It's Sir Julian Hebburn. I'd like to meet with you and discuss what happened at Broughton Stretton. I'll be on my way back to London this evening, so if you could perhaps come back to me with a convenient time later this week, so that we can meet and discuss, I would be grateful."

He'd then packed his small case, thrown it in the boot of 'Oz', locked the house securely and set off for a final day's driving. He stopped for lunch at Yarmouth and enjoyed a walk around the harbour where he sat and watched the boats and the people and the sea. He would tell all to Zoe Carlson this coming week and then he would return to Ryde and make plans to sell his London apartment and retire to his island home permanently. As he watched the boats bob gently in the harbour, he wondered whether he could learn to sail. The idea grew in his head and he was now picturing himself captaining his own small sailboat out around the Solent. He wondered how much a boat would cost.

At 3:30pm he drove the Austin into Fishbourne and into the waiting area at the ferry terminal. There was already a queue of cars in front of him and several articulated lorries waiting for the ferry from Portsmouth. Around twenty minutes later he watched the ferry arrive at the terminal and dock. The vehicles then filtered out onto the terminal and out up the slip road to the road out to Fishbourne. It was all executed very efficiently. Whilst he watched, one of the ferry terminal staff made his way from vehicle to vehicle in the queue checking boarding tickets. Sir Julian had pre-booked his and brought the printout with him when he came to the island. He now displayed it on his dashboard for the terminal official to inspect and scan through the windscreen.

By 4:10pm Sir Julian had driven onto the ramp of the ferry and followed the directions given to him by one of the crew. He parked the Austin Healey on the second deck in the middle space of the middle row. Other cars filtered in alongside him, their drivers giving admiring looks in the direction of Sir Julian's 'Oz'. Once he was parked up and the car locked, he climbed the stairs to the deck of the ferry, moving to the rear to watch the remaining vehicles make their way on board.

At 4:30p the ferry was full, the ramp had been raised and the huge vessel began to make its way out of Fishbourne and into the Solent. In forty-five minutes, it would be docking in Portsmouth and he would be commencing the two-hour drive to his apartment in central London. More people were coming up onto the deck enjoying the view as the island receded and the winter sun began to sink into the sea in the west. Sir Julian walked away from a small group of people who were chatting excitedly and made his way towards the starboard side of the ferry near to the rear. He was behind the wheelhouse here and the setting sun was too low to provide any illumination. He held onto the handrail at the side of the vessel and looked out to sea. As it became darker, the clear winter early evening sky began to glimmer with the pin pricks of a billion stars.

Sir Julian adjusted his scarf and lifted his coat lapels against the chill of the sea air. He wished he'd brought ordinary gloves and not just his leather driving gloves which were currently resting on the passenger seat of the Austin. He sunk his cold hands into his coat pockets and contemplated going inside to the warmth of the seated area. They were now well into the middle of the Solent, so he had another twenty minutes at least before the announcement would be made to return to vehicles. He decided to brave the cold a little longer so that he could continue enjoying the sea air and the beauty of the night sky.

"Excuse me," said a voice.

Sir Julian turned, placing his back against the railings, his hands wedged deep into his coat pockets. A man approached him. He was shorter than Sir Julian, but stocky and solid looking. He looked vaguely familiar. He had a cigarette in his hand.

"Do you have a light?"

Sir Julian shrugged his shoulders. "I'm sorry," he said. "I'm afraid I don't smoke."

The man was closer now. Only a couple of feet away, Sir Julian recognised him now. It was a bit of a coincidence, but this was the man who had said 'Good Evening' to him last night, just as the cat had startled him. He thought that the man hadn't heard his reply to the question, because he continued to approach and was now well within Sir Julian's personal space.

"I said I don't..."

He didn't finish the sentence. Two huge hands were suddenly thrust forward towards Sir Julian. He didn't have time to react. One grabbed his coat at chest height and the other went between his legs grasping his genitals painfully, before lifting him and throwing him over the side of the boat. No-one saw or heard him fall into the water forty feet below. He had been so shocked that he didn't even call out. He just fell, headfirst into the icy cold waters of the Solent, only a few miles away from the island that he had loved for most of his life.

When the ferry docked at Portsmouth, the vehicles exited the vessel in an organised fashion, under the direction of the crew. There was a little delay to some of the vehicles escaping the second deck, because a Colorado Red 1962 Austin Healey sat driverless in the middle of it and despite several tannoy announcements, its owner didn't appear. Once all of the other vehicles had exited the ferry, the staff carried out a bow to stern search of the vessel to find the owner of the Austin Healey, but to no avail. The obvious conclusion was that there was a man overboard. The harbour authority and the police were informed and the many vehicles waiting on the ferry terminal at Portsmouth for their transportation to the Isle of Wight were informed that the ferry had been cancelled.

CHAPTER FIVE

Zoe Carlson was rushing around her apartment holding one shoe in her right hand and searching under table, chairs, and clothes for the other. She'd kicked them off her feet in the midst of the passionate embrace that she had been enjoying the previous evening. The embrace had followed an evening of dinner and then drinks with Harry, a guy she had met at a Fleet Street conference the day before, and it came before some very physical sex on the sofa and then the floor of her apartment. He hadn't stayed the night, instead sloping off just after midnight with some excuse about work the following day. She suspected he was married, and she silently chastised herself for the umpteenth time for not getting to know someone before shagging them.

Her shoe was in the corner of the room. She'd obviously kicked it off with greater force than she had suspected. That's eagerness for you, she thought, as she slid her feet into the black shoes that had just the right amount of heel to create the right kind of interest whilst allowing her to run if she needed to.

She picked up her mobile phone from the coffee table and redialled the number she had already tried several times whilst dressing. It was the number of Sir Julian Hebburn. Yesterday, whilst attending the conference where she had met the lovely Harry, she had switched her phone to silent without noticing that the battery was almost dead. Whilst she and Harry were chatting as they left the conference, heading for the pub across the road, she had gone to switch the ringer back on, only to find that her phone was lifeless. She had meant to ask the cute barman if she could borrow a charger from behind the bar, but Harry must have felt threatened by the possible competition and he had dragged her away, suggesting they go to a restaurant that he absolutely loved in Covent Garden. By the time they had gorged themselves, then undertaken a mini pub crawl and finally made it back to her apartment, she had forgotten all about her phone and was instead only interested in what she was going to do to Harry.

When she had awoken this morning, somehow in her own bed, although she certainly didn't remember going there, it had taken some strong coffee and two Alka seltzer in water before her mind had cleared enough to realise that her mobile phone had not been by her bedside table. When she finally found it in the pocket of her jacket which was curled up in a ball by the wall, she remembered that it had no charge and so she plugged it in whilst she made a second cup of coffee and determined to try and face some food for breakfast.

When the phone sprang into life, she tapped the icon for voicemail and then the icon for loudspeaker and then slumped back on the sofa. The chirpy voice on the phone informed her that she had four new messages and then began to play the first of them. It was an editor for one of the papers that she frequently submitted to reminding her that she was late providing him with an article for review. The second message was the lovely Harry. He was very deliberately speaking quietly, initially remarking on how wonderful last night had been and then very suddenly whispering that he had to go, and he would call her later.

Definitely married. She would have to block his number.

"Miss Carlson. It's Sir Julian Hebburn."

Zoe sprang forward in her seat and stared hungrily at the phone.

"I'd like to meet with you and discuss what happened at Broughton Stretton. I'll be on my way back to London this evening, so if you could perhaps come back to me with a convenient time later this week, so that we can meet and discuss, I would be grateful."

She didn't get to the fourth message, instead grabbing her phone from the table and searching through the contacts list until she found his number. Her hand trembled slightly as she tapped the green telephone symbol to dial and she raised the phone to her ear.

"This is Sir Julian Hebburn. Please leave a message."

Voicemail! Damn!

She tried again but had no luck. Zoe then started scrabbling around the floor for her clothes. She put the phone back on the coffee table and hit loudspeaker and continued to redial as she shrugged out of her dressing gown and clawed on the same underwear, skirt, and blouse that she had worn the previous day.

It was no good. It just kept ringing to voicemail.

She didn't have his office number but figured that she would probably be stonewalled by his secretary anyway, so she pulled on her jacket and hurried out of the apartment, determined to meet Sir Julian at his office. She hailed a black cab and was soon travelling across London to Whitehall. When she arrived, security on the door barred her way. From the outside of the building, it appeared that anyone could simply walk through the open door, but as soon as Zoe entered, she was faced with an interior wall with a glass screen behind which sat a middle-aged man in a security uniform wearing an emotionless face. To his right, Zoe's left, was the real doorway into the building. It was a glass pod, probably reinforced, sealed shut and only opened from the security desk by the impassive security guard. If he was minded to. A small sign on the wall proclaimed that the security level was 'Substantial',

"I'm here to see Sir Julian Hebburn," Zoe said. She smiled her most winning smile.

"Name?" said the security guard.

"Carlson. Zoe Carlson."

The security guard looked on his computer screen, locating the correct phone number, then picked up the receiver on his desk and dialled. "I have a Zoe Carlson for Sir Julian." He listened for a moment, his face still expressionless, then said "Ok, thank you," before replacing the receiver.

"He's not in."

Zoe waited for more information, but none was forthcoming. "Do you know when he will be in?" she asked.

"No."

She looked around the entranceway, not really a foyer, it was far too small, but had she decided to instruct the security guard that she would wait, there was nowhere to sit. So instead, she shrugged her shoulders and went back outside. She tried ringing Sir Julian again, but the call just went to voicemail. Standing on the steps outside the building she wished she had brought a coat in addition to the suit jacket that she wore. The cold November morning was a little too brisk to stand around waiting, so she headed across the road to a brightly lit coffee shop and made herself comfortable inside its warmth, close enough to the window to watch the steps and door of the building opposite.

She was on her second cup of coffee when she saw Sir Julian. Not on the steps leading to his office building, but on the large plasma television screen held on a bracket high in the corner of the coffee shop, just inside the doorway. The screen showed a female reporter, wrapped up warm against the cold, speaking into a furry microphone, a ferry port, and the sea in the background, and a still photograph to the right of the screen with the name 'Sir Julian Hebburn' in large letters beneath it.

Zoe called to the young man behind the counter and asked him to turn the sound of the television on. He smiled and complied. The female reporter's voice competed with the background noises of wind, vehicles and the general hustle and bustle of a ferry terminal.

"Sir Julian's classic motor car was discovered abandoned on the Isle of Wight ferry behind me," she said to camera. "Authorities have not made any official statement, yet, but the fear held by everyone is that he may have fallen overboard during the crossing from the Isle of Wight to Portsmouth. The Harbour Authorities have confirmed that the crossing had been a smooth one, without any significant weather, so it is still unclear how Sir Julian may have fallen overboard. We are awaiting a statement from the Government."

Zoe stared at the screen, speechless and open mouthed. She couldn't believe that her big story may have just taken a permanent bath in the Solent. Her mind raced as she assessed the situation. There was no giving up. She still had a story to tell. The question was how was she to tell it when her main character had quite literally gone overboard.

Picking up her phone, she scrolled through her contact list until she found the number that she wanted and then hit dial.

"News desk," was the reply.

"Hi, it's Zoe Carlson, is Jeremy free?"

"Oh hi, Zoe," replied the voice at the other end of the line. "It's Jess. Long time no speak."

"Jess," said Zoe. "How are you? It has been a long time, you're right. We must catch up soon. Maybe get a couple of drinks in town."

"That would be great," replied Jess. "Maybe later this week?"

Zoe needed to get the conversation back on track. "Yes," she said. "Definitely. But I just wanted to get two minutes with Jeremy, if I could?"

"Sorry, Zoe," said Jess. "He's in meetings all day. It's very much a case of do not disturb."

Jeremy was the Executive Producer at the television news station running the report that Zoe had just watched. She had known him for some years, but never worked directly with him, however, she knew that he would have the background on the story being run. That might be a starting position for her own investigations.

"That's a pity," she said. "Could I not even get two minutes with him? I just wanted a bit of background on this Julian Hebburn story that you are running."

"There's no chance, I'm afraid," said Jess. "But I might be able to help."

"Really?" asked Zoe.

"Yes, I took the original call."

Zoe's ears pricked up. "That's great. Who is the contact?"

"One of the ferry staff called it in after the Harbour Authorities and police had been called. I think he thought he would get a reward for giving us the story. He found the car. It's one of those old flashy types."

"Yes, I know," said Zoe. "Do you have a name?"

"Hang on, let me get my notes." There was a moment's silence, then "Michael Frazier. I've got a number for him if you want?"

Zoe scribbled down the name and number and thanked Jess, promising to call her later in the week to arrange drinks, but knowing that was very unlikely to happen. She hung up and then rang the number that Jess had given her.

"Hello?" the voice that answered sounded suspicious.

"Mr Frasier?" said Zoe.

"Who is this?" was the even more suspicious reply.

"Mr Frazier, my name is Zoe Carlson. I'm a freelance journalist and I have been writing a piece on Sir Julian Hebburn. I understand that you may have some information about what happened to him on the ferry."

"I've already spoken to your lot," came the surly reply. "You need to talk to each other."

"I don't work for the television news, Mr Frasier," said Zoe. "I'm freelance. I work for myself. If you have information, and it proves useful, I may be able to cover some of your expenses incurred in providing it."

"What expenses?" replied Frazier. "I haven't got any expenses." He sounded confused. "I just work on the ferry."

"I understand that, Mr Frazier, but, in my line of work, if someone provides information that assists my reporting, it may be the case that I have to pay for that information. Now, clearly, it is not going to be appropriate for me to be offering rewards, as such, to people such as yourself who might help me out in my investigation into a story, but it may be appropriate that I can reimburse you for any expenses that you might incur in getting that information to me."

Slowly the penny dropped. "Oh, I see," he said. "Well, yes, I reckon that it's probably cost me fifty, no a hundred quid, what with having to hang around and wait for the police and the Harbour guys. You know, I would have, like, extra parking charges and, erm, well I'd have to get some food and stuff."

"Absolutely," said Zoe. "I think a hundred pounds to reimburse you for your inconvenience is entirely appropriate. Tell me, is the ferry still out of service?"

"For now," he said. "But they'll have her back out on the water within the next couple of hours, I'd have thought. They'll be moving his car shortly."

"Before they do, would you be able to take some photographs for me?" she asked. "Inside and outside of the vehicle?"

Michael Frazier laughed. "Already ahead of you, love," he said. "I took photos before we called the Harbour guys. I'll want paying, I mean, my expenses, before you can have them though. I'm not just going to send them to you."

"Absolutely," she said. "You give me your account details and I can send the money across straight away."

"Cash," said Frazier, flatly.

"Oh. Ok," she said. "I would have to come down to see you, though. Wouldn't it be easier for me to send the money electronically and you can then email me the photos?"

"No. Cash only," said Frazier. "I'll throw in a tour of the boat if you want. That other woman off the telly wasn't interested."

Zoe thought about it for a moment. "Ok," she finally agreed.

"I'll have to check on the trains. Can I send you a text to let you know what time I'll arrive?"

"Sure. I'll pick you up from the station if you want."

After she had hung up, she used her phone to search for train times and stations. It would take her two hours from London Victoria to Portsmouth Harbour. She left the café and hailed a taxi to take her to the station.

Whilst she waited for the train, she sent Frazier a text message with her expected time of arrival. The train was late, of course, and by the time she arrived at Portsmouth Harbour there wasn't much daylight left. The station was small, with only two platforms and as she left through the ticket turnstiles and headed out to the steps at the front, she could see a large, three mast sailing ship moored on the other side of a short stretch of water. It was old, the hull predominantly black with a red keel. The fresh smell of the sea air filled her nostrils.

"HMS Warrior," a voice said. Zoe turned to see a tall, slim man wearing a heavy coat and a beanie hat. Once again, she regretted leaving her apartment in such a hurry that she hadn't picked up a coat. "Britain's first iron hulled and armoured warship. Pride of the fleet, she was."

Zoe noticed a ferry logo on the left breast of his coat. "Mr Frazier?" she asked.

He stuck out his hand. "Michael," he smiled, as he looked her up and down. "I googled you," he said. "That's how I knew it was you. Did you not bring a coat?"

"No," said Zoe, beginning to get quite cold now. "Where's your car?"

"Car?" said Frazier. He turned and pointed over his shoulder. "The terminal is only there."

Zoe could see that the ferry terminal was only about a

hundred metres away. She smiled and followed Frazier as he began to descend the steps of the train station. He turned to the left, away from the direction of the terminal and she paused for a moment, confused, until she realised that he was walking towards an ATM. He stopped by the machine and turned towards her with a smile.

"I figured you'd probably need a hole in the wall for the cash," he said.

Zoe took out her purse and withdrew her bank card, inserting it into the machine before turning and glaring at Frazier until he turned away and wouldn't be able to look over her shoulder to see the numbers that she typed into the ATM. Five twenty-pound notes appeared in the slot at the base of the machine after she had removed her card. She pulled them away from the dispenser and turned towards Frazier who was holding his hand out, a large grin on his face.

"The photographs?" said Zoe.

Frazier dropped his hand and withdrew a large mobile phone from his pocket. A moment later he was showing her several photographs of Sir Julian's Austin Healey. "Beautiful car," he said.

Zoe took the phone from him and swiped through the photographs. There were two that showed the interior of the vehicle and she used a finger and thumb to drag the screen, zooming in to see if there was anything of interest. She could make out a pair of driving gloves on the black leather of the passenger seat, but nothing else of interest. She handed the phone back.

"Send them to me," she said. Frazier set to work sending each photograph to Zoe's phone, one by one. Once that was done, Frazier led her across the road towards the ferry terminal.

"He was on The Marquess of Exeter," said Frazier as they approached the terminal buildings. "She'll be unloading just now, so if we're quick, we can have a look around." He paused for a moment, studying Zoe. "We better get you a coat," he said. "Come on."

They entered the staff area of the terminal. Two employees sat behind a Perspex screen dealing with enquiries and ticket sales and neither paid any attention to Frazier or Zoe as they entered the area that was guarded by a sign saying "No admittance, employees only". Frazier led her through to a brightly lit room at the back of the building that served as a canteen for staff. A coat stand stood in one corner and several large blue coats, similar to the one that Frazier wore, hung off it. He pulled one down and threw it to Zoe.

"That'll sort you out," he smiled.

It was huge. When she put it on, she almost disappeared. She battled with the sleeves, trying to pull them up to release her hands, the material bunching up and making her forearms look massive. An image of Popeye jumped into her head and she chuckled.

Frazier looked at her and smiled again. "I doubt I'll find a smaller one. Come on, we won't have a lot of time."

He led her through the rear entrance door down to the dock and then around to the stern of the ferry where the last of the vehicles was leaving via the ramp. They walked up the ramp and onto the boat. No-one gave them a second glance as they walked across the lower deck to one of the doors in the side wall. Up they went to the second deck and Frazier led her through another door and onto the empty parking area, where he walked to the middle and pointed to the floor.

"This was the spot," he said.

Zoe joined him and looked down at the floor at nothing. She looked up at Frazier and then around the vast space of the second deck.

"There's nothing here," she said.

Frazier looked confused. "I told you that the police were taking the Healey," he said. "They could hardly leave it here, could they?"

"I understand that," said Zoe with a little impatience. "I'm just wondering what was the point in bringing me here? There's nothing to see."

Frazier looked hurt. "I thought you wanted to see where his car was? I can take you back to shore if you want."

Zoe shrugged. "No, I'm sorry," she said. "We're here now. Show me around."

With somewhat less enthusiasm than when they had first boarded the ferry, Frazier led Zoe up to the main deck and inside where the seating areas were. Then he led her through to the outer deck and walked her up to the prow of the boat. The cold tried to fight its way through the heavy coat, and she pulled it closer around her. Turning away from the prow she looked up at the huge glass wheelhouse. It stood high up above the outer deck with floor to ceiling windows all around. Zoe pointed to it.

"Can we go up there?" she asked.

For the first time, Frazier didn't look so confident. He checked his watch and then strained his eyes upward, checking whether there was any movement within the wheelhouse. He checked his watch again. They both heard a rumble as the first of the next set of vehicles began to board the ferry down below.

"We'll have to be really quick," he urged. "Follow me."

He led her to an iron ladder that climbed above the interior passenger deck and up to a steel platform that ran around the front of the wheelhouse. Once they arrived at the top, Frazier peered through the windows to check that no crew were in there. His heart was beating fast because he knew that bringing Zoe up here was pushing his luck a bit too far. A door stood in the glass to the port side of the wheelhouse and Frazier tried the handle. It was locked.

"Can't get in," he said.

Zoe was taking in the view from their vantage point. She turned to look through the huge glass panels at the wheelhouse.

"How could nobody see him?" she said.

Frazier shrugged. "Dunno. You can see pretty much everywhere on the top deck from up here."

He looked down towards the deck craned his neck at an angle. "I suppose if he was down there," said Frazier, pointing almost vertically. "He might have been in a blind spot."

Zoe looked over the guard rail that ran around the platform in the direction of where Frazier was pointing. "Show me," she said.

Frazier led the way as they climbed back down the iron ladder to the deck. The noise of vehicles boarding the vessel was now a steady rumble. He looked again at his watch.

"We need to be quick," he said.

They walked around to the starboard side of the boat and up to the rail that ran around the edge of the deck. It was starting to get dark now and the shadows of the wheelhouse stretched out over the side of the ferry and onto the dock. Zoe looked up towards the glass windows of the wheelhouse. They were smaller on this side, higher up on a wall and not running floor to ceiling.

"I think you could be right," she said to Frazier. "I don't reckon that you would be seen if you were stood around this part of the deck, particularly if it was dark."

A whistle blew somewhere below.

"That's us," said Frazier moving away. "Come on, she'll be sailing shortly."

Reluctantly, Zoe followed him back through the interior passenger deck and down to the ramp at the stern. They hustled down the ramp and onto the dock just before the hydraulics began groaning into action and the ramp began to rise. The deck hands closed the barriers until they were flush with the ramp, sealing the hull against the water. Moments later The Marquess of Exeter pulled away from the dock and headed out into Portsmouth Harbour toward the Solent. Zoe watched it glide away, wondering about the blind spot behind the wheelhouse and what, if anything, it meant.

"Michael?" said Zoe without turning towards Frazier, maintaining her gaze on the ferry as it powered away. "Are there cameras on there?"

"What, you mean CCTV?" said Frazier. "Yes, all over the vessel."

"Do you have access to it?" she turned and smiled at him.

Frazier thought about that for a moment, then he returned the smile. "I'm sure I could have," he said. "If the price was right."

"I thought you might say that," she said. "Another hundred. But I want the footage from inside the Captain's driving room."

"The wheelhouse," corrected Frazier.

"Yes," said Zoe. "How soon can you get it?"

Frazier thought for a moment. "Tomorrow should be possible," he said.

That pleased Zoe. "I better find a hotel, then. Call me when you have it."

CHAPTER SIX

She found a hotel easily enough. There were plenty of them situated around the harbour and she checked in for two nights just in case Michael Frazier produced anything of interest. First thing in the morning she called the editor that she had been avoiding and apologised for the delay in providing the piece he was expecting but hinting to him that she was working on something that had the potential of being headline news. He wasn't particularly persuaded by her excuses and warned her that she was at risk of losing the column that had been reserved for her if she didn't get something to him soon.

She'd spent most of the previous day without eating and so today she enjoyed a hearty breakfast before venturing out to the shops to purchase a change of clothes. One of the large chain stores was near to the hotel, the type that sell inexpensive clothes, probably manufactured abroad, and intended to be worn only a dozen or so times before being discarded. She bought a pair of jeans and a sweatshirt, along with some sensible, casual footwear. A warm duffel coat was her final purchase before she headed back to the hotel.

She took the time to shower before changing into her new purchases and then settling down on the bed with a cup of coffee and streaming twenty-four-hour news on the wall mounted television. It wasn't long before Sir Julian's face appeared on the screen. Zoe turned up the volume.

"Authorities are still investigating the sudden disappearance of Sir Julian Hebburn from an Isle of Wight Ferry," the news anchor read from the autocue. "Initial thoughts were that by some terrible accident he may have fallen overboard, but sources from Whitehall are now suggesting the possibility of suicide."

Zoe sat forward, staring at the screen, her brow furrowed.

"Speculation that Sir Julian was potentially facing disciplinary action in relation to his alleged covering up of a minor biological leak at the notorious Broughton Stretton experimental facility, and the thought of public disgrace has led some in Government to speculate that the long serving senior civil servant felt compelled to take his own life."

"Bollocks," said Zoe to the screen.

For the following couple of hours, the story was repeated every half hour as the news programme declared its leading story for the day. Zoe made a few phone calls to journalist friends and colleagues, trying to discover where the suggestion of suicide had come from, but there was nothing to substantiate the claim. The consensus seemed to be that this was simply a story being run by the Government and not the police or other investigating authorities.

Repeatedly, as the story on the television ran throughout the morning and Sir Julian's car was shown on screen, she would call up the photographs on her phone that Frazier had sent to her, zooming in to the interior of the vehicle, looking for anything that might suggest that Sir Julian had intended to take his own life. But there was nothing. The news story and the line from the Government, if that is where it hailed, was pure and unsubstantiated speculation.

Why would he have left her a message asking to meet if his actual intention was to kill himself? Bollocks! was all that came to mind.

Or was that it?

Did he want to set her on a path to investigate his suicide? Maybe there was some substance to the story after all. Could it be, that the biological leak at Broughton Stretton was more serious than the official story from Government. So serious that it might have caused Sir Julian such serious embarrassment as to render life not worth living. She shook her head. Bollocks, remained her primary opinion.

Her phone rang. Michael Frazier's name flashed on the screen. "Michael," she said as she answered it. "What have you got for me?"

"I've got the footage," came the reply. "I've downloaded it to one of those flash drive thingies. I had to buy one, so I'll want reimbursing for that."

Zoe sighed. "Of course," she said. "Do you have a computer that we can look at it on?"

There was silence for a moment before he replied. "No." A few moments more of silence and then he spoke again. "We can use one at the library."

She asked him for the location, which was walking distance from her hotel, and they agreed to meet an hour later. She hung up the phone as the news ran its headline story again, a different anchor this time, but the same unconfirmed report that Sir Julian's death was suicide. Zoe scrolled through the list of contact numbers on her phone and selected one.

"Switchboard," answered a voice.

"Daniel Tomlinson, please," said Zoe.

"I'm afraid Mr Tomlinson is unavailable for unsolicited calls," was the flat reply.

"How would you know?" asked Zoe.

"I'm sorry?"

"How would you know whether or not my call is unsolicited? You didn't ask who I am. Or is it Downing Street policy to block any attempt to call Mr Tomlinson?"

There was silence for a moment before the voice replied. "Who is calling, please?"

Zoe smiled. "Zoe Carlson. I'm a freelance journalist."

"One moment, Miss Carlson." The line went silent. A minute or so passed by before the voice returned. "I'm afraid that Mr Tomlinson is unavailable."

"Do you know when he will be available?" asked Zoe.

"I'm afraid not," came the reply.

Zoe hung up. She hadn't expected him to answer, but she wanted to be certain that Tomlinson knew her name and that she was asking questions. That way, if there was any formal statement to be made, there was a chance, remote admittedly, but nevertheless a chance, that he might do her the courtesy of contacting her first.

She thought for a little while longer and then scrolled through her contacts again before dialling another number.

"Ministry of Defence," said another voice, male this time.

"Sir Nigel, please," said Zoe.

"Who shall I say is calling?"

"Zoe Carlson. He knows who I am."

"One moment, please." The line again fell silent. The silence was much longer this time before the male voice reappeared. "I'm sorry, but Sir Nigel is not taking calls today. Can anyone else help?"

"I doubt it," said Zoe. "Could you try him again, only this time tell him that I am investigating Sir Julian Hebburn's alleged suicide along with the somewhat suspicious death of Benjamin Sharp. I'm just wondering whether he has any comment on the possible link with Broughton Stretton."

"As I said, Miss Carlson," came the reply. "Sir Nigel is not taking calls today."

"Please try again," she insisted. "I think you'll find that he will speak to me if you tell him what I am investigating."

A moment passed before the voice said "One moment, please" and the line fell silent once more. "I'm sorry, Miss Carlson," the voice returned much quicker this time. "Sir Nigel is unavailable for comment. Unless there is anyone else that you wish to speak with?"

"No, that's ok," said Zoe. "Goodbye."

Zoe checked her watch. She still had plenty of time before she needed to set off for the library to meet Michael Frazier, so she settled back on the bed, leaning against the pillows that she had upturned against the headboard, as she watched the scrolling news stories on the television screen. She gave it fifteen minutes before again scrolling through her contacts and selecting a number. Fifteen minutes should have been enough time for Sir Nigel Beswick to have made some calls, one in particular, she hoped. She was confident that Sir Nigel didn't have the wherewithal to deal confidently with a troublesome, nosy reporter like her. He would need help from someone with a much more devious mind.

"Switchboard."

"Daniel Tomlinson, please. It's Zoe Carlson."

"Miss Carlson, I've already explained that Mr Tomlinson is

not available."

"Please try him," said Zoe. "I believe that you will find that he is available now."

The line went silent.

"Miss Tomlinson. Zoe," said a male voice, after a few moments. "How can I be of assistance?"

"You've had a call from Sir Nigel, then, Mr Tomlinson?"

"I speak to many people, Zoe," said Tomlinson. "I'm now speaking to you. What can I help you with?"

It was the first time that Zoe had actually conversed directly with Daniel Tomlinson. She had heard him speak on many occasions, although not very often answering questions, particularly from reporters. His voice sounded different when he was speaking just to her. It was different to when he was speaking to a room or packed auditorium. Lower, more.... menacing.

"I've not heard an official line, yet," she said. "But I wondered what your views are on the speculation that Sir Julian Hebburn may have committed suicide and what your thoughts on his motive may have been."

"There isn't an official line, yet, Zoe. The Government is waiting on the facts."

"Yes, I thought that would be the case," said Zoe. "But I figured that you may have an opinion, particularly given that the death of Benjamin Sharp was as a result of some leak from Broughton Stretton and the fact that the leak was a toxin being developed by the Ministry of Defence." She thought she would chance her arm with that line of questioning, although she didn't really expect the very experienced Daniel Tomlinson to fall for it.

"I don't know where you are getting your stories from, Zoe," said Tomlinson. "But I'm afraid that is all they are. Stories. You were at the Press conference when the explanation about what happened at Broughton Stretton was provided and it really is somewhat unprofessional of you to try and embellish on that explanation in order to sensationalise what was only but an unfortunate accident. That kind of misconceived reporting is one of the reasons that the Press and certain journalists are losing the trust of the general public."

Zoe riled a little at his comments. Which was no doubt exactly what he had planned. Tomlinson's style was to cause agitation and anger in order to misdirect from the subject matter.

"That's funny," said Zoe. "You see, Sir Julian was going to tell all. He contacted me to arrange a meeting and he was going to tell me all about the dirty little secrets held at Broughton Stretton and exactly what happened to Benjamin Sharp."

For a moment Tomlinson was silent. "You spoke with him?" he asked eventually.

Zoe faltered. "Well, not exactly. He left me a voicemail. But that alone is quite damning," she lied. "And I'm in Portsmouth right now investigating exactly what happened on the ferry. I only wanted to give you the opportunity for a comment before I complete the investigation and run the article."

"You've had your comment regarding Broughton Stretton," said Tomlinson. "It was given to you at the Press briefing. If there is to be any formal statement about Sir Julian's death, it will be given in the same fashion, but I can only strongly suggest that you take care that you do not impede any investigation that the Authorities are currently undertaking. Good day, Miss Carlson."

The call was disconnected. Zoe smiled to herself. Well, that had rattled him, she thought.

CHAPTER SEVEN

It took her around ten minutes to walk to the library. Michael Frazier was stood outside waiting for her. He was leaning against the wall with one foot raised up behind him and pressed against the brickwork. A cigarette hung from his bottom lip. Zoe's look must have been one of disapproval, albeit unintentionally, because he removed the cigarette from his lip and threw it into the gutter.

"I'm trying to give up," he said.

"Don't mind me," smiled Zoe. "Shall we go in?"

The interior of the library building was straight out of the nineteen seventies with the exception of a bank of computer screens against the wall. They were the only modern items in the room. It was surprisingly busy, and all the computer stations were in use, so Zoe and Frazier sat on a bench in the middle of the room waiting for one to come free.

As soon as one was available, Zoe rushed to it, before anyone else might have had the opportunity. Frazier joined her, remaining standing. Zoe held out her hand.

"Can I have the stick?" she asked.

"We discussed a fee," replied Frazier.

"I know," she said. "We can go to the bank straight after this." He didn't move. "Don't you trust me?"

Frazier puffed out his cheeks in thought for a moment and then drew his hand out of his pocket and opened it. The USB stick rested on his palm. Zoe took it from him and inserted it into the hole on the computer tower.

"We don't need any special software for it, do we?" she asked.

"Shouldn't do," replied Frazier. "I've not seen it. A mate of mine downloaded it all from the office computer and I'm pretty sure that doesn't have any special software."

When she finally accessed the memory stick, a number of files appeared on the screen. Each was labelled MoE with a number following the prefix. She remembered that the ferry name was the Marquess of Exeter. She double clicked on the first of the files and a video sprang into life of the rear of the vessel, its ramp lowered and vehicles trundling over it. The video was in black and white, but she didn't have any trouble identifying Sir Julian's Aston Martin as it drove off the dock at Fishbourne and onto the boat. There was only a glimpse available of his face as he came into view on the camera, but it was expressionless and told her nothing.

She worked her way through the other videos until she came to the one inside the wheelhouse. It gave a panoramic view through one hundred and eighty degrees, showing the prow of the boat and the front deck through the windscreen. The pilot was sat in front of a small wheel looking ahead. For a long time, she couldn't make out anything of interest and then, just as she was beginning to get bored, she made out a tall, slim figure, turning away from the prow of the boat as other passengers started appearing on deck.

That's him, she thought, leaning forward, and squinting at the screen. It wasn't a very clear picture, but she was sure that the man on the screen was Sir Julian Hebburn. He moved towards the bottom right of the screen and then disappeared from view. Zoe paused the video with a click of the mouse and then moved the search bar back until Sir Julian reversed into view. She paused it again and stared at his face. It was expressionless. She sighed and clicked play again, watching the man on the screen move out of view once more.

Zoe began to wonder what her next move would be. So far, her investigation into Sir Julian's death had proved fruitless but expensive. She hadn't really known what to expect from the video coverage. It was just a lead, a hunch.

Someone broke slowly away from the main group on the deck and began walking in the same direction that Sir Julian had taken. She watched him disappear from view at the same place where Sir Julian had and then moments later reappear and walk back towards the group at the front of the ferry. Patiently, she waited to see whether Sir Julian would appear, but he didn't, so she rewound the recording again to the point where this new man started moving in Sir Julian's direction. It took a few attempts, but by moving forward and backwards through the frames she finally managed to pause the screen on a relatively clear shot of the man's face.

"Who are you?" she asked out loud.

Frazier leant over her shoulder and studied the picture. "Who's that, then?" he asked.

"Good question," replied Zoe. She pulled her mobile phone out of her pocket and took a picture of the screen, zooming in as close as she could on the face of the man on the deck of the ferry.

"You could go back through the boarding video and see if you can pick him out of one of the vehicles," said Frazier. "The cameras are set to record at windscreen level, so he should be easy enough to find."

That was an excellent idea, she thought, as she clicked again on the first file that she had opened. "How many vehicles does the ferry hold?" she asked.

"Sixty-five cars," said Frazier. "Fewer if there are lorries on board."

Zoe was pleasantly surprised at how quickly they found him. He was driving a small van. She paused the video again and took another photograph with her phone. An idea came to her and she rewound the video until the registration plate of the van was in view, then took another photograph of the image on the screen.

"Now I just need a way of getting into the DVLA database," she laughed.

"What for?" asked Frazier.

"To check his number plate and find out who he is," she replied.

"No need for that," said Frazier. "It will be on the manifest."

Zoe looked puzzled.

"You can't take a vehicle onto a ferry unless it's recorded on the manifest," explained Frazier. "They all have electronic tickets with vehicle registration plates and names and addresses. I can have a look for you if you like?"

"Absolutely!" said Zoe, removing the memory stick and handing it back to Frazier. "Can we go now?"

"Just me," he replied. "I'll have to go in the office and access the system. I'll have to do it on the QT, so best if I went alone."

They left the library and found a cashpoint. Frazier wasn't willing to do anything more until he had been paid. Then Zoe headed back to her hotel to wait for him, having given him instructions to call her as soon as he had located the record of the mystery driver.

It was a couple of hours later before Frazier's name flashed up on her phone. He explained that he had found the name and address listed against the registration plate of the van. "It's John Smith," he said.

"Well that's a made-up name," said Zoe, the disappointment clear in her voice.

"Do you think?" replied Frazier. "I know a few John Smiths. It could be real."

"Whatever," said Zoe. "What about the address?"

"That's an odd one," said Frazier. "I don't quite know how he managed to get that through the system, but it's a van rental company in Portsmouth. I do have something else that you might be interested in, though," he teased.

Zoe sounded a little impatient. "Michael, I am not drip feeding you money for snippets of information. Particularly when they don't lead anywhere."

"Who said anything about money?" asked Frazier. "I'm quite enjoying this detective work. I might be willing to give you this information for free."

"Go on then," said Zoe. "What have you got for me?"

There was silence for a moment. "Fancy a drink?" he said.

"Really?" sighed Zoe. "Michael, I'm not on holiday. This is serious stuff and I'm not in the mood for messing around."

"Go on," said Frazier. "I'll buy. And I'll tell you what other information I've found."

It didn't take much persuasion. She could do with a drink after building up her expectations to find evidence that would lead to an award-winning piece of journalism only to have her hopes dashed by a video recording that revealed nothing of any use. He gave her the details of a pub overlooking the harbour and they agreed to meet just after six. She could have a couple of drinks and then head back to the hotel for some food before going to bed in preparation for her trip back to London tomorrow. She resolved that next time she felt the urge to jump on a train to somewhere she would remember to bring her laptop so that she could at least do some work.

The pub was busy when she arrived. It was full of drinkers enjoying 'early doors' after a day at work before they headed home. Frazier was stood at the bar, pint in hand, looking out for her. He waved enthusiastically when she entered and called her over to join him at the bar. She ordered a large glass of wine and looked around for a table, finding one that had just been vacated and instructing Frazier to follow her. The noise of the pub was a pleasant buzz of chatter, interspersed with laughter.

"So, come on then," she said, shrugging out of her coat and sitting down after hanging it over the back of the chair. "What have you got for me?"

"Well," said Frazier. "I was a bit surprised at finding the address for John Smith to be a local van hire place. A bit disappointed as well, to be honest. I thought our security checks were better than that. If you want, I can go and check out the van hire place tomorrow and see whether or not he really does live there?"

Zoe shrugged. "I'm not sure it would serve any purpose," she said.

Frazier looked a little disappointed. "Well, anyway," he said, perking up a little. "Seeing as how I couldn't find much about John Smith, I thought I'd scroll the video back and check the number plate of your missing Lordship."

"Knight," said Zoe. Frazier stopped midsentence at the interruption, looking confused.

"He was a Knight," said Zoe. "A 'Sir', not a Lord."

Frazier thought about that for a moment, but the distinction was lost on him. "As I was saying," he continued. "I looked for his number plate and checked the address details on the manifest for his vehicle."

"He lives in central London," interrupted Zoe. "Same as me."

A smile spread across Frazier's face, just a little bit smug.

"What?" asked Zoe.

"The address your Lordship, Knight, or whatever, for his Aston Martin is listed as Ryde."

Zoe leaned forward. "Where?"

"Ryde," repeated Frazier. "On the island."

The words hung in the air for a moment as Zoe tried to take in their meaning. "Not a hotel?" she asked. "He wasn't staying at a hotel?"

"Nope," the grin on Frazier's face grew wider. "He's got his own place on the island."

Zoe's mind raced. "Let's not get ahead of ourselves," she said. "It could be an air b and b, or a holiday let."

"But he's registered his car at that address," grinned Frazier. "He's got a house on the island. Well, he did have."

Zoe looked at him questioningly.

"He's dead, now, isn't he? So, technically, it's not his anymore."

"Idiot!" smiled Zoe, playfully hitting his arm. "This could be important," she said. "If he's got a house on the island and a place in London, why would he commit suicide by jumping off a ferry?"

"I don't follow," said Frazier.

"Why not do it at home?" continued Zoe. "On the Isle of Wight? I knew this didn't feel right. He left me a message telling me that he was going to meet with me to discuss the case I'm working on. If that wasn't true and if, instead, his intention was to take himself away somewhere to kill himself, why not do it at home, with some sleeping pills and a bottle of whisky or something? No, there's more to this and I've got a feeling that John Smith has something to do with it."

"Do you want to go and see it? The house?" asked Frazier. "We could go tomorrow?"

Zoe sat up straight and looked at Michael Frazier with an expression that a child might have in the moment when it had been offered a visit to the zoo by mum and dad.

"Really?" she asked. "Could we?"

"Of course," beamed Frazier, pleased with himself at eliciting this reaction from his new 'friend'. "I can get us a couple of walk on tickets for the morning ferry and we can have a wander over to Ryde, or get a taxi if you're too lazy."

Zoe beamed from ear to ear. "It's a date!" she grinned, lifting her glass, and chinking it against Frazier's. He blushed. Just a tiny bit.

She relaxed for the rest of the evening, enjoying two or three more glasses of wine than she had intended to before heading back to the hotel, alone. She wasn't sure whether or not Michael Frazier had any designs on her, but if he had, it wasn't going to happen. He hadn't appeared to be disappointed when she had told him that she had to get back to the hotel and that she would meet him in the morning, but who could tell? He was a man, after all.

The following morning was bright, sunny, and cold, with

just a hint of a breeze when she met him at the ferry port. She had checked out of the hotel following a swift and lighter breakfast than the previous day. The outfit that she had been wearing when she had travelled down on the train to meet Frazier was screwed up into several balls, bulging out of her handbag, whilst she held the shoes by the straps in one hand.

"We should get you a bag for them," remarked Frazier when she approached him.

They boarded together, Frazier having already purchased, or perhaps just arranged, the tickets, and they stood together at the front of the boat as it set off across the Solent towards the Island. Zoe enjoyed the crossing. The brisk, salty air caressed her skin and the cold of the autumn sea wind tried to tickle its way between the folds of her coat to touch her. Everything around her was beautiful. The sea was a little bit choppy, but nevertheless relatively calm for the time of year, and it shone in the glare of the morning sun making her feel, well, alive. The low sunlight glanced off the windows of the buildings on the island ahead of them as they approached the port at Fishbourne, and Zoe felt a little disappointed that their little 'sea cruise' was almost over.

Frazier was watching her expression with knowing interest. "It's good, isn't it?" he smiled.

Zoe looked up at him and pulled the collar of her coat closer around her ears, nodding slightly. The ferry slowed and came to a stop at the port and Frazier led Zoe down to the shore and up to the road at the top of the Ferry Terminal.

"You know," said Frazier, pointing back the way that they had come. "If we took the coastal path, along Millionaires' Way, it would be a lovely walk. A bit longer, but ever so pretty."

"How much longer?" asked Zoe.

Frazier shrugged. "Couple of hours, maybe."

"Let's get a taxi," said Zoe, shaking her head.

The taxi journey to the address that Frazier gave the driver took about fifteen minutes. Zoe paid, obviously, and then climbed out of the car, and looked towards where Frazier, who had decamped from the vehicle as soon as it had halted, was standing. In front of him was an attractive two storey cottage, its front door and one window framed by the autumn bare branches of a Wisteria. A single, shallow gravel driveway, guarded by two iron gates stood at the front, bordered by a path which itself was bordered by a small patch of lawn. She joined him at the gate.

"Do you think anyone else lives here?" she asked him.

Frazier shrugged. "Dunno. Nice, though, isn't it?"

Zoe nodded, imagining Sir Julian stood in the doorway waiting to welcome them into his idyllic little cottage. She turned so that her back was to the building and looked out across the choppy November waters of the Solent and thought how beautiful it was.

"I bet he loved it here," she murmured.

Frazier opened the waist high iron gate and the two of them walked down the short path to the solid looking wooden front door. There was no doorbell, but a large brass knocker hung at head height on the door and Zoe lifted it and banged twice. Best to make sure that no one was in before looking around, she thought. There was no answer. She moved to the window and peered inside. The front room looked cosy and comfortable, with a deep red sofa, an expensive looking coffee table and a bookcase, full to the brim, standing against the back wall. Everything looked neat and tidy. Moving back to the front door, she decided to try the door handle. Nothing ventured and all that, she thought. He might have left it unlocked.

He hadn't, of course.

The two of them walked around to the side of the house, where a narrow path led from the gravel drive to a large wooden gate. The handle on the gate turned easily and Zoe opened it, walking through to a tiny cottage garden at the rear of the property. A brasserie table and two chairs sat on a small lawned dais in front of a wall of rock rising at least thirty feet, providing perfect privacy. Zoe turned and looked at the back of the house. The rear door to the property was bright red with a large clear glass window displaying the small kitchen beyond. Frazier was trying the round doorknob, but to no avail.

"Shall I break in?" he suggested.

"Absolutely not!" said Zoe. To the right of the building, against the high, feather board fence, was a terracotta pot upturned and quite obviously deliberately placed where it was.

"Anyway," she smiled. "I'll bet..."

She walked over to it and lifted the pot. Beneath it was a mortis key with a wooden key fob. She chuckled. "Just like my nan used to do," she said as she picked up the key. It fitted the lock on the backdoor to Sir Julian's cottage and within moments, they were inside the little kitchen. Everything was clean and tidy. A wooden kitchen table dominated the room with two stools hiding beneath it. No pots or pans had been left out, all the surfaces were clean, and every utensil was in its place.

The internal kitchen door led to a small hallway and Zoe wandered through. Immediately to her right was the small front room that she had seen through the window when they had arrived at the property. Now she was inside, she saw two easy chairs on either side of the window, in addition to the sofa.

She noted that there was no television. This room was also spick and span, with nothing out of place.

Back in the hallway, the foot of the stairs was right by the front door, probably blocked by the door itself, when open, she thought. The stairs creaked as she climbed them and faced the open door to a small bathroom, which, like the other rooms that she had been in, was spotless. There were two bedrooms, one at the front and one at the back of the house. The rear room was tiny, with a single bed and a small wardrobe. The front bedroom was only a little bit bigger, but it could fit a double bed, neatly made, a small bedside table next to it. A paperback book was open with the pages face down so the reader could pick up where he had left off easily. The front cover was red and the title 'Change of Plan' beneath what looked like a keyhole stared up at her. She moved to the foot of the bed and looked out of the window. The view was glorious. Clear and bright and panoramic, the sea frothing in the autumn sunshine.

"Wow," she murmured.

Beautiful as it all was, however, the view, the pristine house, the lovely walled garden, none of it provided her with any information as to what had really happened to Sir Julian Hebburn. She looked in the wardrobe and guiltily teased open the drawer of the bedside table, but there was nothing out of the ordinary anywhere. So, she retraced her steps down the creaky stairs and back into the kitchen. Michael Frazier was sat on one of the stools that he had pulled from under the table, and he was biting into an apple as he looked at a piece of paper from a notepad laying on top of it.

"Where did you get that apple?" asked Zoe.

"In the fridge," answered Frazier.

"Bloody hell, Michael," said Zoe. "Don't be taking things.

The police will be looking over this place as part of their investigation."

He paused mid bite, considering whether he should return the half-eaten apple to the bottom drawer of the fridge, then thought against it and continued to munch into the fruit.

"I thought this fella topped himself?" said Frazier with a mouthful of chewed apple.

"That is the line that seems to be coming out of Government, or somewhere," said Zoe.

"So why has he left a shopping list?" asked Frazier, looking down at the sheet of paper.

"What?" said Zoe.

Frazier turned the paper one hundred and eighty degrees so that it was readable for Zoe as she approached the table. "He's left someone called Margaret a shopping list."

Zoe's heart raced as she picked up the piece of notepaper and read it.

Dear Margaret.

I'm sorry I dropped in unannounced last week. Things at work were beginning to get on top of me and I needed to take a break. Anyway, I'm feeling much better now, and I expect to be spending a lot more time over here.

I have to nip back to London for a few days but will be returning soon. Could I be a pain and ask that you get a few bits in for me in advance of my return? I know it's cheeky of me, but I doubt I will have time to get the essentials before coming back. I'll make it up to you. It must be my turn to buy the ice creams! Make sure you let me know how much I owe you. I've listed some things overleaf.

See you soon.

Julian

X

Zoe's mouth hung open. Frazier finished the last of his apple and looked around for a bin in which to deposit the core.

"This is proof!" said Zoe. "He didn't kill himself. He was coming back here, and it reads like he was coming back here permanently. He was going to resign!"

Frazier opened a cupboard under the sink and a flip lid bin appeared in view, its lid rising automatically. He dropped the apple core into it.

Zoe had her phone in her hand and was taking photographs of the handwritten note. "My God!" she beamed. "This is gold! I need to ring my editor," she said.

Frazier smiled. "I bet you want me to go to the van hire place now, don't you? Make some enquiries about John Smith?"

"Yes," beamed Zoe as she raised her phone to her ear.

CHAPTER EIGHT

The Downing Street Chief of Staff is widely recognised as the most senior, non-elected position in Government. The holder of the position has the ear of the Prime Minister and, no doubt, exercises a great deal of influence over the decisions made by the actual most senior and elected member of Her Majesty's Government. The Chief of Staff is a 'spad', a special adviser and is usually a career civil servant who is both personally and professionally close to the Prime Minister. Whilst the position is an aspiration of many career civil servants, the office holder is more often than not reviled by all of those that have not had the good fortune to be appointed to the position.

Daniel Tomlinson was the current incumbent and had been for the previous three years. He had been generally disliked before he was appointed, so it followed that, when the Prime Minister announced the appointment of his new Chief of Staff, a collective groan had rumbled through the buildings of Whitehall. Not that he cared. He had little regard or concern for the opinions of others, particularly when that opinion related to him. In fact, to some extent, he enjoyed being disliked, particularly when he had the power to effect changes that caused upset to those who disliked him.

Tomlinson was donning his coat and his favourite grey Irish linen flat cap before leaving his office.

"I'll be back in a couple of hours," he told his secretary as he marched past her desk and headed down the corridor to the stairs at the end. Within a couple of minutes, he was outside in the cold air, walking briskly to the nearest Tube station.

He had just finished a telephone call with the senior political editor of a national newspaper who was inviting him to comment on the apparent recently acquired evidence that Sir Julian Hebburn had not committed suicide off an Isle of Wight ferry, given the fact that he had left for his cleaner (or someone) a shopping list before heading back to the mainland. The editor had taken a very much unhidden smug delight in giving this information to Tomlinson, whose reaction, quite clearly caught off guard, had given away his ignorance of the letter. The editor had gone on to inform Tomlinson that one of his journalists was in possession of a recording from Sir Julian announcing that he was to become a whistle blower in relation to the incident at Broughton Stretton, photographs of the letter to his cleaner, and photographs and video surveillance of a man who they suspected was involved in Sir Julian's death. Tomlinson's gruff response to the editor was that, if what he was being told was true, it would be a matter for the police and not something on which he would be drawn to comment.

"Oh, I can assure you," said the editor. "The moment that the story is ready to go to print, copies of all of the evidence will be handed over to the police."

Tomlinson was fuming. He'd known this editor for many years, and they had a very mutual great dislike of each other. In fact, he couldn't decide if the guy was genuinely trying to get a comment, or just revelling in giving Tomlinson bad news.

And it was bad news. The balls up at Broughton Stretton had a very firm line drawn beneath it, especially with the demise of Sir Julian. The last thing that Tomlinson wanted was for it to rear its ugly head again.

He trotted down the steps of the Tube station at Embankment and used his Oyster card to pass through the turnstiles. Once he was on the platform, he checked his surroundings and waited for the Circle Line. Only a couple of moments later he could feel the rush of air through the tunnel in advance of and announcing the approach of the coming train. It slowed to a halt and the doors all opened simultaneously, sliding into hidden cavities as a robotic voice ordered him to 'please mind the gap'.

At that time of the day, the underground wasn't terribly busy and there was plenty of room on the train to sit, but Tomlinson chose to stand, looking out from under the brim of his cap at the few people occupying seats, ensuring that he didn't recognise anyone and, perhaps more importantly, that no one recognised him.

Three minutes later, the train slowed to a halt at Westminster Tube station, where Tomlinson alighted and crossed platforms to the escalator leading further underground and down to the Jubilee Line, all the while maintaining a watchful eye on his surroundings and the people around him moving to and fro. Once on the train. he occupied a position in the doorway, standing again, despite the many empty seats. The train stopped at Waterloo, where a couple boarded and sat together, deep in conversation. Then to Southwark, London Bridge, Bermondsey, and Canada Water, where he slipped through the doors of the train as they slid open and walked to the end of the platform before turning through one of the arches and heading to the escalator.

The moving stairway climbed slowly and laboriously as he stood to the right-hand side, leaning on the moving arm. Once at the top of the steep climb he walked out to the platform for the overground train. When it arrived, he climbed on board and this time, he took a seat at the back of the train, just in front of what would be the driver's cab if it had been heading in the opposite direction. Within a quarter of an hour the train arrived at his final destination, Brockley rail station.

Once he was outside, he set off purposefully in an easterly direction. It took only a few minutes before he arrived at his destination. A café. At its front, on the pavement, were several tables and chairs, covered by a large black awning that provided shade in the summer, but the cold autumn day meant that the outside seating held little attraction for customers, other than the one huddled over a cup of tea or coffee and smoking a cigarette. Tomlinson opened the glass panelled door and entered.

The inside of the café was huge. Deceptively so from what could be seen on the outside. It was also busy, considering the time of day. There were booths and benches down one wall and round metal tables and metal chairs filled the floor, most of them occupied, mainly by youngsters. On the right-hand side, as he entered, was the counter, displaying cupcakes and huge oatmeal biscuits under a glass dome. A modern coffee machine hugged the wall behind the counter and two staff members fought each other for space as they prepared orders and served customers. Tomlinson ordered a coffee and found a table, one of the round metal ones, close to a wall. In a corner of the café was an old fashioned and noisy pinball machine.

Next to that was a Wurlitzer juke box, straight out of a 1950's movie. He couldn't tell whether it was real or reproduction. In the opposite corner was a bright red London telephone box. It was an original, George V phone box, with a letter box on the back, displaying the G R symbol of George Rex. The café owners had positioned it so that the letter box was on display, but the phone box could still be accessed. It was the phone box that was the reason he had undertaken his journey.

Tomlinson had discovered the café a few years previous. He had been in Brockley attending a meeting with a group of campaigners who were trying to put together a strategy to overturn some local Planning decisions. His reputation as a focussed strategist with many successful campaigns under his belt had led them to make contact, hoping to persuade him to come on board and help them gain the level of public support needed to make the Local Authority revisit their decisions. The only problem was that, as soon as their meeting touched on the specifics of the matters that they wanted addressing, Tomlinson had made it clear that they were wasting their time, and his, for that matter, not the least because he agreed with the Planning decisions.

Needless to say, they were extremely unhappy with him and were quite vocal and somewhat threatening as he left the room and the building. Tomlinson was not a fighter. He wasn't a coward. Quite the opposite. He was well known for confronting anyone on any issue of which he had an opinion. He was a capable and competent advocate and could argue a point and present a case better than most. If there was an argument to be had, Tomlinson was the person who was likely to win it. But he wasn't a fighter. He never had been and on those relatively rare occasions where someone that disliked him squared up to him, once he realised that he could not talk, discuss, or argue his way out of the situation, he would retreat and find a way to escape. On that particular day he had managed to escape, but only after being jostled and pushed by a couple of the larger men in the room. He had been a little shaky and trembling on adrenalin as he had headed back towards the station and when he saw the café with its interesting name of 'Sinatra's', he took the opportunity to get a coffee and a seat and calm down.

And he had been intrigued by the telephone box. When he investigated it, he had discovered that it held a working pay phone inside. In a world where almost everyone had a mobile phone almost permanently glued to their hand, the idea of someone still using a payphone amused him.

But it had also given him an idea.

Given his general unpopularity, particularly within the walls of Westminster, he was fairly certain that his communications were monitored. It could be MI5, Whitehall, the Press, or, for all he knew, all of them, but in an entirely non-paranoid fashion, he was sure that his mobile, office and home phones were all regularly listened to. He was also fairly sure that, on occasion, he was followed, which meant that, if he chose to use a public phone box anywhere near his office or his home, there was a chance that he would be observed and that particular phone would then be compromised and, no doubt, listened to on some future occasion.

But the phone box in Sinatra's gave him a sense of security and anonymity. Since first discovering it, should he need to make a call to someone and should he need to be certain, well, as certain as he could be, that no one was listening, he would travel south of the river, by various means, although the Tube and the train were the simplest, and he would use the George V pillar box red call box to do so. The phone itself was the latest British Telecom version of payphone, not the old-fashioned slot style device that accepted 2p and 10p coins. It didn't matter. He always ensured that he had the correct denomination to use in the machine.

He followed his usual routine. When he had finished his coffee, he returned to the queue at the counter and ordered a fresh one, before moving to a different free table to drink it. He had been his usual cautious self while travelling, but this seemingly innocuous manoeuvre within the café allowed him the opportunity to check further whether anyone was paying any attention to, or interest in him. By the time that he had finished his second coffee, he was confident that he hadn't been followed to the café.

He stood and walked to the phone box, opening the heavy door, and letting it swing slowly shut behind him as he entered. He lifted the receiver and dropped a pound coin into the opening at the top of the phone, before dialling a number that he had committed to memory and never written down.

Moments later, the call was answered with a disinterested "Hello."

"It's me," said Tomlinson.

"I'd gathered," came the reply, the voice holding a faint Scottish accent. "I can't think of anyone else that would use a landline these days."

"We have a problem," said Tomlinson.

"We?" was the response. "There is no 'we'. There is you and there is me. You ask me if I am willing to do a job and, if I am, and the money is right, the job gets done. When the job is done, it is done. No 'we'. Just 'you' and just 'me'".

Tomlinson bristled at the man's arrogance. "Well therein

lies the problem. The job is not done," he said, his tone clearly angry, but his voice not raised.

"From everything that I have seen on the various media outlets," said the voice. "I would say that the job is very definitely done. And by the way, just in case this is what you are angling at, I don't do refunds."

"Don't be an idiot," said Tomlinson. "That's not why I'm calling. You didn't check his house on the island. There was a note. A shopping list."

The phone was silent for a short while and Tomlinson watched the numbers on the phone count down in pence and reached into his pocket to find another pound coin to top up the meter.

"How do you know?" came the reply, eventually.

"A reporter. Zoe Carlson. She's been sniffing around for a few weeks and somehow she has got hold of this note and also claims to have a recording from him telling her that he was coming back to London to spill the beans for her."

"I don't see how that is my problem," was the reply. "As I've said. The job is done."

Tomlinson bristled again. "The job is not fucking done if it doesn't look like a suicide, and as far as I know, most people planning to commit suicide don't leave a fucking shopping list for their cleaner."

The line was silent again.

"There's another issue," said Tomlinson. "She claims to have a photograph of you."

The silence was longer this time. "Go on," the voice eventually said.

"I don't know the details," said Tomlinson. "I've had a call from her editor, but I don't think he has the details either. She's freelance, so she will no doubt be holding onto everything until she's ready with her story, but he's talking about disclosure to the police."

"I thought that you could deal with that kind of shit?" said the voice.

"I can," said Tomlinson. "The police are the easy part. What I can't control is her publishing a story, with photographs of you."

The pause was so long this time that Tomlinson had to deposit a third pound coin into the machine to avoid being cut off.

"It will be a new job," said the voice.

"Oh, come on!" said Tomlinson.

"A new job," he repeated. "If you want this sorting, the same terms as the last will apply."

"Fine!" said Tomlinson, angry with himself for not anticipating this. "I've got a rough idea where she lives...", he was cut off by the interruption.

"Don't worry about that," the voice said. "I can find her. I only need a name."

The line went dead, and Tomlinson replaced the receiver. He looked around the café once more from the inside of the phone box, making one final check that he wasn't being observed, before opening the door and then leaving the café, heading back to the train station and his return journey to his office.

CHAPTER NINE

Zoe was on the train back to London. Michael Frazier had accompanied her to the train station at Portsmouth Harbour and had waited with her near to the barriers until the details of her train flashed up on the television screens hanging from the walls, high enough to be well out of anyone's reach. She had then given him instructions about what questions to ask at the van hire company, before leaning in and giving him a quick peck on the cheek. It hadn't meant anything. It was almost reflex. But Michael Frazier beamed with pleasure as he watched her walk through the turnstile and out towards the platform.

She'd missed the quicker train. This one took forty-five minutes longer to get into Waterloo, but she spent the entire journey in a state of excitement. She was planning out the details of her article in her head, again regretting that she hadn't picked up her laptop when she'd left the apartment. Benjamin Sharp had clearly been poisoned by something from Broughton Stretton. Something that would cause the Government embarrassment, so they had attempted to cover it up by issuing some ridiculous story about a small biological leak that had now been cleaned up and fixed. Sir Julian Hebburn, one person who would, without question, know whether or not that story from the Government was true, or just a steaming pile of bullshit, had obviously taken himself away for a few days of, no doubt, guilt ridden contemplation, before deciding that he had to come clean and blow the whistle about the cover up. He had chosen Zoe as the one to whom he intended to spill those beans and she had the telephone message that proved, well, in her mind it proved, that his intention was to spill the beans and give her the full story. And that's when someone had found out about his intentions and decided to remove Sir Julian from the picture, trying to make it look like either a tragic accident or a suicide. Something that Zoe was now confident, given the note left on Sir Julian's kitchen table, was not suicide, or an accident, but a killing. A murder. A hit.

But who?

Who would a 'dastardly deeds' story about Broughton Stretton hurt the most?

It had to be Government. It was unlikely that such a story would be so damaging to DEFRA, though. Sir Julian was a principled man and, Zoe was confident, was not the type that would condone, or permit any unscrupulous activity anywhere, and certainly not at the widely scrutinised and mistrusted Broughton Stretton, about which various activists had made all manner of frightening allegations over the years.

Now, Sir Nigel Beswick, on the other hand. That oleaginous head of the Ministry of Defence. Zoe could readily imagine that he would have his slimy hands in some nefarious activity at the mysterious scientific facility. And he would be absolutely horrified at the very idea that he might face public scrutiny and any embarrassment that might come about because of it. Yes, she thought. He wouldn't have any qualms about having the scientists develop some dangerously toxic substance, or the like, and, furthermore, he wouldn't suffer any guilt pangs about an innocent member of the public being harmed by whatever it was that had been developed.

No, Sir Nigel Beswick wouldn't take time away to contemplate on the rights or wrongs of whatever he might have been responsible for. His only interest was power.

As was that of the other potential player in her scenario, Daniel Tomlinson. The unelected Civil Servant who was the puppet master of so many individuals in high-ranking positions, whether in business or in Government. Nobody doubted that Daniel Tomlinson had full knowledge of everything, approved or otherwise, that went on behind the doors of the various Government Departments. It followed that, if the MoD, or Sir Nigel, were getting their respective hands filthy, Daniel Tomlinson would know all about it. He might even be the one directing it. At the very least, there would exist an implied permission from him that Sir Nigel and his team could do whatever it was that they were doing. If he didn't want it to happen, it just wouldn't happen.

Her editor had called her gleefully after speaking with Tomlinson that morning and joyfully recounted the reaction of Tomlinson when it was disclosed that there was evidence that Sir Julian had no intention of committing suicide.

"It was fabulous!" he'd said to Zoe when he called. "I could hear his teeth grinding when I told him that you have a recording of Hebburn announcing a 'tell all'. And I bet there was steam coming out of his ears when I mentioned the photos of your suspect. I tell you, Zoe. I would love to get one over on that arrogant prick. If he is mixed up in this, even only a little, I want to see him finished."

Zoe was confident that he must be mixed up in it. She recalled how quickly he had become 'available' when she had telephoned Sir Nigel, having been fobbed off by Tomlinson's, or Downing Street's secretary, whichever it was. The only thing that she struggled to believe, was that either Tomlinson or Sir Nigel would order a kill. That was the stuff of spy stories, wasn't it? Was it credible that a senior Civil Servant would sanction the killing, the assassination, of another senior Civil Servant? She struggled with that.

Eventually, the train rolled into Waterloo station and Zoe made her way down the platform, through the turnstiles and down to the Underground, where she took the Jubilee Line to Bond Street, from where she walked the rest of the way to her apartment building. She lived in an affluent part of the City, the street immediately to the front of her building was pedestrianised and lined with pop-up stalls selling all manner of expensive products. The entrance to Zoe's building was situated behind one of these pop-up stalls. It held a large, wide, white front door, slightly recessed in a small archway, with buzzers for the eight apartments fixed to the stone of the arch, and letterboxes for each, neatly spaced in the centre of the wood.

As she entered the building, closing the door behind her, she opened the letterbox assigned to her apartment. She used her key, but even as she turned the lock, she could see that she hadn't closed it properly last time she had looked in it and the flap at the top was not secured down. It was fine, though. There was nothing in it.

Her apartment was on the third, and top floor. She rushed up the stairs, excited at the prospect of opening her laptop and commencing her writing. She was beginning to wonder whether there was enough information and speculation for her to serialise the piece, thereby gaining greater notoriety and impact as it ran over a couple of editions. Or could it be a couple of weeks? The excitement built.

She slid her key into the lock on her apartment door and pushed it open.

Straightaway she could see that she had been burgled. The front door opened into an open plan living area where she could see that cushions had been strewn around the floor, the sofa upturned and slashed open from the bottom by a knife or other sharp instrument, her small bookcase lay face down on the floor, although the books were strewn around the room and her vinyl records, her favourites, her prized possessions, lay in and out of their sleeves, dotted and broken around the wooden floorboards.

Zoe's mouth fell open in shock. She dropped her small bag and rushed through the rest of the apartment. Every room was the same. Furniture was overturned, drawers were pulled out of units and upturned on the floor, the chairs, the bed. Her clothes were strewn around the floor. The whole place was ransacked. She was both furious and dismayed that someone could do this to her. Back and forth she went, retracing her steps into each room with disbelief at the mess and seemingly wanton damage. Eventually, she had the presence of mind to call the police. After confirming with Zoe that the burglar was not still on the premises, the police despatcher informed her that it could be a few hours before anyone could attend. Apparently, they were busy and dealing with various serious incidents and, so long as she wasn't in any imminent danger, she wouldn't be prioritised.

She returned the sofa to its correct position and sat down,

elbows on her knees and her head in her hands. She looked around the living area and shook her head in frustrated disbelief. Then she stood and walked to the front door, certain that it had been locked. There was no damage to the door or the lock, so, whoever had gained entry either had a key or could pick locks. Zoe swore to herself a couple of times and closed the door, before returning back to the sofa and the same position with her head in her hands. Eventually, her thoughts turned to her laptop. Jumping to her feet and remembering that it had been in the bedroom, she moved quickly to check that it was still there.

It wasn't.

"Fuck!" she shouted, lifting up items of clothing and bedding to see if anything was underneath, then dropping to her knees and looking under the bed. No good. It was definitely gone. She searched the whole of the apartment, but the laptop was nowhere to be seen. Oddly, though, nothing else appeared to have been taken. The more she searched, the more certain she became that the only thing missing was her laptop computer.

An idea began to formulate in her mind, and she telephoned her editor. She wanted to know more about what he had said to Tomlinson.

"Don't go there, Zoe," said Eric, her editor. "You can't be accusing someone like Tomlinson of burglary without some pretty compelling evidence. He'll have you for libel."

"But who else could it be?" she said. "The only thing missing is my laptop and you told Tomlinson that I've got photos and a recording. It would be reasonable for him to think they would be stored on a computer. He doesn't know they're on my phone. Why else was nothing taken?"

"Seriously, Zoe," said Eric. "Not a good idea. Write your story based on the evidence you have. Come into the office tomorrow and I'll loan you a laptop. You can make your inferences and suggestions about what happened to Hebburn but stick to that story. If you start making allegations that the Prime Minister's Chief of Staff has somehow broken into your home to steal your computer, not only will you be vilified by him, but you'll undermine the real story."

She knew he was correct. After the phone call, she began to tidy up, until there was a knock on the door and two uniformed police officers came to take her statement. One of them, the male, looked around the apartment, whilst the female talked to Zoe. The police officers were kind and understanding, but they were also disappointingly honest as they explained to Zoe that the likelihood of recovering her property, or catching the burglar, was slim, to say the least. When they left, she went to the fridge to seek out wine or other alcohol. But the fridge was bare.

"Looks like it's the pub, then," she said to herself. She changed into fresh clothes, once she had picked most of them up from the floor and donned a hat and coat before heading out to her most regular haunt. The pub occupied the corner spot of two roads and was a ten-minute walk from where she lived. It was popular with diners and drinkers and when she entered, was busy with couples hunched over menus preparing to order dinner and groups of office workers standing around the bar and debating whether or not to have another one before heading home for the evening. Zoe squeezed past a group of them and wedged her way into the corner of the bar, just by the hatch. She hitched herself up onto the barstool and surveyed the bar. The barman recognised her and when she nodded in reply to his silent mouthed "The usual?", he poured her a large glass of white wine and placed it on the bar in front of her.

A faint hint of heartburn as she took a swig from the glass reminded her that she hadn't eaten anything since breakfast, and so she caught the eye of the barman once more and asked for a menu. One of the pub's well known large, crusty sandwiches would do. She'd liked this place for a number of years because it weirdly offered anonymity in a bustling, friendly and welcome environment. She could sit quietly and alone, and no one would bother her, yet at the same time she felt like she was a part of the groups of people. If she thought about it, she was fairly confident that she had never been hit on in there. Well, apart from the faintest of flirting from the barman, who seemed to be working every time she visited the place. The customers were, in the main, couples, or groups of friends, or those dropping in as part of a daily routine that formed part of the commute. Zoe had frequently sat at the bar with her laptop resting on top of it, typing away furiously and fuelling her thought processes with a couple of glasses of the House white, whilst the rest of the world, or at least that part of London, milled around her without paying her any heed.

She was on her second glass by the time that the sandwich arrived. She didn't ordinarily drink so fast, but her emotions were high today. She was excited about the story and at the same time feeling angry and violated by the break-in of her home. A number of times her hand went to her jeans pocket and tapped the bulge of her phone, reassuring herself that she still had the evidence that would justify the article that she would produce. If Tomlinson was responsible for the removal of her laptop, and the more she thought about it, the more she was convinced of it, he would be disappointed when he found that there was nothing of relevance to this case on there, apart from some preliminary notes of the conversations with Eloise Sharp and Dr Emery of the HazMat team. But it still made her angry. She finished a third large glass of wine and beckoned for a fourth.

"Is it a celebration, or something?" asked the barman with a smile. Zoe frowned questioningly. "That's your fourth."

"Just a bad day," said Zoe. Her tone of voice told the barman that she wasn't in the mood for chatting, so he cleared away the plate that held just a few crumbs of the sandwich she had eaten and left her to her thoughts. And wine.

She contemplated a fifth, but thought better of it, particularly after almost taking a tumble at one point when she left the barstool to go to the toilet. She'd looked in the mirror over the sinks in the toilet and chastised herself for being pissed. The barman had to remind her that she had a bill to pay as she was about to leave, so she knew it was a sensible time to call it a night. The cold night air didn't sober her up, as such, but it shocked her brain into a sharper focus than it had enjoyed in the warm buzz of the pub. She stood in the doorway for a moment, preparing to walk back to her apartment, but still fuming over the break-in.

A sudden resolve took hold of her and she turned away from the direction of home and marched purposefully towards the taxi rank. A short drive later saw her climbing out of the black cab and onto the pavement of a quiet street of expensive town houses. They all had steps leading up to the front door and others leading down to cellars. These kinds of properties were all over London and the majority had been turned into flats or apartments, but in this street, in this very affluent area, the residents enjoyed ownership of the whole building, rather than a couple of converted rooms. She stood at the foot of the stairs leading up to a polished black front door of one of the houses, contemplating what she would say.

It was the house of Daniel Tomlinson. She, like most of the media, knew where he lived, not the least because there would often be a pack of them waiting on the street right where she now stood ready to shout questions and, sometimes, ridiculous accusations at him as he left his home to head for work. They would jostle up against him, almost hugging him, as he fought through them to the car that would be waiting for him and they would still shout questions and take photographs, cameras flashing, even as the vehicle drove away. Zoe had always been above that hyena like method of journalism and had never been one of the pack, pressing up against someone and shouting pointless questions in the certain knowledge that they would not be answered.

But she nevertheless knew where Daniel Tomlinson lived. And the light peeking through a gap in the curtains of the downstairs bay window told her that he was home. With an angry determination, she climbed the steps to the large black door. There was a doorbell, but that wouldn't give her the same satisfaction as pounding on the wood with the side of her fist, so that's what she did, stopping for a brief moment in order to listen for any sign that someone was coming, before resuming her pounding again, this time interspersed with her shouting his name.

"Tomlinson!" she shouted, the side of her hand beginning to hurt. "Where's my computer? I know it was you." Her voice lowered as she completed the sentence with a quieter "Bastard."

She heard footsteps on the other side of the door, followed by the sliding of a well-oiled bolt, before the door opened inwards. Tomlinson stood on a parquet floor just inside, glowering at her.

"I have children in bed, Miss Carlson," he said through his teeth, recognising her immediately.

"You broke into my home," she snarled back at him.

Tomlinson stiffened and stood up taller. "I beg your pardon?" he said.

Zoe blew air through pursed lips. "Don't play the indignant innocent with me," she said. "I know it was you. You broke into my home and you stole my computer."

A voice in the house called to enquire who was there. "Nobody," called back Tomlinson, half turning his head, before again facing Zoe, and lowering his voice. "Just some drunk." He smiled annoyingly.

"I want my computer back," said Zoe, her voice a little slurry now, almost as if Tomlinson had reminded her that she had been drinking.

"I'm afraid that I have no idea what you are talking about, Miss Carlson," replied Tomlinson. "Now do yourself a favour and leave before I call the police."

"Call them," she retorted. "They can arrest you for breaking into my apartment. Bastard." Her voice raised as she uttered the insult and Tomlinson stepped forward over the threshold.

"I've already told you," he snarled. "I have children in bed. Now lower your voice and leave."

"Pah!" was all she could muster. She turned and took the first step down towards the pavement, wavering a little and reaching out for the iron rail that descended alongside. "You won't find anything on it, anyway. I've got the evidence I need on you and when I tell the police about the letter in a certain cottage on the Isle of Wight, I think they'll be paying you a visit, Mr Tomlinson."

She stopped at the foot of the stairs and turned a smug smile in his direction. He was smiling back at her. "I really don't think that is very likely, Miss Carlson," he said, before stepping back over the threshold of his home and closing the front door.

Zoe was confused as to why her threat hadn't resonated more with him. She walked slowly away from the house, weaving a little now and then. She had to walk for quite a while before she saw a cab that she could flag down to take her home. As she sat in the back and thought about everything that had happened over the previous days and her anger with Tomlinson, a worrying idea occurred to her. Taking her phone out of her jeans pocket, she searched for the contact details of Michael Frazier and pressed dial. It rang for a long time before his sleepy voice answered.

"Michael," said Zoe. "You need to go back to that house and get that letter."

"I thought we were leaving it for the police," he said.

"Not anymore," replied Zoe. "You need to get it and keep it somewhere safe."

"It will have to be tomorrow, now," said Frazier. "I'm in bed, and anyway, there aren't any crossings at this time of night."

"First thing," commanded Zoe, before hanging up.

CHAPTER TEN

The man in the picture, captured on Zoe's phone, caught by the cameras on the ferry as he drove his van aboard the boat and when he had walked across its deck, following Sir Julian Hebburn, was not called John Smith. His real name was Andrew McDermott, although for this particular assignment, he used the name John Smith. He had used it before on several occasions and had the necessary identification documents to serve as proof that he was, in fact, John Smith, in the same way that he had the necessary identification documents for his other pseudonyms, his Derreck Stone, Carl Manson and Phillip Greenwood, to name but a few. The alias chosen generally depended on a number of factors, not the least who was commissioning his services, but also where in the country, or abroad, he was required to travel and, in some cases, what his particular mission was. In most cases, his client would know which name to instruct, based on their own understanding of what was required for any specific job.

Some of his aliases had very specific qualifications and even, for a limited few, credible reputations which served to ensure that he could insert himself into the right location and situation that was required for the task at hand. Others were simply a nobody, employed to carry out a short duration role and then disappear into the unknown again.

John Smith was such a nobody. Whenever McDermott, or one of his clients, called upon John Smith to be his alias it was to carry out a job of short duration, intended to stir up little or, preferably, no interest from other parties, particularly the Authorities. He was an 'in and out' man whose aim was to neutralise a target quickly and then walk away whilst passers-by thought they were witnessing a heart attack, or an unfortunate accident. For example, the man on the packed rush hour Underground train, bodies squeezed like sardines in a tin all around him as the smallest of needles, unobserved by anyone, pressed into his thigh and injected a substance that would bring on convulsions within the hour and death minutes later. Or the woman in her car, driving on an icy road in the dark, returning from her lover, heading home to her husband, and nudged ever so gently, at just the right angle from the rear, to cause the vehicle to skid, for her to lose control, and her life, as her car smashed nose first into a tree.

Everything he did he planned out meticulously, devising bespoke plans to fit the circumstances of his surroundings, so that the job always went smoothly, and he was never called back to clean up any mess or fallout.

Never.

That's why he was so angry about this particular job. An instruction from a new client, who he had vetted and re-vetted and then led through a myriad of checks and traps to ensure he wasn't being set up, had ended with a perfect result. There had been an element of good fortune about it, that had actually meant that he had completed the task sooner than expected. He remembered the pleasant surprise that he had felt as he had watched his quarry cross over to the darkened side of the ferry returning from the Isle of Wight to the mainland. Even at that point he hadn't determined what exactly he was going to do.

As Smith had followed him across the deck, surreptitiously checking that he wasn't being observed, he had quickly formulated the idea that he could just throw him overboard, so long as his body positioning was in Smith's favour. When his target had turned towards him, half leaning against the railing, John Smith realised immediately that the stars were aligned and, without thinking more about it, took a single step, his left hand grabbing at chest height, his right at the groin, his knees bending and then a lift and a forward step, pushing upwards and forwards, and the man was gone.

It was inspired, silent and perfect.

Or so he thought. He hadn't expected a nosy reporter to start searching through CCTV footage from the ferry.

When Andrew McDermott had determined that it would be John Smith who would undertake this particular assignment, there hadn't been a plan to set things up to look like a suicide. The problem that had arisen subsequent to what he thought was the completion of his task was that his target had been high profile, unlike so many of his others, and the media had devoured the story of the man falling overboard. The story of a possible suicide and any associated scandal had made the Press positively salivate, which meant that, if any evidence came to light that it hadn't been a suicide, the Press and other media would devour that as hungrily as the first story and add to it, embellishing it, feeding the perceived need of their viewers and readers, that it must be a conspiracy, there must be something horrible going on in the darkest corridors of power. The fact that they might be accurate in their assessment was neither here nor there to him.

McDermott couldn't care less. He couldn't give two shits about politics, conspiracy theories, the Press, or anything else, for that matter. He was a professional who had a solid reputation for completing whatever task was at hand, without any fallout or unnecessary drama, unless drama was required of course. That was why he was well paid.

When he had completed a job, he fished. He had a small seaside home on the east coast of England, in an unexciting seaside town that had nothing much going for it except a clean beach and a long pier, and he sat at the end of that pier, sometimes during the day, sometimes overnight, with a twelve-foot fishing rod and a sea line and hooks, casting out into the cold waters of the North Sea. That was his true passion.

But now, this time, this new client, new job, and high-profile target, meant that, for the first time in his professional career, there were matters, after the act, to clean up. It was out of his comfort zone. It meant that too many variables were in play, rather than the one single task of despatching his target, the task that normally constituted, for him, an ordinary 'day at the office'.

He had been walking for about fifteen minutes in the bright sunshine and cold air when he arrived at his destination, crossed the car park where twenty or more vehicles were parked and opened the door to the reception area. The room beyond was quite small with a reception desk, rising to chest height, facing the door and a couple of plastic chairs to the left of the entrance, next to a self-service coffee machine, the kind that dispensed drinks in small plastic cups, normally too hot to handle when full.

McDermott walked straight to the desk and placed his driving licence on the top, displaying his unsmiling face and his name, John Smith.

"I need a small van for twenty-four hours," he said bluntly. "One of the VWs or the Fords will do. I've used you before."

One thing neither McDermott nor John Smith were renowned for was small talk.

The man behind the reception desk looked at McDermott and then at Smith's face on the driving licence and then turned to the large flat computer screen to one side of the desk. He moved the computer mouse and typed something with the keyboard below the top of the reception desk and out of sight from the customer side of it.

"Oh, yeah," he said. "Here you are. You had the little Courier last time." It wasn't a question, but a statement of fact without any obvious need for confirmation. "Same one is available if you want it. Same price as well."

"Yes," said John Smith, flatly, as he took a wallet burgeoning with cash out of his pocket, opened it, removed the necessary amount of notes and deposited them on the counter."

The young man looked at the wallet with wide eyes. "Wow. Balling!" he said.

Smith had no idea what the man meant. "Do you have something for me to sign?" he asked.

"Oh, sorry, yes," said the young man, clicking somewhere on the screen to print the paperwork and then reaching behind himself to the printer that shoved the paper out in stunted motions. He marked the sections requiring a signature with a squiggly cross and turned the papers around for Smith, offering him the pen. As Smith scrawled a well-practiced signature on each of the necessary parts of the form, the young man watched him intently. "I could let you have some information as well," he said. "You know, if you made it worth my while."

Smith pushed the signed forms, the pen resting on top of them, back across the counter to the man. He stared at him, saying nothing.

The young man began to feel nervous, deciding that he had stepped over a line with this scary looking stranger. "I'm sorry," he stuttered. "I didn't mean to ... well, nothing. I didn't mean nothing."

Smith continued to stare at him. "Keys," he said, eventually.

The man spurred into action. "Shit!" he said. "Sorry, didn't mean that. To swear." He turned to a large board behind him that held lots and lots of single ignition keys attached by small pieces of white string to cardboard fobs displaying registration numbers in black felt tip. When he found the one that he needed he turned and placed it on the counter in front of Smith. But John Smith didn't pick up the key and instead stood looking at the young man in silence, waiting.

Eventually, terrified that this situation was going to end very badly for him, the young man started talking.

"Some guy came in asking about you," he said. "He knew your name and he had a picture of you, and he was asking questions like, have I seen you before and, do I know anything about you and, why did you hire the van..." his voice trailed off in fear, whilst John Smith's face remained completely expressionless.

"He works on the ferries," the man continued, lamely. "Michael Frazier. He asked me to call him if I saw you again." The man's voice began to tremble. John Smith's expression had not changed at all throughout, almost as if he hadn't been listening. Except that his eyes told a different story. They were murderous and the man behind the reception counter at the van rental hire company quite literally began to tremble in fear. His hands began to scrabble around his clothing, in and out of pockets, until he found a small piece of paper and with a look of palpable relief, he placed it down in front of Smith.

"There you are," he almost gasped. "That's him. That's his number."

Smith looked down at the piece of paper, then picked it up and put it in his pocket. He picked up the ignition key for the van and dropped that into his trouser pocket, before turning and beginning to walk away. Then he stopped, much to the terror of the man behind the reception counter, before turning around again, drawing out his wallet, opening it and extracting two notes and dropping them on the counter in front of him.

"Say nothing," Smith commanded. The young man nodded furiously, grabbing the money, and shoving it into his own trouser pocket.

As Smith drove towards the ferry terminal, he wondered what, if anything, he should do with the phone number that he had just acquired. He wasn't convinced that ringing the number would achieve anything. More likely, it would stir up more interest and suspicion, no doubt leading to further speculation from the reporter, Zoe Carlson, and serving to achieve quite the opposite of what he currently wanted; to tie up loose ends and close the file, so to speak. By the time that he parked the small van in the waiting area at Portsmouth ferry terminal, his mind was made up. He would do nothing with the number. He entered the building at the front of the terminus and bought a return ticket to the island, then returned to the vehicle, placing the printout that had been given to him on the dashboard.

He stood on the deck of the boat as it crossed the Solent, taking in the views and the fresh morning air. Watching the water chopping about, creating frothing rims on the tips of the waves made him miss his little home and his favourite pier and the peace and solitude he enjoyed as he spent hour after hour, often fruitless, fishing from the end of it. He wondered whether this job and the fact that he had something to clean up for the first time ever in his career, was an omen, a sign, that perhaps, now was a good time to think about retirement. After all, he could afford to retire. He was still young, only in his late forties, and had accumulated quite a substantial amount of money over the years, safely deposited in various accounts, pensions and other investments, including properties, both at home and overseas, providing regular rental incomes, or just accumulating value as time passed by. All of his assets were spread across various aliases, just in case the day came when he might be compelled to explain his wealth, or risk losing it under some of the new laws that had been implemented by Government to restrict proceeds of crime.

It was a serious consideration over which he pondered as the vessel approached Fishbourne and he heard the tannoy instructing all passengers to return to their vehicles. It started to become more than a consideration as he drove from the boat and onto the island, heading up to the main road and turning left towards Ryde. The thought in his head was now becoming a desire, a plan, a determination. He'd never really given any serious thought about what he would do once he decided to stop killing people for money. It wasn't as if he enjoyed what he did. It was just something that he was exceptionally good at. And he didn't suffer from any remorse, or feelings of guilt about what he did. Each job was just that, a job, and it was his responsibility to complete the job to the best of his ability. He didn't question the jobs. They were undoubtedly deserving targets, whatever they may have done, but, in any event, someone, on each occasion, had their own valid reason for wanting another person dead. It wasn't random, or terrorism, something that he would never be involved in, it was targeted, reasoned and rational.

Smith parked the van at the end of the lane that led to Sir Julian's cottage. He sat and watched for a while, ever cautious, always looking for any indication that he was under observation, or that something was out of place, suspicious. Once he was happy that he hadn't been followed and that everything looked ordinary and as it should be, he climbed out of the vehicle and walked down the narrow footpath that led to the front gate. The lane was deserted. Nevertheless, he paused and looked carefully in each direction before he was satisfied that it was safe to enter. He headed straight for the passageway that led around to the back of the house. He remembered the layout of the front and rear gardens from when he had first looked around, when he was formulating his plan as to how and when he would kill Sir Julian. He'd considered doing it at the house, perhaps a fall downstairs and a broken neck, but he hadn't finalised the plan in his mind before the unexpected opportunity had presented itself on the ferry. Once more he questioned whether he had made a mistake in taking that opportunity, instead of waiting and watching and finalising a methodology that would not have prompted some nosy journalist to start investigating.

Smith stopped dead in his tracks. The rear door of the property was wide open, the key still in the outer lock. He swivelled his head instinctively, scanning the small rear garden, ensuring that no one was out there. Satisfied, he stepped quietly over the threshold, his intention being to find the handwritten note and then leave before whoever was in the house saw him. His problem was that he didn't know whereabouts in the house the note was. He stepped into the kitchen and cast his eye quickly over the work surfaces and the kitchen table, but there was no note in sight.

He paused and listened for any noises or movement within the property. He couldn't hear anything, so he quietly moved into the hallway and then into the front room. That was also empty and looking around the room, there was no sign of a note.

Somewhere in the house a floorboard creaked, and John Smith stiffened, immediately standing still, and listening intently. Footsteps began to descend the stairs, so Smith stepped further into the front room and behind the door so that there was no chance of being seen from the hallway. The footsteps arrived at the bottom of the stairs and Smith could hear them turn at the front door and pause. Perhaps, whoever it was, would leave via the front, rather than retracing their steps through to the back of the house. That would save John Smith having to confront them and instead leave him at liberty to search the place for the note that he had come looking for.

But the front door remained closed and instead, he heard the footsteps move past the front room and down the hall to the kitchen. A moment later he heard the rear door close. He waited for what felt like an eternity, listening intently for any sign of the footsteps returning, and then, satisfied that the other person had left, he moved from behind the door and stepped into the hallway.

A man stood motionless in his way, startling Smith in a manner that he was very unused to.

"Who the fuck are you?" asked the man.

Instinct and training took over and Smith sprang into action, stepping forward quickly, his right hand clenching into a fist as his powerful right arm lashed forward, his knuckles connecting with the man's windpipe, causing him to bend forward, his hands clutching at his throat. Smith grabbed the man's head, his huge hands grabbing the ears and pulling the head down with force whilst at the same time stepping forward with his right knee raised, slamming the man's face into his knee, the nose being crushed under the force and blood spurting out in a starburst. The impact sent the man reeling backwards, still clutching at his throat, gargling and gasping noises coming from his mouth.

Smith stepped over the man and leant down, grasping hold of the thick collar of his blue coat and then, standing upright, dragged him along the short hallway and into the kitchen. The man's legs flailed about, trying to gain some purchase to enable him to stand, one hand still clutching at his throat, the other slapping and grabbing at Smith's hand, trying to break its grip of his collar. Smith dragged him across the tiled kitchen floor towards the cupboards and work surfaces, on which the kitchen knife block stood that he had observed when he had first entered the house. With his free hand he pulled one of the knives from the block, then he turned, released his grip on the man's collar and, crouching down grabbed the man's hair with the same hand, pulling his head back and then with the other hand swiftly and dispassionately drawing the knife across his throat. Blood appeared, but the knife was not very sharp and hadn't sliced as deeply as Smith had intended.

Adrenalin was now driving the thrashing body of the man on the ground as Smith frowned at the blade before leaning in to try a second slice. But the man broke free. Scrabbling away on his back and then flipping over to his front and rising up on his knees, one hand desperately holding his bleeding throat, still gasping and gargling from the earlier punch to the throat and knee to the face. His terrified eyes stared at Smith who had stood from his crouching position, knife in hand and was moving towards him. The man tried to stand, but couldn't make his legs move normally, so he ended up falling backwards into a sitting position in which he scrambled backwards until his back was against the wall. Still his legs thrashed as he tried to stand, to push himself upright and still Smith advanced, closing the gap between them in the small kitchen.

Finally, Smith stood over the man, one foot either side of his legs which had stopped thrashing. The man's hands had dropped away from his bloodied throat and lay by his sides. His breathing was still gurgling and rasping, and his eyes stared up at Smith with terror. Smith bent over, knife in hand and lifted the man's chin, before resting the blade against his jugular, preparing to slice it open. The man's mouth opened and suddenly, unexpectedly, he leant forward and grabbed Smith's thumb with his teeth, clamping down as hard as he could, teeth breaking through flesh and tendon, down to the bone. At the same time, he threw his hand up with as much force as he could muster, straight into Smith's groin.

Smith roared with a mixture of anger and pain. He stepped back, dragging his now bloodied hand away from the man's mouth, the pain in his groin throbbing through his genitals and up to the pit of his stomach.

"You fucker!" he roared at the man who sat unmoving, but smiling through bloodied teeth, a large red V shape forming from his neck down to his shirt. Smith looked at his thumb. It was a mess, skin and flesh hanging off and the bone clearly visible. He shook his hand furiously as if that would ease the pain, then stepped forward once more, this time bringing his right foot down hard on the man's knee and bending down so that his face was inches from the other.

"Fucker!" he repeated, then thrust the knife as hard as he could through the man's shirt and chest, through his ribs and directly into his heart, all the way to the handle. The man threw back his head, his chest pushing forward, a half breath of agonising pain slipped from his throat and he died.

Smith stepped away from the body and slipped a little in a pool of blood on the kitchen tiled floor. He looked around for something that he could use to stem the blood flow from his hand, pulling out drawers from the kitchen units and letting them fall to the floor. He eventually came across one with several tea towels folded neatly inside and used one of them, tearing it into small pieces and using one to tourniquet the wound on his thumb. Once he was satisfied that it was working, he leant back against the sink and surveyed his 'work'.

What a mess, he chastised himself. He was becoming convinced that this job was cursed. His breathing began to return to normal, although the throbbing in his thumb would not subside. Moving back to the body leaning against the wall, the knife handle protruding from the chest, blood pouring from the wound, Smith crouched down and started searching through his pockets. The man's wallet had a large amount of cash in it, but no identification. There was a mobile phone in his trouser pocket and Smith tried using the man's thumb print to unlock it, but it didn't work. He cast the phone aside on the floor. In the inside pocket of the man's bloodied jacket was a piece of paper with a handwritten message on one side and a shopping list on the reverse. Smith shoved it into his own pocket and then stood up. He looked around the room again and contemplated cleaning it up, but then thought against it. There was no way he could get rid of the body. Instead, he opened the back door of the property and stepped outside, pulling it closed behind him. The key was still in the lock, but he didn't bother locking the door. Instead, he headed back to the front of the property and, having satisfied himself that no one was about, he headed back to his van.

He had some serious thinking to do. He was angry with himself that events had taken a turn in a direction that he had not planned. Things were too messy, and he still had Zoe Carlson to deal with.

CHAPTER ELEVEN

The taxi pulled to a halt outside the house and the driver looked in his rear-view mirror and rather unnecessarily read out the fare on the meter that was clearly visible from the back seat.

"Would you mind waiting?" asked Zoe. "I'll only be a minute. I've just got something to pick up."

The driver frowned. "Sorry, love. I'm not allowed to do that. Too many people do a runner."

Zoe half laughed. "Really?" she said, pointing at the house. "I'm only going there. I'll be in and out in no time."

"Sorry, love. No can do."

"Oh, for God's sake," she muttered as she opened her bag and removed her wallet. She handed cash over to the driver. "Can you at least wait for me," she said. "You can leave the meter running if you want."

The driver nodded. "Ok," he said, pocketing the notes without any consideration of the change that his passenger was due. He'd assumed the excess to be a tip.

Zoe climbed out of the back seat and crossed the road to the house. She had just put her hand on the gate when she heard the engine noise of the taxi increase and she turned around just in time to see it drive off, the cabby waving as he did so.

"Wanker!" she said quietly to herself. It was only about five thirty in the afternoon, but it was already dark, and she wanted to get back to Fishbourne as soon as she could, once she'd collected the note from the kitchen table in Sir Julian's Isle of Wight home.

She was annoyed at Michael Frazier. Well, to be fair, she was annoyed at herself for getting pissed the night before and ringing Frazier up at Lord knows what time, instructing, nay demanding, that he retrieve the handwritten note from the kitchen table. She realised that she must have sounded like a real bolshy cow, knowing what she was like when she was angry drunk. Why the bloody hell had she thought it would be a good idea to go to Tomlinson's house and confront him? It had been a rooky move. It was bad enough that her editor had already told Tomlinson about the note, rather than keeping quiet about it until they were ready to call the police, but why on earth had she felt the need to try and rub Tomlinson's nose in it.

She promised herself that she wasn't going to drink like that again. Her head felt awful, like someone had sandwiched it between two pieces of solid wood and then began pounding on them. Her mouth was dry, and her eyes were puffy and bloodshot. That's probably why the taxi driver hadn't wanted to stay. She looked pretty bloody rough and he was obviously suspicious that she was still intoxicated. She probably was.

And her stomach! Oh my God, it felt like she'd been beaten up. Her abdomen was swollen, and her insides hurt like a bastard. She must have drunk about a gallon of water throughout the day, trying to rehydrate, but the only effect it had was to make her pee a lot. She had woken late and after throwing up dry air in the toilet and trying to force down a cup of black coffee, she had remembered that she had called Frazier the night before. Not in the mood for engaging anyone in conversation and feeling a little guilty about how she had probably spoken to him at whatever ridiculous time of night it had been, she sent him a text message.

"Did you get it?"

Then she staggered into the bathroom, threw up the small amount of black coffee that she had managed to swallow, and took a hot shower. When she'd finished, she wrapped a towel around her body and another around her hair and stumbled into the bedroom, collapsing face first onto the bed. She dozed, her breath exhaling in dry puffs, blowing her lips apart and closing them again between each one.

Eventually, after an indeterminate period of time, she groaned and forced herself over onto her back and then into a sitting position. The towel on her head half unravelled and she stared at the white material as it bobbed in front of her nose. Groaning, she stood up slowly and allowed both towels to fall to the floor. Then she looked for some clothes to wear. The drawers in her bedroom were still upturned and her clothes scattered around the room. She hadn't finished tidying up before she had left for the pub last night and it crossed her mind, as she bent and picked up items of clothing, groaning at each bend, that the room wasn't going to be tidied today either.

Eventually, she was dressed in jeans and a jumper and she went back into the living room and checked her phone. Frazier hadn't replied.

She thumbed two ?? on the screen and hit send again, before flopping onto the sofa and closing her eyes. The room span and her head throbbed. Her whole body began to ache. Annoyed, she leant forward, her elbows on her knees and looked at the mobile phone on the coffee table. It remained silent. With a sigh, she picked it up and pressed dial at Frazier's number. It rang out, without an answer until eventually dropping to an automated voicemail message.

"Michael," said Zoe. "I'm sorry if I was a bitch last night, but please call me back and let me know that you have it."

She put the phone back down on the coffee table, leant back, closed her eyes and dozed. It wasn't for long and it didn't make her feel any better. She leant forward again, picked up the phone and pressed dial once more. Again, it rang to voicemail.

"Bloody hell," she muttered.

Over the next hour, she tried calling Michael Frazier multiple times, but each call only rang to voicemail. By noon, she had decided that he was either tied up on something else, work probably, or he was simply pissed off with her because she had called him so late and so wretchedly drunk. She couldn't even remember exactly what she had said to him, only hoping that it wasn't vile. She could remember most, not all, of what she had shouted, had she shouted? at Tomlinson, but all she could remember from her call to Frazier was telling him to get the note.

So, given that he was either working, or ignoring her, and given that she was genuinely concerned that Tomlinson would have someone go to Sir Julian's cottage and take the only tangible evidence that existed which could rebut the notion that Sir Julian had committed suicide, Zoe donned her coat and shoes and headed out to Waterloo, her intention to get the note herself.

A few hours later, she was walking off the ferry at Fishbourne and up towards the front of the taxi rank, explaining to the man behind the desk that she didn't know the address, but she could direct the driver to it, and now, she was pushing open the gate to Sir Julian's front garden, determined to get what she came for, but wondering how she was going to get back. She ignored the front door, remembering where the key for the back door was hidden and made her way through the pathway leading to the back of the house. It was very dark at the back and she had to fumble for her phone and find the torch app to light her way. She flashed it onto the rear door of the property and her eye fell upon the key in the lock. She paused, surprised that it should be there and not in its hiding place. For a moment, the thought crossed her mind that Frazier may have already arrived and was either inside collecting the note or had already left but forgotten to replace the key. Her mood lifted a little at the thought that, despite having to travel for hours, suffering the worst hangover that she had suffered for a long time, the note was safe and sound.

She pressed down the handle and pushed the door, following it as it opened inwards easily and noiselessly. Her phone torch light illuminated the room insofar as that kind of technology can, but also to the extent that her mind wasn't prompted to reach for the light switch by the door and to turn on the kitchen lights. Instead, she stepped into the darkened kitchen in the partial light from her mobile device. It lit up the wooden kitchen table and she could immediately see that it was bare. No note.

She lowered the phone slightly, not deliberately, just a natural movement and the light caught a large dark patch of something on the floor and then a foot, encased in a large boot came into view. Zoe jumped backwards in shock, a strange half scream coming from her throat as she nearly dropped the phone. Recovering slightly, but her heart now racing, she stepped forwards again, slowly and deliberately, arching the phone light down to the left and to the foot again and then moving it slowly and with trepidation up the leg and towards the torso.

Stepping forward, she moved the direction of the phone light quickly upwards to see who it was on the floor, but her foot suddenly slipped in whatever the dark patch was and one leg slid away at an awkward angle, causing her to tumble forwards and sidewards, almost completing the 'splits', sliding through the sticky substance on her knee and falling forward over the extended legs of the body face first, her hands flailing out in front of her, the phone sliding away under the kitchen table. She yelped, in shock, more than pain, and rolled to her right, away from the body and off the legs, trying to sit up, her hands flailing in the sticky stuff on the floor as she pushed herself away, her backside skidding on the floor.

Heart pounding, Zoe scrabbled for her phone. Reaching out, she leant to her side, sliding in the substance on the floor, until her fingers closed over the device and she pulled it close to her body before slowly, terrified, she raised it high again and let the torchlight fall onto the face of the body hunched over, leaning against the wall.

A gurgling wail came out of her throat as she recognised him. "Michael" she cried. Zoe could tell that he wasn't breathing and now she saw the brown wooden handle of the kitchen knife sticking out of his chest, with not a millimetre of the blade in sight. Her hand went to her mouth.

"Oh my God!" she cried. "Michael."

The sticky stuff was on her hand and now she had managed to get it on her face. She looked at her hand and shone the phone torch to it. Realising that it was blood, another strange noise came from her mouth and she began to wipe her face with her hand, trying to remove the blood, but only managing to spread it further over her jaw and cheek.

Horrified at the sight of Michael Frazier, bloodied, grey and dead, head hanging forward, chin on his chest in an almost sleep like pose, Zoe tapped 999 on her phone with her thumb, more of the drying, sticky blood transferring to the screen.

"Emergency, which service do you require?" said a voice.

Zoe raised the phone to her ear. "Police," she half whispered. "My friend has been stabbed."

"What's the location?" asked the voice.

Zoe looked around the kitchen fruitlessly. "I don't know the address," she said. "It's in Ryde. Up on the hill. A cottage. Number twenty, I think."

"What's your name, Miss?" asked the voice.

"Zoe," she replied, staring at Frazier. "He's dead." She started crying.

"Ok, Zoe," said the voice. "I've got help on its way to you, but I need you to help me to help them to find you."

Zoe nodded as if the voice on the line could see her.

"Can you go outside, Zoe? Can you look for a street name? Would you be able to do that?"

It took a moment for her to manage to tear her gaze away from Frazier. "Yes," she eventually said, as she put her hand to the floor and pushed herself upwards, bending her legs under her and finally managing to stand upright. Gingerly, she moved towards the back door, pressing herself up against the kitchen units as she did, her hand leaving a blood trail streaking across the edge and the surfaces, until she was past the body and at the back door.

She half ran out of the house and down the passage at the side that led to the front garden. She flung open the front gate and ran onto the street, turning left blindly and crashing into an elderly man walking his dog.

"Woah! Take it easy," shouted the man, whilst his dog, an old looking Collie, barked in surprise. The man recovered from his shock and took in the sight of Zoe, a sharp intake of breath leaving him lost for words for just a moment. "Are you ok, love? What happened?"

Zoe still had the phone pressed to her ear. The voice on the line asked if someone else was there and suggested that Zoe pass the phone to the other person. Slowly and without explanation, she did so, and as the old man took it, his mouth hanging open in shock, Zoe slumped to the ground, sitting with her back against a low garden wall and her knees bunched up to her chest, her arms wrapped around them as she sobbed.

She was still there, with the old man and his dog, when two police vehicles arrived and four uniformed officers in Hi-Viz jackets approached them. She vaguely heard the old man explaining that 'that was how I found her' and 'covered in blood, head to toe'. Two of the officers went around the back of Sir Julian's house, whilst the other two stayed with Zoe and the old man. She heard radios stutter into life and one of the officers turned away, speaking in reply.

Eventually, he turned back towards her and squatted on his haunches in front of Zoe.

"Zoe," he said. "Can you tell me what happened?"

It dawned on her that she must be in some state of shock. She struggled to think straight, or to fully understand what was happening or what was meant by the question.

"He's dead," she said, a silent tear running down her cheek

and glistening over the browning blood stain on her face.

"Who's dead, Zoe?" asked the officer.

Again, it felt like an age before she could answer. "Michael," she said.

"Who's Michael?" asked the officer. "Is he your husband?"

She shook her head.

"Boyfriend?"

Again, she shook her head.

"Can you tell me what happened, Zoe?" asked the officer. She stared blankly into the middle distance.

One of the police officers who had gone into the house re-emerged and asked to speak with the officer that was talking to Zoe. After a brief discussion, he crouched down in front of her again.

"Zoe," he said. "What happened in the kitchen? What happened to Michael?"

"He's dead," was her reply.

"I know Michael's dead, Zoe. I need you to try and remember what happened. Were you arguing? Was he trying to hurt you?"

Zoe shook her head vigorously. "No, he was like that when I found him."

Another police car pulled up next to the other two, its blue lights flashing silently and bathing Zoe and the police officers on the street in a cold strobe effect. The officers talked quietly to each other and some went inside the house and then returned, and others came out of the house and then went back in. Their personal radios chattered busily as they went.

"Zoe," said the same police officer. She continued to stare ahead. "Zoe, I need you to listen to what I have to say to you, ok?"

Zoe didn't respond.

"Zoe," he said again, placing his hand on her arm. She turned and looked up at him, her eyes glazed. "I'm going to have to place you under arrest until we find out what has happened, ok?"

She began to shake her head. "What? No," she said, realisation of what was happening beginning to dawn on her. "No, he was like that when I found him."

"You can explain all of that later, "said the officer, gently. "Right now, we need to get you off the street and to a place of safety. So, Zoe, you need to listen very carefully. I'm arresting you on suspicion of murder..."

"No!" her voice became louder. "You don't understand. I didn't do this. He was dead when I found him."

"You do not have to say anything, but it may harm your defence..."

"No," she sobbed.

"if you do not mention, when questioned, something that you later rely on in Court..."

"Please," she cried. "You don't understand. You're not listening to me."

"Anything you do say may be given in evidence. I need you to stand up for me now, Zoe," said the officer, sliding one hand up the inside of her arm and up to her armpit, then gently, but deliberately, raising her to her feet. She began to sob uncontrollably, taking in great gulps of air and expelling them with the most mournful of noises.

"I'm going to search your pockets, Zoe. Do you have anything sharp on you or anything that might cut me?" Another officer joined him on the other side of Zoe, who shook her head, still sobbing. Once he had checked the pockets of her jeans and her coat, he reached behind his back and unclipped his handcuffs from his belt, at the same time, taking hold of Zoe's wrist.

"I'm going to handcuff you for your safety and mine," he said gently.

"No!" wailed Zoe, her distress pouring out of her. "I didn't do anything."

The other officer gripped her other wrist, as the first brought the handcuffs around and gently pushed one bracelet over a wrist, before snapping the other in place over its twin. She began to sink, sobbing and wailing to her knees and both officers had to hold her up as gently as they could and lead her to one of the police cars. A third police officer opened one of the rear doors and they manoeuvred her into the back seat and then closed the door. The one that had opened the door stood guard whilst the arresting officer and his colleague went into the house, which was now lit up on the interior by what may well have been every light and lamp within.

When they had finished whatever it was that they were doing, the arresting officer and his colleague returned to the vehicle and climbed inside.

"Zoe," said the first, starting the car's engine. "We're going to go to the station now and then we'll talk through everything that's happened, ok?"

She had stopped crying. She was staring into space, not really aware of her surroundings or what was being said to her. As the car pulled away from the curb, she only vaguely comprehended what the feeling of movement meant.

When they arrived at the police station in Ryde, the car turned into the little car park at the side of the building and drove through to the area at the rear where the back entrance to the station was, which was used as the way into the custody suite for prisoners. Zoe was eased gently out of the back seat of the car by the police officer that had arrested her and led up two steps to the locked glass doors. The officer pressed a buzzer and moments later the electromagnetic lock was released, and the officer pulled the door open with his left hand, whilst he placed his right onto Zoe's back and gently moved her inside. The other policeman followed them in.

The custody suite was lit brightly by fluorescent light strips, gleaming off the white walls and floor and temporarily blinding Zoe, who flinched back momentarily.

"This way, Zoe," said the officer, as he gently directed her towards the custody Sergeant, a large, bearded man, stood behind a tall counter with a Perspex screen separating him from her and the police officers. An opening in the screen where it met the top of the counter was large enough to pass items through if needed. For the first time, Zoe noticed that the second police officer was carrying her bag and he placed it on the counter at the opening.

"Name?" said the bearded Sergeant. Zoe looked up at him through the screen, her expression vacant. "Miss," said the Sergeant. "What is your name?"

"Zoe Carlson," she mumbled.

The Sergeant turned slightly and began to tap the keys of a keyboard in front of him, whilst looking at a large flat screen to his right.

"Address?" And so it continued, date of birth, age, occupation. Then he turned to the arresting officer. "Reason for arrest?"

The officer explained that they had been called out to an incident at a domestic property following a three nines call. When they arrived, they had discovered Miss Carlson at the front of the property with an elderly gentleman and his dog. He went on to describe how it was apparent to him that Miss Carlson was in shock and given the fact that her clothes, hands and face were covered with blood, he realised that a serious incident had taken place.

At the mention of blood, Zoe looked at her hands, confusion spreading over her face. She then looked at her jeans and saw that they were smeared with blood, turning dark brown as it dried. She couldn't understand how she was covered in so much blood.

The Sergeant's fingers typed away busily as the officer continued.

"Colleagues had already entered the property, and, after some initial questioning of Miss Carlson, I entered the rear of the property where an unknown male was deceased, likely cause of death, stabbing."

"Michael Frazier," whispered Zoe.

The Sergeant stopped typing and looked at her. The arresting officer paused in his account.

"His name is Michael Frazier," repeated Zoe.

The Sergeant began typing again and the arresting officer continued.

"Scenes of Crime and the Coroner were informed, after which I returned to Miss Carlson and cautioned her, before placing her under arrest and then attending here."

"Reason given for arrest?" asked the Sergeant.

"Suspicion of murder," replied the officer, his tone matter of fact.

Zoe looked up again. "I didn't," she whispered. "He was already dead."

"Miss Carlson," said the Sergeant. "You remain under

caution, do you understand?"

Zoe looked at him blankly.

"You have the right to remain silent, Miss Carlson. You will be interviewed shortly and that will be your opportunity to explain your version of events. For now," he reached under the counter and produced a large brown paper bag, almost a sack, which he pushed through the gap in the Perspex before continuing. "I require you to change into these clothes and deposit the clothes that you are currently wearing in the same bag. This officer will take you to a cell where you can change. Do you understand?"

She didn't reply. She just stared at him.

"Number three is free," said the Sergeant to the arresting officer.

Zoe was led down a short, brightly lit corridor, to an open cell door and directed inside. The officer removed the handcuffs and handed her the paper bag and instructed her to change into the clothing. He stood in the doorway, his back to her to afford her a little modesty, as she complied, automaton like. When she had finished, now clothed in grey sweatshirt and joggers, her feet bare, she folded up her clothes, still sticky to the touch, and pushed them into the paper bag.

"Ready," she whispered, holding out the bag to the officer as he turned to face her.

He looked at her bare feet. "What size are you?" he asked.

She looked down at her toes. "Five," she said.

A few moments later he returned with some paper slippers before suggesting she make herself comfortable and closing the door. Zoe heard a heavy lock slipping into place as the key handle on the outside of the door was twisted.

CHAPTER TWELVE

She didn't know how much time had passed before the door opened again and the same officer stood in the entrance.

"Come with me, please, Zoe", he said politely.

She wasn't quite as dazed as she had been earlier and the shock that she had suffered was beginning to wane a little. She followed the police officer as he led her out of the custody suite and up a short flight of stairs to the only interview room in the small police station. He opened the door and pointed to a chair next to a table.

"Sit there, please Zoe," he said. "I'll be back in a minute."

When he returned, he was accompanied by a woman. She wore a plain, dark trouser suit, with a white blouse. Her long black hair was pulled fiercely back from her forehead and tied into a ponytail. She smiled as she entered, dropping an A4 pad of paper on the desk before the two of them sat down. The male officer had two sealed cassette tapes with him, which he opened before slotting each tape cassette into the two tape slots on the black recording device at the end of the table. Once he had closed both drives, he pressed the large red button in the centre of the machine, which then emitted a long, loud single tone beep. The digital display next to the button began to count in a red digital display.

The woman then spoke. She announced the date and time first.

"Interview with Zoe Carlson. Present in the room are Detective Sergeant Daniels," she paused and looked at her colleague.

"PC Lock," he said.

Daniels looked at Zoe. "Could you say your name for the tape, please?"

She hesitated for a moment. "Zoe Carlson," she said timidly.

"Ok," said Daniels, shifting in her chair to make herself comfortable. "Zoe, you remain under caution, do you understand?"

Zoe nodded.

"For the tape, please, Zoe."

"Yes, sorry, yes, I understand."

"Right. Earlier this evening, Zoe, my colleague PC Lock found you at," she looked down at the pad for a moment and read out the address of Sir Julian's house. "Just to confirm, Zoe. That is not your house, is it?"

She shook her head.

"For the tape?"

"No, sorry, I'm not used to this kind of thing."

"Do you know whose house it is?"

"Yes. Sir Julian Hebburn," said Zoe.

"Do you know Sir Julian?" asked Daniels.

Zoe nodded. "Sorry, yes," she said. "Well, I knew him. He's dead."

"So I understand," said Daniels. "Did you have permission to be at the property?"

"No," said Zoe. "I was going to get the note."

"What note?"

"Sir Julian left a note," she said. "It was a shopping list. It's proof that he didn't commit suicide."

Daniels paused for a moment. "Did you find the note?" she asked.

Zoe shook her head. "I didn't get chance. I saw Michael." Her hand went to her mouth, trembling, until she saw the dried blood on it and pulled it away, looking up at Daniels and then putting her hands under the table, as if they hadn't already been seen by her and Zoe was hiding them.

"It was horrible."

"Who is Michael?" asked Daniels.

"Michael Frazier. He works on the ferries. He was helping me."

"How was he helping you, Zoe?"

"To look for the note."

"Ok," said Daniels. "So, you both went to the house. What happened then?"

"No, we didn't go together," said Zoe, looking up suddenly. "He went before me. I phoned him last night and asked him to go, but he didn't call me back and wouldn't answer my calls, so I travelled down from London to go to the house myself. I thought he might be angry with me."

"Why was he angry with you, Zoe?"

She shook her head again. "I don't know if he was. I was drunk." She stopped and looked up at the two police officers. "Not today," she corrected quickly. "Last night when I called him. I was drunk and I was probably a bit," she paused, looking for the right word. "Abrupt."

"Go on," encouraged Daniels.

"I asked him to go to the house and get the note and then, this morning, I sent him a text message, well, I sent him a few, asking if he had got it, but he didn't reply. I tried phoning him a couple of times, but he didn't answer."

"This note," said Daniels.

"There's a picture on my phone," said Zoe, suddenly remembering. "If you get me my phone, I can show it to you."

"How do you have a picture on your phone, Zoe?" asked Daniels.

"Last time we were here," she explained. "I took a picture of it then."

"With Sir Julian?" asked Daniels.

Zoe looked confused. "What? No. Sir Julian was dead at that point."

"Just to be clear," said Daniels. "After Sir Julian was dead, you went to his house and took a photograph of a shopping list?"

"Yes," nodded Zoe, insistently. "It was on the kitchen table."

"How did you gain entry?" asked Daniels. "Do you have a key?"

"No. There's one under a plant pot in the back garden. It was in the door when I got there tonight."

"And how did you know it was under the plant pot?"

Zoe shrugged. "A guess. My gran used to do the same thing."

"Was Michael Frazier with you that time? The first time that you went."

"Yes."

"What is your relationship with Michael Frazier?"

Zoe again looked confused. "My relationship? I don't have a relationship with him. I contacted him for information about Sir Julian after the news ran the story of Sir Julian disappearing off the ferry. I'm a journalist. I got his name from an editorial desk after he had contacted them claiming to have information."

"And what was the information that he had?"

Zoe couldn't figure out where this line of questioning was going. "He said that he had pictures of Sir Julian's car. Then, when I spoke with him, he told me he could show me the boat, er, the ferry, that Sir Julian had disappeared from."

"Is that all?" asked Daniels.

Zoe shifted in her chair. "Well, no, obviously," she said a little indignantly. "He managed to get me CCTV footage from the boat, the ferry, and then later he found out that Sir Julian had a house on the island."

"How did he find that out?"

"I believe that he checked the registration number of Sir Julian's car and found it to be registered there. Here," she corrected.

"Is that when you decided that you would break into the house?" asked Daniels.

Zoe sat up straight. "Hang on!" she objected. "We didn't break in. The key was under the pot and I opened the door. We didn't do anything wrong or take anything."

"No?" said Daniels. "So where is the note?"

"I don't know," said Zoe. "I presume it's in the house, on the floor, or somewhere. I didn't get chance to look because of.... Michael."

"Did he try to stop you taking the note?" asked Daniels.

Zoe's indignation showed again. "No!" she repeated. "He was dead when I got there. It shocked me. Frightened me. I didn't go searching for anything. I called you lot!"

"Why were you covered in blood when PC Lock arrived, Zoe?"

"I fell over," she cringed. "When I went in the back door, I slipped in his blood and fell over."

"Did you stab Michael Frazier, Zoe?"

"No!" she cried. "He was like that when I got there."

"Zoe, did you and Michael Frazier have an argument?"

"No, we couldn't. He was dead!"

"Was it about this note? This shopping list?"

"No."

"I suspect that something like that is probably worth a lot of money in the right hands. In the hands of a journalist with a story to tell?"

"No! Ok, yes, it's worth something, but that's why I took a photo of it. I deliberately left it on the table for when we called the police, you guys."

"We?"

"Me and my editor."

"Not you and Michael Frazier?"

"What?" Zoe was confused again. "Why would Michael call you? He isn't a journalist."

"No, so you said. Did you pay him for the photos?"

Zoe hesitated. "Yes," she said, eventually.

"Anything else?" asked Daniels.

Again, she hesitated. "Yes, the CCTV footage."

"Sounds like he was quite the entrepreneur."

Zoe shook her head, sadly. "He was just making a few extra quid for helping me out."

"More than a few extra quid, if his wallet is anything to go by," said Daniels. "There must be a couple of hundred in there. Was he demanding more?"

"What?" indignant again. "No, of course not."

"Did Michael Frazier get violent with you, Zoe?"

"No, of course not. Why would you even think that?"

"When you paid him for the CCTV footage, how did he supply it?" asked Daniels.

Zoe thought for a moment. "It was on a memory stick," she said. "We used one of the computers at the library to play it."

"And where is the memory stick now, Zoe?"

Again, she paused. "I gave it back to him," she said.

"Really?" said Daniels, feigning surprise. "But you'd paid him for it. Why give it back?"

Zoe shook her head. "I ...I don't know," she said. "I'd taken pictures on my phone. I suppose I didn't give it further thought."

Daniels paused for a moment and looked into Zoe's eyes, before looking away and gently shaking her head.

"Let me run something by you, Zoe, and then you can tell me your thoughts. As I said, Michael had his wallet with him and in that wallet was more than two hundred pounds in cash. His phone was in the kitchen with him, and we've been able to look at his phone records, but even without looking at those, we only had to touch the screen on his phone to see text messages and lots of missed calls, all from you. He doesn't appear to have responded to those messages or answered those calls.

You have then travelled all the way down to the Isle of Wight, from London, on the same day that you have sent these text messages and telephoned Michael. Travelled to somebody else's home, not yours, not Michael's, and then, what I believe has happened, is that you and Michael have argued over something, perhaps this note and the memory stick that you've talked about, maybe he was demanding more money, but anyway, you argued over something.

I think that the argument became heated and you have lashed out. You said you were angry. I think you have grabbed a kitchen knife and stabbed him. It might have been frustration, or anger at his betrayal, demanding more money, or maybe, you tell me if it was so, maybe it might have been that he was coming at you. Maybe he was the one that was angry. Perhaps he was the one attacking you and you grabbed the knife in self-defence? That would be ok, you know. You're allowed to defend yourself. Which was it, Zoe?"

Her mouth hung open in disbelief. "You're not serious? I found him like that. Why would I kill him?"

"Come on, now, Zoe. Think this through. You were covered in his blood. Still are," said Daniels, pointing at Zoe's hands. "Forensics are checking the knife. It's got a nice, clean wooden handle has that knife. The kind that makes taking fingerprints really easy, and when those prints come back and then we take yours and compare them, it's going to be a match and you will have lost your opportunity to give us your side of the story. Like I said, Zoe, if he was attacking you and you were defending yourself, that's self-defence. But we need you to tell us exactly what happened."

"He was like that when I found him!" said Zoe angrily. "Yes, ok, perhaps we shouldn't have been in the house without permission, but I was looking for evidence to show that Sir Julian hadn't committed suicide. I'm writing a story about something that happened at a Government scientific facility and Sir Julian was going to give me a scoop. I've got a message on my phone from Sir Julian confirming just that. But then Sir Julian allegedly fell off a ferry, on his way to spill the beans to me, and now Michael is stabbed to death in Sir Julian's house. Don't you see? It's all part of the same conspiracy."

Daniels exhaled loudly and sat back in her chair, folding her arms. "Conspiracy, eh? So, who is behind this conspiracy,

Zoe?"

Zoe sat up straighter, determined to look confident and serious. "I believe it's the Government."

Daniels laughed derisively. "Really? The Government?" she said. "Can you hear how ridiculous that sounds, Zoe? We find you in someone else's house, covered in someone else's blood, that same someone stabbed to death in the kitchen, and you're seriously telling me that it was the Government that is responsible?"

"Yes," said Zoe firmly.

"Ok," laughed Daniels. "Who in the Government stabbed Michael?"

Zoe hesitated. "Daniel Tomlinson, the Prime Minister's Chief of Staff."

"You're not serious?" said Daniels.

"Well not him, in person," said Zoe. "He got someone to do it. I've got a photo of him. It's on my phone. If you'll just get my phone for me, I can show you. He's called John Smith."

Again, Daniels laughed. "Oh, really? John Smith, eh? I'm sure he'll be easy to track down."

Zoe became bolder, the initial shock of finding Michael Frazier dead in Sir Julian's kitchen was beginning to wear off and her thoughts were becoming clearer, sharper.

"Shouldn't I have a solicitor?" she asked suddenly.

Daniels sighed and looked at PC Lock. "You are entitled to a solicitor if you want one," she said, turning back to Zoe.

"I want one," said Zoe.

"Interview suspended," said Daniels. She looked at her watch and read aloud the time and PC Lock turned off the tape machine. He ejected the two tape cassettes and wrote the date, time, and Zoe's name on them, before inserting them into their respective cases and handing one over to Zoe.

"That's for you," he smiled.

Daniels stood up. "PC Lock will take you back to your cell, whilst we arrange for a solicitor. Do you have anyone in mind? Or shall I call the Duty solicitor?"

Zoe thought for a moment and then told Daniels that she was happy with the Duty solicitor. PC Lock then escorted her back to her cell.

Detective Sergeant Daniels took the stairs back to the second floor and the small CID office. She slipped out of her jacket and hung it on the back of her chair, before sitting down and logging into her computer. She was immediately distracted by an email that she had received regarding a burglary that she had been investigating in East Cowes. Midway through reading it, her desk phone rang.

"Daniels," she said, as she answered it.

"Suzie, it's Graham," came the response.

"Hi Graham," she said to the Duty Sergeant downstairs in the Custody Suite. "I was about to call you. Zoe Carlson wants a solicitor. Could you check the Duty roster and give them a call?"

"Will do," replied the Duty Sergeant. "I was calling you to let you know that SOCO have got the prints back off the knife in the Frazier stabbing."

"That was quick," smiled Daniels.

"They're in the system," he said.

Daniels' heart dropped. She'd already carried out a search on Zoe Carlson before interviewing her and she was unknown to the police, no record at all. If the prints were in the system, that meant that they weren't Zoe's.

"Bugger!" she said. "I was sure it was her."

"That's not all," said the Duty Sergeant. "They're flagged."

Daniels sat up straight. "You're kidding?"

"Nope. Sorry, Suzie. I've had to let the Yard know."

Daniels understood. If fingerprints were flagged on the Police National Computer, it was because the individual to whom they belonged was someone that only Scotland Yard could deal with, usually in relation to a witness protection program.

"Bollocks," cursed Daniels. "That will be the end of that, then."

"It's looking that way," said the Duty Sergeant. "Do you still want me to arrange the Duty Solicitor for Miss Carlson?"

"I'm not sure that there is any point, now," she said. "I presume I'm going to get a call?"

"They said within the hour," replied the Duty Sergeant.

"Ok. Hold off until then and I'll let you know," she said and then hung up.

It was sooner than she had expected. Within about ten minutes or so her desk phone rang again, this time with a double ring, indicating an outside line.

"CID, Detective Sergeant Daniels speaking," she said as she answered.

"Sergeant," said a deep voice on the other end of the line. It resonated authority and gravitas. "Chief Superintendent Langley, Scotland Yard."

"Hello, sir," replied Daniels with suitable reverence.

"I understand that the prints from one of your suspects has been flagged."

"Well, kind of, sir," said Daniels.

"I don't understand, sergeant. What do you mean 'kind of'?"

"Well, sir," continued Daniels. "The suspect that we have

in custody isn't in the system. The fingerprints are not hers. They were prints taken off the murder weapon, sir."

"I see. So, you don't have the flagged suspect in custody?"

"No, sir. We have a female who was found at the scene and was our original suspect, although she has been insistent that it was a third party who killed the victim. Unfortunately, the prints on the knife seem to back up her story."

"What has she said about the third party?" asked Chief Superintendent Langley.

"To be honest, sir, it's a little farfetched. She has tried to pin the blame on someone in Government, a..." she looked at the pad that she had used in the interview. "Daniel Tomlinson. Chief of Staff to the Prime Minister, if you can believe it."

There was silence from the other end of the phone, so Daniels continued. "The suspect..."

"Her name?" Langley interrupted.

"Oh, yes, Zoe Carlson, sir. She has alleged that this Tomlinson bloke has hired someone to murder the victim and that it was all over nothing more than a shopping list left in the house by the deceased owner."

"Name of the deceased owner?" It was an authoritative demand, more than a question.

Again, Daniels looked at her pad. "Julian Hebburn. A Sir Julian Hebburn, if you don't mind," she half laughed.

There was a long pause. "And has this Carlson given any details about the alleged perpetrator?"

"You won't believe it, sir," said Daniels. "She says he's called John Smith. I mean, how ridiculous. She claims to have a photo of him on her phone, but we haven't checked on that yet."

"And you're not going to, are you Sergeant Daniels?"

"Sir?" asked Daniels.

"You understand protocol. This case, the fingerprints, have been flagged. That means you must cease your investigation and hand everything over to me. I want the knife securely bagging and the personal effects of both the victim and Zoe Carlson putting in a secure box and transported directly to me here at the Yard. I'll need that to be done with immediate effect and I expect to receive the box within twenty-four hours. Is that understood?"

Daniels was a little put out by Langley's authoritative tone, but she confirmed her understanding, nevertheless. "What would you have me do with Miss Carlson?" she asked.

"Release her," said Langley. "Just ensure that her address details are in the evidence box."

"Understood, sir," said Daniels. The line went dead without Langley engaging any further. "Pompous prick," muttered Daniels as she replaced the receiver.

She rang down to the Duty Sergeant and passed on the instructions and a short time later, PC Lock opened Zoe's cell.

Zoe looked up expectantly. "Is my solicitor here?" she asked Lock.

"No," he replied. "There's no need. You're being released."

Her expression was full of surprise, followed by suspicion. "Why?"

"Just my instructions, Zoe," said Lock. "I don't know the reasons. Now, if you want to come with me, I'll take you down to the Duty Sergeant and get you processed and then you can get out of here."

She continued to look suspicious. "Are you charging me, then?"

Lock shook his head. "No," he said, gesturing with his hand for her to come forward and follow him. "You're being released without charge."

Cautiously, Zoe followed PC Lock out of the cell and down the short corridor to the brightly lit Custody Suite. The same Duty Sergeant was behind the Perspex screen, busy typing into his computer.

"Ok," he said, looking up from the computer screen and smiling at Zoe. "Miss Carlson, you are being released without charge. There are no bail restrictions attached to your release, however, if you are contacted by the police and asked to attend a police station for further questioning, please do so without delay. Do you understand?"

"Not really," said Zoe, shaking her head. "I've no idea what's going on. Where's my stuff? My clothes and bag?"

The Duty Sergeant pushed an A4 size piece of paper through the gap in the Perspex screen, a biro resting on top of it. "Your belongings are being held under the Police and Criminal Evidence Act 1984. If you could check the list and then sign to confirm that it is accurate, your belongings will be returned to you after the investigation is completed."

Zoe was incredulous. "You are joking, aren't you? What about my wallet? My money? How am I supposed to get home?"

Another thought crossed her mind.

"What about my phone?"

The Duty Sergeant tapped with his forefinger at the line on the document where her signature was required. "PC Lock will drive you to the ferry and make arrangements for onward travel on the train to London. Your belongings will be returned to you once the investigation has been completed, but only if you sign here to confirm that the list is correct."

She was fuming. She scribbled her signature on the document, at the same time muttering how ridiculous this was.

"Before we set off," said PC Lock, gently. "Can I suggest you use the sink in the loo and wash that dried blood off your face and hands. Stop you getting any funny looks on the journey."

Zoe looked at her hands and then up and down herself at the grey joggers and sweatshirt that she was wearing, and she laughed sarcastically. "You don't think I'm going to get funny looks dressed like this, then?"

PC Lock shrugged and then looked down at her feet in the paper slippers. "Sarge," he said, without looking up at the duty desk. "We're going to need a pair of size five trainers."

Once she had finished washing herself, PC Lock drove her to the ferry terminal at Fishbourne. His first intention had been to make arrangements for her to cross as a foot passenger, but he took sympathy on her predicament and instead boarded the ferry with her in the car. When they disembarked at Portsmouth, he went with her to the train station and organised her one-way travel to London, informing British Transport Police in order to avoid any difficulties.

As he was about to leave, Zoe touched his arm.

"Thank you," she said, meaningfully. "I know you were only doing your job, but you were.... kind."

PC Lock smiled. "Take care, Zoe," he said.

CHAPTER THIRTEEN

Chief Superintendent Bob Langley sat behind his large, modern desk, in his corner, glass walled office at Scotland Yard, one window overlooking the Chindit Memorial, the other across the Thames at the huge round wheel of the London Eye. He leant back in his expensive, high backed, leather chair and then swivelled it so that he was looking out across the river. The Eye was moving slowly, the pods filled with people and queues on the ground waiting for their turn wrapped up in winter clothing but, no doubt, baking in the bright, clear winter sunshine.

He swivelled the chair again and pressed a button on his phone.

"Yes, Chief Superintendent?" came a female voice.

"Dorothy, would you get hold of Daniel Tomlinson at Downing Street and have him come over to see me, please."

"Right away, Chief Superintendent."

He turned again to watch the people on both sides of the river. The tourists were enjoying themselves, taking photographs, laughing and pointing. He might have smiled. If he had been that way inclined.

But he wasn't. He was a career police officer who was profoundly serious about, not just his work, but life in general.

And he had not finished with his aspirations yet. He was young enough, still in his early fifties, to pursue further career advancement in either enforcement or security. MI5 was a serious consideration, especially with the contacts he had already made and built upon throughout his career so far. It was unlikely that he would get the top job in the Met. That role was secure for its incumbent for some time, he thought. So other, linked career paths were the obvious next steps.

Just so long as people like Daniel Tomlinson didn't cause problems along the way.

His desk phone rang, and he spun around, leaning forward, and pressing a button.

"Chief Superintendent," said Dorothy's obedient voice. "Mr Tomlinson is unavailable to meet today but has suggested that he may be able to accommodate a telephone conference at some point in the forthcoming week. Would you like me to arrange an appointment?"

"Dorothy," said Langley. "Please call Mr Tomlinson back and politely inform him that, unless he is in my office within the hour, I will have two armed police officers escort him here under threat of arrest."

"Very good, sir," replied Dorothy. He could hear the smile in her voice.

The hour was very nearly up when Tomlinson was finally shown into Langley's office by Dorothy. Langley was certain that Tomlinson had delayed for as long as he dared before setting off, with the childish intent of simply pissing him off.

"Bob," said Tomlinson as he entered, removing his cap, and throwing his coat over the back of one of the chairs. "Was that really necessary?"

"Sit," said Langley, without getting up from his chair to

greet him. Tomlinson paused and looked at the Chief Superintendent with a puzzled expression.

"Bob?" he questioned.

"Sit," said Langley, more forcefully this time.

Tomlinson sat in one of the chairs opposite Langley, his coat beneath him.

"Talk to me about Zoe Carlson," said Langley.

"What about her?" asked Tomlinson, suddenly nervous.

Langley leaned back in his chair and studied Tomlinson's face for a moment. "Zoe Carlson was arrested on the Isle of Wight at the home of Sir Julian Hebburn," he said.

Tomlinson frowned.

"She was arrested," continued Langley. "On suspicion of murder. The victim, Michael Frazier, worked on the Isle of Wight ferries. He was stabbed to death in Sir Julian's kitchen."

Tomlinson was confused. "Why would Zoe Carlson kill someone?" he asked, more to himself than Langley.

"She didn't," Langley replied.

"I'm sorry, I don't follow," said Tomlinson, leaning forward. "I thought you said that she has been arrested."

"She was," said Langley. "But she's been released now, because the evidence at the scene confirmed that it wasn't her who stabbed the victim."

Now Tomlinson started to get a feeling for the direction in which this conversation was going, and his nervousness increased.

"There was a very clean set of fingerprints on the knife used to stab the victim. But those fingerprints are already in the system and, worse than that, they are flagged. Do you know what that means, Tomlinson?"

"I don't think I do, Bob," said Tomlinson, cautiously.

"Details are flagged on the PNC in order to protect the individual to whom they belong," said Langley. "Those individuals might be in a witness protection program, or they might be long term undercover police officers, for example."

He looked pointedly at Tomlinson.

"They are also sometimes flagged in order to protect the identity of certain," he thought for a moment. "Shall we say, special, individuals. Individuals that might be used for... occasional unusual activities that need to be undertaken in a somewhat clandestine manner. Individuals such as John Smith."

Tomlinson's heart sank and his eyes dropped away from Langley's down to his own hands, which were twisting his cap involuntarily.

"I can explain," he said shortly.

"I should bloody well hope you can!" shouted Langley. "You lied to me, Tomlinson."

"Well, not strictly lied," Tomlinson squirmed in his chair.

"Don't bullshit me," shouted Langley. "You told me that you had been instructed to provide the Prime Minister with a list of the covert, irregular assets under our control. You told me that it was an issue of National Security and an instruction that came directly from the Prime Minister."

"It was," said Tomlinson. "It was an issue of National Security."

Langley stared furiously at him. "But not an instruction from the Prime Minister?"

"Not directly," said Tomlinson, awkwardly.

Langley sighed loudly.

"Look, Bob" said Tomlinson in the best conciliatory tone he could muster. "There was a serious issue, one which could have caused untold damage, not only to the PM, but to our security as well. It wasn't Hebburn's fault, or wrongdoing, but he was primed, all set to talk to the Press. The scandal would have rocked the Country. It would have destroyed this Government, and you know damn well what would happen if we ended up with the Opposition in power. But also, particularly if there was a power switch, our National Security would have been put at the utmost risk. MI5, and probably MI6, and without any shadow of a doubt, your 'irregular assets', if the Opposition came to power, would be at best shackled and made toothless, or, at worst, dissolved altogether. Even if MI5 survived, your assets wouldn't.

"I had to make a swift call. A decision that others would have hesitated to make, in order to protect the best interests and safety of our Nation. So, yes, I admit it, I utilised your asset."

Langley was speechless for quite a while. He was so angry that he had to stand up and pace back and forth along the glass walls of his office. Eventually, he stopped mid-stride and turned to face Tomlinson.

"How?" he demanded. "How did you 'utilise' our asset? I gave you his confidential details, not a fucking introduction!"

Tomlinson shrugged. "I phoned him," he said calmly.

Langley stared at him for a few moments more. "You phoned.... You phoned him?" He was incredulous.

"Well, yes," said Tomlinson. "Once you had provided access to the file, all of the contact information was available for me to use."

Langley walked back to his desk and flopped into his chair, leaning back, and staring at the ceiling in disbelief. "You phoned him," he said again, shaking his head.

"Oh, don't worry," said Tomlinson, leaning forward in his

chair. "It wasn't easy. He was extremely distrusting and very suspicious."

Langley stopped staring at the ceiling and lowered his eyes to stare into Tomlinson's. "But you managed to persuade him, anyway," he said, his tone heavy with sarcasm.

"Well, yes," smiled Tomlinson. "I am the Downing Street Chief of Staff."

"You do realise that you have probably written off a perfectly serviceable asset? You need to tell me exactly what you did and what you had him do. Now."

"Bob, I really don't think that there is a need for you to take that tone," said Tomlinson.

"Now," insisted Langley, leaning forward on his desk.

Tomlinson sighed. "Very well," he said. "His mission was to silence Hebburn, which he did, rather well, I thought. Clever of him to make it look like a suicide. The second time I used him..."

"Second time?" said Langley. "You instructed him twice?"

"Well, yes," said Tomlinson. "Don't worry. Every contact was made from a secure location that nobody knows about. I was very discreet. Anyway, his instructions on the second occasion were simply to retrieve the note from Sir Julian's house on the Isle of Wight. It was the only thing that could cast any serious doubt on his suicide. There was no new target. His instructions were clear. All I can suggest, if he killed someone else, is that he went rogue."

"How did you pay him?" Langley asked angrily.

"What, the second time? I didn't. I told him it formed part of the first job. I mean, come on, he's supposed to be a professional, but he makes the suicide look doubtful by not cleaning up properly. A bit shoddy in my book. I wasn't going to pay him a second time. I didn't say as much, of course. He's probably still waiting for payment."

Langley stared at Tomlinson, open mouthed. He couldn't get over the arrogance of this man.

"How did you pay him?" he repeated, in a low and angry tone. "What method of payment did you use?"

"Oh," smiled Tomlinson, understanding the question for the first time. "I was quite cute with that. I had him on a kind of retainer. Once he was satisfied that I wasn't part of some sting operation and he had indicated his willingness to work with me, I set up a small, third party contract arrangement via one of the Departments at Whitehall. It was only a hundred thousand, so it could be spread out very easily and paid in instalments into a shell company that then moved the funds in one payment to his chosen account as soon as he accepted instructions. Such a small amount wouldn't raise any eyebrows. It's less than most MP expenses, for God's sake."

"Please tell me that you didn't use your own name to create that company," sighed Langley, holding his head in his hands.

"Of course not," smiled Tomlinson. "Completely fictitious name. Well, kind of. The Director's name is a composite of the first names of my children. Fortunately, I've set the registered address as a Post Office Box Number."

"That's very smug of you," replied Langley. "Except, the only way you can do that is by providing the actual registered address of the company to Companies House."

"I'm ahead of you," laughed Tomlinson. "It's registered at the address of a small Accountancy Firm in South London. "I'm covered."

"And the PO Box?" asked Langley.

"Sorry?"

"The PO Box. What address is that registered to?" Tomlinson fell silent, his brow furrowed. "You used your own address, didn't you?" continued Langley.

After a short while, Tomlinson nodded.

"Fucking idiot!" said Langley. "This needs clearing up immediately. First, I want details of this 'secure' phone that you think you have used. Second, you will close that PO Box, after giving me its details, so that I can have it removed from the register, and third, you speak to that Accountant as soon as you leave this office and have that shell company wound up. Give me the name and I will ensure it is removed from the records. And fourth, please heed some grown up advice. You may think that you are a big fish in a little pond, with lots of power and control, but you are not. You might think that you are the Puppet Master, but you are wrong. You are just a single cog, in a machine of a thousand cogs, all of which are replaceable and, trust me on this, Tomlinson," Langley leant forward, his forearms leaning on his desk as he looked Tomlinson directly in the eyes. "You are very replaceable. Easily. Swiftly. If you ever pull a stunt like this again, I will personally ensure that you are found floating in the Thames somewhere. Do I make myself clear?"

Tomlinson's usual cocky arrogance had left him. For the first time in a long time, he was genuinely scared. "Completely," he said.

Langley handed him a pad and a pen, and he wrote down the information that had been demanded, after which, he left, head down slightly.

Langley stood and paced back and forth, watching the tourists through the windows. Eventually, he returned to his desk and opened the top drawer, removing a small, nondescript box, with a short white cable and USB connector at the end which he plugged into one of the USB ports on the underside of his desktop phone. Three small lights illuminated on the box and began to flash red, then yellow and then, one by one, they turned green, at which point, Langley picked up the handset and dialled. He didn't hear the usual ringtone at first, but instead a series of clicks and electronic noises before the familiar double beat tone that indicated the line was ringing.

"Carter," said a voice as the line connected.

"Mark, it's Bob Langley at the Yard."

"Oh, hi Bob. Are we green?"

Langley looked at the three green lights on the USB phone scrambler on his desk.

"Yes, Mark. That's confirmed."

"What can I do for you, Bob?"

"We have a bit of a problem with an asset. It's partly my fault. With hindsight, I rather foolishly agreed to disclose the details of an asset to a high ranker at Downing Street and, well frankly, it's come back to bite me on the arse."

"Tell me more," said Mark Carter.

The phone call took a long time and, for Langley, was painfully embarrassing at times. He knew, before he had to explain his actions, that he should not have revealed anything to Tomlinson when he had come to his office so long-ago asking questions about assets. He should have stuck to the Intelligence line that no such assets existed.

If he was honest with himself, part of his willingness to provide some limited amount of the extremely confidential information in his possession, was his forward career planning and aspirations. Being well thought of by those that held the real power within Government, no matter which Political Party was at number 10, could only be advantageous for his future prospects. He just hadn't expected that one of those power holders could be so immeasurably fucking stupid.

When the call was over, he gratefully replaced the receiver and unplugged the scrambler, silently reassuring himself that he wasn't going to allow himself to be placed in such a similar predicament ever again.

His next call was to the Tech Team after which, having received from them the assurances that he required, he instructed a uniformed officer to return Zoe's belongings to her.

When she opened her front door and was presented with a cardboard archive box containing her possessions, she excitedly signed for them and rushed inside to open the box and find her phone. It was amongst the ochre-coloured blood-stained clothing and she pressed her thumb on the button at the bottom of the screen. It lit up as it came to life, but her heart sank when it displayed the 'Welcome' message of a phone that had been cleared and returned to factory settings.

CHAPTER FOURTEEN

The glow on the horizon signified the coming of the dawn and as it began to stretch into the morning sky, like an early riser climbing out of a cosy bed, it pushed the bright twinkling spots of star light further into the nothingness of space, until they disappeared altogether when the first darting ray of sunlight knifed across the surface of the calm sea.

Andrew McDermott leaned back in his fold up chair and stretched his legs out to their fullest extent, the toes of his warm boots tapping against each other. Once his muscles had confirmed that they were awake, he pushed himself out of the chair and stood up, his eyes devouring the glorious sunrise.

"You callin' it a night, Scotch?" asked an old, bearded man to his right. His clothing was similar to McDermott's. Waterproof trousers and jacket that covered several layers of warm, woollen clothing and a woollen hat on his head, the kind with flaps at the side that looked like a bloodhound's ears. He leant against the guardrail at the farthest end of the pier, two, twelve foot long fishing rods secured into stands on either side of him, the line from each stretching out in the morning air into the distance and the cold water of the North Sea.

"I think so," replied McDermott, clasping his hands above

his head, and pushing them up as high as he could until he felt, and heard parts of his spine and chest crack pleasantly. His own two rods pointed out in a direction sixty degrees to the left of the old man. He looked in the bucket next to one of his rods. Half a dozen Mackerel glistened in the morning light and a couple of seabass lay amongst them. They were disappointingly on the small side.

Around him, several more fisherman began stretching and yawning and discussing their overnight tallies, before lifting rods and spinning reels, drawing in their lines and hooks. McDermott did the same. It wasn't a speedy process by any means. Once the lines were in, poles were either separated or collapsed into the telescopic housing of the more expensive ones and then encased lovingly in specially made holdalls. Thermos flasks that had been filled with coffee, or perhaps something a little stronger, were sealed up and the metal cups screwed tightly onto the top, before they were placed into rucksacks next to now empty Tupperware boxes that had once held sandwiches and biscuits and chocolate.

Rucksacks were shrugged into, holdalls hung by straps over shoulders, freeing one hand to carry the folded-up chair and the other to carry the bucket with the spoils of the night, ready for the freezer when they got home. Then they all began to move, almost as one, away from the sea, from the end of the pier, towards the land, passing the wooden clad shops and stalls that were open during the summer months, but closed and locked away when winter came, until they passed under the metal archway entrance with the name of the pier engraved into it and out onto the pavement.

Some walked towards cars, whilst others set off for the walk home, each nodding a tired farewell, looking forward to the warmth of home and the comfort of a bed, or a sofa, for a few hours, at least, of sleep.

McDermott didn't have far to walk. He'd bought a little stone cottage some years previous, just a short walk from the pier, with a front door that opened almost directly onto the sand dunes, but for a short path to a small wooden gate. He loved the sea and this pretty cottage had been a steal when it had come onto the market. There were many days and evenings, particularly in the winter months, when he would sit in a rickety old chair in the window and watch the foam on the water as the waves crashed into each other.

He pushed open the green wooden front door and leant his foldup chair against the inner wall in the hall. He placed the holdall containing his fishing rods into an umbrella stand and then shook the rucksack off his back, before struggling out of his heavy, waterproof topcoat, which he hung on the coat stand. He moved to the foot of the stairs and sat on the second to bottom, before battling with his boots and removing them from his feet. Finally, standing up, he was able to slide out of the elasticated waistband of his waterproof trousers.

Shuffling along in his grey woolly socks, he carried the bucket of fish through to the kitchen at the back of the cottage and opened the chest freezer which dominated the tiny room. It was already well stocked with fish and he poured his catch on top, resolving to cook a couple of the mackerel once he had taken a nap. He'd managed to grab a couple of hours during the night, even on the cold, exposed end of the pier, so he only needed a couple more hours on the sofa before he would be fully refreshed.

Continuing to shuffle, he made his way into the front room and arranged the cushions on the sofa to use as pillows and then lay back with a satisfied sigh, pulling the crocheted blanket from the back of the sofa over his body. He felt better now. A night's sea fishing had reduced the stress levels brought about by the happenings on the Isle of Wight. He had been quite angry with himself for making what he considered to be an error of judgment. He'd approached the task too quickly, not taking his usual measured approach of assessing all of the possible outcomes before taking action. Instead, he had been annoyed with Tomlinson for his criticism of the original job and his insistence that there was more to do. His annoyance had meant that he had rushed things, instead of planning and taking a measured approach.

But it was done now. He drifted off to sleep.

Around mid-morning his phone pinged and vibrated at the same time in his trouser pocket. McDermott stirred and opened his eyes. He stretched and then took the phone out and looked at the screen. An email from an automated sender told Mr John Smith that his hotel reservation had been confirmed. McDermott sat up, swinging his legs around and dropping his feet to the floor. He tapped the screen on his phone and the full message appeared. The reservation was confirmed for the following day at a hotel in Norwich.

McDermott sat up straight. When Tomlinson had contacted him, he had broken all protocol and used the telephone. That had initially aroused suspicion in McDermott and it had taken some time and some background digging before he was satisfied that he wasn't being set up and was instead receiving a genuine instruction. The hotel reservation method was the correct protocol for assigning a job and, to some extent, he was pleased that the normal procedure was once again being followed. But his instinctive caution caused him some concern. What had happened on the Isle of Wight was messy. McDermott didn't follow the media news and couldn't be certain whether or not the killing had been reported yet, but sooner or later it would be. And no doubt Tomlinson would see what had happened as a mess. One which might be difficult to clean up.

So would they use him again, so soon? Or even at all?

Of course, it might not be Tomlinson this time. After all, the correct protocol was being used. In fact, Tomlinson had been the only one to have ever used his own name when he had instructed McDermott. Every other instruction had come using the hotel booking confirmation method, which suggested that this was coming from one of his usual clients. The one that used him the most. The one with significant power.

That might also explain the use of John Smith. No successive instructions ever used the same name. His client knew the various aliases that McDermott used and, on occasion, would even create a new one for him. The process was simple enough. He would receive an automated hotel reservation confirmation and would check in on the designated date. Once in his room, he would open the hotel safe using a master code contained within the body of the email, normally a reference number. The safe would contain his instructions and target and occasionally, new identification for a new alias.

If his client were unaware that Tomlinson had instructed John Smith, they wouldn't think twice about using the same name for a new instruction. But that also made him cautious. He had believed that Tomlinson was authorised to use him. To be authorised, except for a few rare private clients, the main client would have had to have given him the ok. That would mean that they would know, or at least should know, that John

Smith had undertaken the most recent job.

He stared at the message long and hard, remembering his thoughts of retirement when he had been on the ferry crossing to the Isle of Wight. He thought about the errors that he had made on this job that Tomlinson had given him. It was so unlike him. He didn't make mistakes. Perhaps it was time to hang up his boots and call it a day, finally.

The message displayed the phone number for the hotel, and he tapped it before raising the phone to his ear. It was only two rings before the call was answered.

"Good morning," he said. "My name is John Smith; I have a reservation for tomorrow."

"Oh yes, Mr Smith," was the reply. "You should have received an automated confirmation by now."

"Yes, I've received it," he said. "But I'm going to have to cancel, I'm afraid."

"That's not a problem, sir," said the happy sounding voice. "I've noted that on our system. Is there anything else that I can help you with?"

"No, that's all, thank you." He pressed the red button on his phone and disconnected the line. For a long time, he sat and pondered over his decision. He wondered whether there could be any repercussions. After all, it wasn't an ordinary career with the prospect of an ordinary retirement. When he thought back in time, there were only two or three occasions that he could recollect when he had cancelled a reservation. The reasons for doing so had been genuine. There were times when, for whatever reason, one might just not be available. The cancellations had never been questioned, so it followed that this cancellation shouldn't be questioned either, but he felt an odd, misplaced pang of guilt, for not taking the job when he wasn't prevented from taking it by other obligations or commitments.

He changed into some more comfortable clothes and a sturdy, but well worn in and comfortable pair of walking boots and went for a hike up the coast. It was a beautiful, clear and sunny day. Cold and brisk, but beautiful. At the top of the coastal walk stood the ancient lighthouse, no longer in use, but maintained by the town, through charitable donations, owing to its long history and its dominating position on a corner of the rise, overlooking the sea and the local area, where it invited attention from tourists, artists, and anyone with an eye for history, culture and design.

Turning right at the lighthouse led down a cobbled street into the main area of the small town. It was blessed with two pubs, both of which he regularly frequented, particularly in the winter months, when the tourist families were not taking up all of the space with loud children and empty crisp packets or sweet paraphernalia cluttering tables, or worse, in the beer gardens, being blown around by the wind and ignored by those that had discarded them.

He was often tempted by the delicatessen on the high street and the 'ginger pork sausage rolls' made on the premises and as he approached, his stomach grumbled, almost as an instruction not to forget to drop in and buy one. Or two, if he felt inclined.

Before he considered entering the shop, he heard the ping and felt the vibration of his phone in his pocket again. He paused in his stride and took it out to look at it. A new message informed him that his reservation at the same hotel in Norwich the following day had been confirmed. McDermott frowned. Whatever the job was, it must be important. But, even so, his mind was made up. He was retiring.

Well, it was half made up. The thought of 'going out' on an untidy ending of the last job played on his mind. He'd never considered himself to be egotistical, but then, what assassin or serial killer would? But he wondered now whether his hesitation over simply repeating the cancellation was a subconscious admission that, in reality, he craved the work and the power it made him feel.

He walked on past the delicatessen toward the church at the end of the high street and entered its grounds before tapping the phone number on the screen of his mobile and dialling the hotel for a second time.

The call was short and, once completed, he returned in the direction that he had come, back down the hill, past the lighthouse and the pier, to his pretty little cottage, so that he could pack a bag and prepare for his trip to Norwich on the following morning.

CHAPTER FIFTEEN

McDermott had been to Norwich on a number of occasions, mainly for pleasure, rather than business. He particularly enjoyed the Cathedral, with its large cloisters and its huge spire. He enjoyed the City's medieval charm, with its cobbled streets and ancient, half-timbered houses.

But today, he wasn't here as a tourist, or as a person with an interest in history and architecture. Today, he was here to work.

The hotel was situated in the centre of the City, on the river, in sight of the Cow Tower, an ancient artillery tower built in the 1300s to defend the City. It was a modern, new build hotel, part of a large chain of hotels and it had faced rather a lot of opposition when the planning application had been submitted to build a new hotel right on the bank of the river. Nevertheless, the consent had been granted and the building went ahead. It wasn't unattractive, but some thought it a little too contemporary to be situated beside some of the ancient constructions which were its neighbours.

McDermott checked in as John Smith and asked whether there had been any messages left for him. There were none, so he carried his holdall to the lift, which he took to the sixth floor and his room. He used the key card to open the door and once inside, with the door closed behind him, he closed the security latch, preventing anyone from entering. He slung his holdall onto the bed and then opened the built-in wardrobe, which was the most likely place for the safe to be housed within. Sure enough, it sat at the bottom of the wardrobe, a gunmetal grey colour, about a foot in width and half a foot in depth, secured to the floor by unseen bolts. McDermott crouched down and then paused.

This wasn't right.

The door of the safe was open, the square, numerical keypad now redundant and a red digital zero displayed on the screen. McDermott frowned and crouched down so that he could look inside. The interior was dark and invisible, so he took out his mobile phone and activated the torch app, shining the bright light into the casing.

Empty.

McDermott sat back on his haunches and carefully considered why the hotel safe might be empty. He thought it through, mulling over in his mind the different scenarios that he had considered. He began to pace, slowly, back and forth, as he pondered the situation and stopped when he arrived at the sliding window doors that opened to the balcony outside. He pulled aside the net curtains, sliding them along their runner until they hung delicately at one end of the window, then he slid open the glass balcony door. Stepping out into the cold air, he looked across the river at the medieval brick Cow Tower, then left and then right, in each direction of the slowly moving water. It was all very beautiful and peaceful.

He leant on the rail that ran around the small balcony and looked down to the river. McDermott wasn't scared of heights, but his stomach nevertheless performed a gentle somersault as his eyes took in the sheer drop from the balcony to the water below. He continued to stare downwards in silent punishment of his stomach that had dared to show fear, and then, taking a final look at Cow Tower, he turned and stepped back into his room, pulling the sliding door closed behind him, but leaving the bunched-up net curtain hanging at one end of the window.

Sitting on the end of the bed he waited and thought and waited a little longer, eventually using the phone at the side of the bed to call reception.

"It's John Smith in 603," he said. "Have I had any messages?"

"I'll just check for you, sir," said the happy receptionist. A moment later she spoke again. "I'm sorry, Mr Smith, but no, there haven't been any messages for you."

He thought for a moment. "No packages?"

"No, sir," came the reply. "If you are expecting something in particular, I will make a note to call your room as soon as it arrives." It was almost a question.

"Yes, ok, thanks," he said, replacing the receiver.

He continued to wait on the end of the bed, still thinking. Eventually, his stomach called him to action by reminding him that he had only eaten in the morning, missed lunch and was now at risk of neglecting dinner. It was just starting to go dark outside, so still early, given the time of year, but he decided to head out and stretch his legs and find somewhere to get something to eat.

He walked into the centre of the City, towards the castle, where there was a host of bars and restaurants. The streets were lit for the autumn evening and were busy with shoppers and tourists and early finishers from work. He took some enjoyment from just walking and watching and studying the people and did so for some time so as to avoid eating too early. When he finally decided it was time for sustenance, he settled on a small Italian restaurant and opted for a table at the back, away from the window, where he could see the entrance clearly and anyone coming and going.

He took his time over dinner, enjoying the food and a half bottle of red wine, whilst watching the people, the couples revelling in each other's company, the families celebrating some occasion or other and the attentive staff, smiling and engaging, adding to the warmth of the environment. When he had finished, he walked around the centre of the City, people watching again and taking in the architecture and history that he had enjoyed on previous visits. The night was getting colder and he decided to head back to the hotel. As he walked through the entrance lobby, he was attracted to the buzz of noise from the bar to his left and decided to have a nightcap before returning to his room. The bar was clearly popular, and very busy, no doubt because of the pleasant ambiance and the views over the river. McDermott sat at the end of the bar, his back against a pillar, and drank an Irish whiskey with a single cube of ice, whilst he took in the noise of his surroundings and watched the people intently.

Even though he was relaxing, he was still intently working. He'd been a little put out about the lack of instructions in the room safe but had considered that his earlier cancellation might have had something to do with that. So, he had maintained an acute awareness of his surroundings and the people within them just in case the instructions would come in a different manner. He was also playing over in his mind the other thought that had been running through his brain on the previous day. The thought that plagued him the most.

Nothing presented itself to him, and, feeling comfortable and confident about his plans, he treated himself to a second whisky whilst he continued to watch those around him in the bar area enjoying their evening. Eventually he decided that it was time for bed, and he headed back to his room, pausing at the front desk to ask again whether any messages had been left for him and receiving the same negative answer. Once in his room, he checked the safe again, just in case a delivery had been made whilst he was out, but it remained empty, the door ajar.

Finally, he made his preparations for bed and retired.

He was a light sleeper. Always had been and the slightest noise or disturbance would almost always have him wide awake in an instant. It was useful for his night fishing. He could drift off to sleep, even in the cold and the wind, but a part of his brain seemed to ever be awake, ready to nudge him into action as soon as it heard a reel begin spinning. It was also useful in times of potential danger.

Like now.

The intruder in the room was trying to be stealthy. No doubt the intention was to enter unheard and carry out his task in silence, without waking his prey. McDermott had deliberately failed to apply the security bar when he had closed the bedroom door, but the electronic 'click' of the door lock hadn't caused him to awake. It was the noise made when the intruder stumbled over the carefully positioned overnight bag, left on its side, just far enough inside the entrance to enable the door to be fully opened without it touching the obstacle. The intruder did not fall over the bag, but instead stumbled over it, his left hand reaching out to the doorframe of the bathroom entrance just within his grasp, supporting himself and preventing any further forward momentum which might have resulted in a fall. He paused and listened, staring intently ahead of him. The net curtains at the window were pulled to one side and moonlight slipped into the room forming shadows and shapes. One of the shapes was formed under the quilt on the bed and the intruder stood motionless for a few moments, watching, and listening, trying to determine whether the shape under the covers had heard him.

It didn't move, so, confidence returning, the intruder stepped further into the room and moved silently around the foot of the bed and to its side, at the same time drawing out of his inside jacket pocket a jet injector, the type used to administer drugs without the need for a hypodermic needle, instead delivering them by a piston powered by gas. He stepped closer to the bed and, right hand with the jet injector held at the ready, he reached out with his left hand in order to gently pull back the covers and reveal the neck area of his victim. The drug inside the injector would have an almost immediate effect, at first causing paralysis and then heart failure. His target would be found by the hotel cleaning staff the next day and he was confident, that when a doctor was called, the cause of death would be determined as a heart attack.

Slowly, he pulled back the quilt.

Before his mind had time to recognise that the shape underneath the quilt was not, in fact a person, but rather a pile of clothes and pillows formed up to make the shape of a person, a rabbit punch to the base of his skull sent him flying forward onto the bed, pain like a lightning bolt firing both up into his head and down his spine simultaneously. The injector gun fell from his hand and he felt a crushing weight on his back and then another punch, this time on the back of the skull, followed by a third to his left temple. Stunned, he passed out.

It was only for about thirty seconds, but when he regained consciousness, he realised that Andrew McDermott (or John Smith as he knew him) was sat across the top half of his back, knees pinning his shoulders down. Lying face down on the bed could make it easier to remove McDermott, the 'give' beneath him would allow him to squirm and wriggle and perhaps get free, but he had no intention of trying to do that. He could feel the cold round tip of the jet injector pressed forcibly against his neck.

When McDermott had telephoned the hotel for the second time on the previous day, it wasn't to cancel the room, as he had done the first time, but it was to check whether there was an adjoining room, the type that has a pair of internal doors joining the rooms together. His instincts had told him that something didn't feel right and had there not been an adjoining room, or had he not been permitted to book it in addition to the existing booking, he would have cancelled for a second time. But there was an adjoining room. It was already booked, but the helpful hotel staff were willing to move the couple who had booked it, and who were checking in on the same day as McDermott, to another room.

When he had checked in, he had been given key cards for both rooms, and the cards also unlocked the adjoining doors. On discovering that the safe in his pre-booked room was empty, he was fairly confident that this was a trap and then he felt assured in his intuition and his plan for taking control of whatever act was going to play out.

His evening out, walking around the City, dining in the restaurant and then sitting in the bar served two purposes.

One, it was to try and identify whether or not he was being followed and, two, it was to give the impression to anyone who may have been following him, irrespective of whether or not he had noticed them, that he was relaxed and not on guard. When he had returned to his room, he had emptied his overnight bag and positioned it deliberately within the entrance of the room, so that anyone entering, in the dark, was likely to trip over it. He had deliberately left the security bar on the door free, so that it could be opened with, as he expected, a master key, and then he had gone about arranging his clothes and the pillows underneath the bed covers to resemble as closely as possible a sleeping body. He left the curtains open deliberately, so that the moonlight would frame the bed and the shape within it, drawing the immediate attention of any intruder to it and not to the stumbling block of the overnight bag, positioned so purposefully.

He had then gone to bed in the adjoining room, leaving the door to the pre-booked room open by an inch, but the other, inner door to the adjoining room wide open, satisfied that he would hear anyone entering the other room. He had already taken the precaution of securing the entrance door to the adjoining room with the security bar. When his subconscious heard the intruder trip over his bag, he had awoken instantly and slipped off the bed silently. He had laid fully clothed on top of the bed, so he made no noise getting up and he moved silently to the open adjoining door and looked through the gap of the door that was ajar into the other room. The intruder was staring intently at the shape in the bed, his left hand leaning against the doorframe of the bathroom. McDermott watched him move slowly and silently into the room and around the foot of the bed and to its side until he had his back to McDermott who wondered whether, had their roles been reversed, would he have paused and checked the adjoining doors.

Of course he would. He was meticulous.

He watched as the intruder withdrew something that looked like a gun from his inside pocket, before leaning forward slightly and reaching out with his left hand for the bed cover. McDermott knew instinctively that was the time to strike. He didn't have a weapon, but then, he didn't need one. He was a competent and efficient fighter and was perfectly capable of disabling a foe in a couple of strikes. This one took three, but only because of the fact that his prey had fallen onto a bed and not a more solid base.

He pinned him down with his knees and picked up the gun, immediately recognising it for what it actually was. He studied the vial on the top of the device, wondering what solution was inside and guessing at two that immediately came to mind. As the body beneath him began to stir, he pressed the nozzle against the neck of the man who had come to his room with the undoubted intention to kill him.

"Name?" said McDermott, menacingly. "Who sent you?"

"I don't know," said the man. "Come on, you know the score. We never know. I just got the instructions."

"But you knew I'm an operative?" asked McDermott, no less menacingly.

"Yes," replied the man. "There were some additional instructions telling me that you are on the Team. It's nothing personal. You must know that. It's just a job."

"I need a name," said McDermott, pressing the nozzle of the jet injector more firmly against the man's neck.

"I swear to you, I don't have a name," he replied. "I get a text message confirming a hotel booking and then the instructions are in the safe in the room. I never speak to anyone. You must know that? You're on the Team?"

McDermott considered what the man said. It made sense. What he described was similar to the method by which he received his own instructions; except for on one occasion. Tomlinson. He was the only one that had ever made contact in person.

"Look, Smith," said the man. "We could just go our separate ways. I could say that you weren't here, or something. You can leave and I can leave, and no one needs to know any different. Like I said, it's nothing personal. It's just a job. You know that. I mean, how long have you been in the game?"

McDermott looked down at the back of the head of the man. "Too long," he said, before pressing the trigger on the jet injector. The man convulsed, his back rising and lifting McDermott, almost pushing him off the bed, before dropping back to the quilt, twitching momentarily, and then, finally falling still, a huge, single exhalation of air pronouncing his death.

"Nothing personal," said McDermott drily, as he shuffled backwards off the man and the bed and stood up. He walked to the window and slid open the door, stepping out onto the balcony and into the cold night air. He placed both hands onto the cold metal rail and closed his eyes, breathing in deeply. His mind worked through the problem that now quite literally threatened his very existence and he tried to develop a solution. Eventually, he opened his eyes and looked around at the lights of the City and then down below at the flowing water of the river. That at least presented one solution, he thought.

The man was quite heavy, that deadweight heavy that seems to push down on you with twice the force of the actual weight.

Nevertheless, McDermott managed to get him up off the bed and over his shoulder in a fireman's lift, before carrying him out to the balcony. He sat the limp figure down onto the rail of the balcony before giving him a solid push, causing him to tumble backwards, down and away, until he splashed into the water below and was carried away, silently. Looking left and right into the distance, confident that no-one had seen or heard anything, he then retrieved the jet injector gun from the bed, returned to the balcony and dropped it over the side, watching it disappear into the river.

Then McDermott re-entered the bedroom, closed the sliding door and went to bed.

The following morning, he took his bag with him when he went to breakfast, in order to avoid having to return to his room before checking out of the hotel. Taking a table by the window, overlooking the river, he visited the breakfast buffet and filled a plate, before sitting back down and eating. In the distance, on the other side of the river, an ambulance and a police car were parked at odd angles to each other, the blue lights spinning silently. Two police officers were cautiously descending the stone stairs that led down from a gate fixed in the railings that ran along the bank of the river, to the water itself. Something was snagged against the bottom step, most of it in the water, but part of it hooked or hanging from a piece of metal protruding slightly from the river. One police officer held onto the others forearm as he knelt on one knee to lean over the side from the platform at the base of the stairs and grasp hold of what was stuck. It was obvious that he was struggling because he let go of the other and dropped to both knees, leaning forward, his colleague now joining him and assisting to pull whatever it was out of the river.

It was eventually obvious to McDermott that it was a body. The officers struggled to drag the wet dead weight out of the moving water and onto the platform. One was gesticulating to the ambulance crew above who rushed to the open rear doors of her vehicle and returned with a blanket, treading carefully down the steps to join the two police officers. Even though the body was covered up quickly, McDermott could tell that it was his visitor from the previous evening. It didn't concern him, though. Any bruising on the head would be attributed to a fall into the river and he had no doubt that whatever the drug had been in the jet gun, it would have administered a heart attack and would ensure that the death of his assailant would be classified as an unfortunate accident.

As he left the hotel, McDermott deliberately walked past the spot, but on the opposite side of the river, watching with interest the activity over the water, before heading to the train station, already planning in his head the detail of the next stage of his plan.

CHAPTER SIXTEEN

The phone on the large mahogany desk buzzed loudly and the Prime Minister raised his head from the papers that he was digesting and reached out to press a button.

"He's here, sir," said a voice on the other end of the line.

"Excellent! Send him straight in."

The Prime Minister shuffled together the papers he had been reading through and once they were stacked, he moved them to the side of his desk, before leaning back in his leather Chesterfield Captain's chair, hands settling firmly on the wooden arms and eyes fixed on the oak panelled door to his office. It opened with a flourish and Daniel Tomlinson entered, removing his long coat as he did and then his hat.

"PM," he said, cheerfully. "You asked to see me?"

"Daniel," said the Prime Minister, softly. "Please," he pointed to the chair on the other side of his desk. "Take a seat."

Tomlinson's energetic stride paused momentarily, the PM's formality disarming him a little, before sitting opposite him, coat and hat resting on his knees, straight backed, as if in the Headmaster's office waiting to be told something he didn't want to hear.

"Is everything ok?" asked Tomlinson. "The message said it was urgent."

"Well, it is, really," said the PM. "Langley at the Yard came to see me this morning."

Tomlinson's heart jumped as he frowned, feigning surprise. "What about?" he asked.

"I think you know the answer to that question, Daniel," said the PM. "Is it true? Have you been using a Service asset?"

"Well, I, er..." Tomlinson faltered.

"Good God, man," said the PM. "You don't have authority to be using assets like that. Hell, I'm not convinced even I have the authority. What were you thinking?"

"I was doing it for you, PM," replied Tomlinson, emboldened by his own certainty of the righteousness of his actions. "It was to protect you, and this Government."

"I can't believe what I am hearing," said the PM, his exasperation clear on his face and in his voice. "How can your actions possibly help me or this Government? There is a reason that the use of those kind of assets is done covertly and by only a certain set of people. For God's sake, Daniel, we have very specific Departments for that kind of thing and we as a Government, my God, as a whole damn Parliament, are deliberately distanced from those kinds of activities. We don't know that they are going on. It's called plausible deniability. I would have thought that you of all people would understand that!"

"Yes, of course I do," said Tomlinson. "But that's the whole point. No-one was doing anything, at exactly the point in time when something needed to be done."

The Prime Minister held up his hand, palm facing Tomlinson in a clear instruction to be silent.

"I don't want to know!" he said.

"Hebburn," replied Tomlinson. "Sir Julian bloody Hebburn was what nobody was doing anything about!"

"No!" shouted the PM, standing up and slamming both hands down on the desk. "I don't want to know! Nothing!"

"Hebburn was going to blow the whistle on the Broughton Stretton spillage and the Rinderpest variant," continued Tomlinson, unperturbed by the PM's insistence. "He was going to the Press and he was going to tell them everything. That would have been the end of you. It's chemical warfare. Can you imagine trying to respond to that if it had got out?"

The Prime Minister stared silently, a little open mouthed at Tomlinson, still sitting straight backed, hands resting on the overcoat in his lap. Slowly, he sat back down in his Captain's chair and stared into the middle distance.

"Chemical..." he half whispered; the full potential impact of what Tomlinson was saying to him beginning to register. "But you assured me. Sir Nigel assured me. You said that some of the toxin was held back for the purpose of creating an anti-viral. That isn't chemical warfare." The PM's voice trailed off into uncertainty, his eyes again staring into the middle distance until eventually they returned to focus and settled once more on Tomlinson's face.

"Strictly speaking," said Tomlinson. "That is correct. The idea was to create an anti-viral, but the main thrust was to create something that would cross the species barrier, a zoonotic disease. But that isn't really the point, Prime Minister, is it? The salient point is that Sir Julian Hebburn was going to talk to the Press about what Broughton Stretton had created and that it may have been done so at the behest of the Ministry of Defence. He wouldn't have to say the words 'chemical warfare'. It would be implicit in what he was telling them."

He let that point sink in with the Prime Minister before continuing.

"So, something had to be done. Five weren't interested. They didn't see it as a domestic issue, but more of a political one, and Six had pretty much the same view. And it was pointless talking to Nigel at the MOD. He would have only done or said something stupid without thinking."

"And your choice of action wasn't stupid?" interrupted the PM. "Is that what you are trying to say?"

Tomlinson sighed dramatically. "My choice of action, Prime Minister, was absolutely necessary in order to protect you and this Government."

The PM stared at him in silence for a long time, the effect eventually beginning to make Tomlinson feel uncomfortable.

"Did you sanction the Rinderpest variant?" he eventually asked.

"The MOD are responsible for what Broughton Stretton have created," replied Tomlinson firmly.

"The MOD don't have the authority to sanction such a move," said the PM. "Sir Nigel might, in the most exceptional of circumstances, but I strongly suspect that if I were to call him in right now and ask him whether he sanctioned the research himself, he would tell me that he sought approval before sanctioning it. I know that approval request did not cross my desk, so that leaves the question of who did see it and who approved it. Was that you?"

After what seemed to be an eternity, Tomlinson looked the PM directly in the eyes and confidently and unshakingly said "Yes."

The Prime Minister threw his head back and his hands into

the air simultaneously, exhaling loudly and then standing up and pacing back and forth, his face becoming redder and his hands bunched into fists held rigidly at his sides as he walked.

"Why?" he demanded. "How? You don't have that power! You don't have that ... right!"

Tomlinson remained seated, hands still resting on his over-coat. "You gave approval, sir, vicariously through me."

The PM's face got redder still, as he stopped pacing, wheeled, and stared back at Tomlinson.

"What?" he demanded. "I did no such thing!"

"That is not how the public would have seen it had Sir Julian talked to Zoe Carlson," said Tomlinson. "Even if the disclosure had sparked an internal investigation that determined that it was me that had given the go ahead, I'm your Chief of Staff. Everything that I do is on your behalf. Ultimately, whatever I may have authorised, the buck stops with you, sir. Something had to be done to protect you."

The PM stared at him furiously.

"Get out," he said eventually.

Tomlinson didn't move. Instead, he half smiled up at the beetroot face of the PM and said "Oh, Prime Minister. There's no need for that, now, is there?"

If the PM's head had been capable of blowing steam from his ears it would have done so, as his blood pressure rose a further notch, his anger and frustration reaching previously undiscovered levels.

"Get out!" he shouted, his right arm raised to the horizontal and his forefinger pointing rigidly at the door to his office. "Get out before I throw you out! And don't come back!"

This time Tomlinson was startled, taken aback by the out-burst of rage coming from his boss. As the PM had shouted, he had stood up quickly, almost involuntarily, one hand just managing to grab hold of his coat as it slipped off his lap, the other missing his cap, which fell to the floor. He crouched and retrieved it, staring up at the angry red face of the PM.

"Sir," he almost whimpered. "That is really unnecessary."

The Prime Minister said nothing more and remained in a rigid position, his arm still outstretched and his forefinger pointing at the door. He shook it in a way that reemphasised the instruction to leave. Tomlinson slowly rose from his crouched position and began to walk towards the office door, head swivelling between it and his boss.

"Sir, if you do this, you may come to regret your decision," he said, trying to sound authoritative.

"Don't ... you ... dare!" said the PM, the menace in his face clear to see, shaking his arm and finger again.

Tomlinson opened the door and walked through into the room on the other side, where several secretarial staff were all sat behind their desks staring at him, a couple of them with unashamed smirks on their faces, clearly having heard the shouting that had come from the other side of the door to the Prime Minister's office. Tomlinson faltered for just a moment, then, remembering his reputation and the fact that he could not care less what may be the opinion about him held by these minions, he stood up straight and deliberately and slowly placed one arm into the sleeve of his coat, transferred his hat from the other hand before sliding that one through the other sleeve and shrugged the long overcoat up over his shoulders, then flopping the Irish cap onto his head and adjusting front and back until it was where it was supposed to be. Purposefully and not a little pompously, he marched out of the room. As the door swung to behind him, and as he walked down the corridor, he could hear the unmuted laughter from the room behind him.

He was furious.

As he marched towards the stairs and then down to the front door and the usual security guard who stood by it, he considered that perhaps he should have left Sir Julian to blow the whistle and to hell with them all. He quite clearly was not appreciated by those who should know better. The guard nodded and Tomlinson stepped outside into the cold. The usual Press pack were hovering around behind the movable railings opposite the front door of Number 10. As he turned left and marched away from the building, he was half tempted to stick two fingers up and shout something obscene to the waiting vultures, but common sense and a lifetime in the public eye held him back. They appeared to hold little interest in him, in any event.

Once through the security and the iron gates at the end of the street, he stepped forward and raised his hand to hail a cab. He needed to release the pent-up aggression within him, and he instructed the driver to take him to the sports club where he was a member. Squash was his thing and now was a good time, he thought, to smash a ball around a court for an hour, assuming that he could find a suitable opponent at the club.

It was an exclusive gym, near the centre of London and occupying three underground floors of a glass fronted office high-rise. The first underground floor housed a range of hi-tech gym equipment with high paid gym instructors on hand to offer assistance, training, and tips to improve performance. Below that floor were the squash courts and the deepest and final subterranean area housed the swimming pool, showers and changing area. This being a members only club, the lockers in the changing area were all assigned to individual members and the one registered to Tomlinson always had at least two pairs of shorts, shirts, and socks inside, as well as a pair of trainers, just in case he came straight from work. The club offered a premium laundry service which meant that he always had fresh, clean kit to change into when he visited.

When he descended the stairs from the reception area of the high-rise and walked through the entrance lobby to the gym, one of the instructors was sat behind the desk entering something into a computer. She looked up and smiled as Tomlinson arrived and gave him a courteous welcome. He grunted in response and pushed open one of the glass doors leading into the gym itself. Looking around he saw that it was sparsely populated today, and he only vaguely recognised some of the people sweating heavily over walking machines or bending and stretching under weights. Another of the instructors recognised him and raised a hand in greeting.

"Anyone in the courts?" asked Tomlinson, pausing momentarily in his stride towards the stairs in the far corner that led down to the next floor. The instructor shook his head.

"Good!" said Tomlinson. "Fancy a game?" He'd arrived at the top of the stairs and turned to face the other man.

"Sure thing," replied the instructor. "Go and change and I'll be down in five."

Tomlinson bounced down the stairs and then the next flight to the lowest floor and the changing rooms.

When he met the instructor on one of the squash courts, they spun a racquet to decide who would serve and then the game commenced. Tomlinson was a skilled player and when he was angry, rather than his ire negatively affecting his ability, it instead honed his precision and seemed to improve his strength and skill. He punished the ball with every strike, lashing out with precise force and speed. His opponent was also an accomplished player but could not keep up with Tomlinson this time. They both spun and sped around the court, racquets slicing viciously through the air, the shrill, high pitched squeaking of their shoes mixed with their grunting and panting as with each rally they tried to outdo each other.

Tomlinson won 11-9, his final shot causing the instructor to overreach and miss, tumbling over onto the floor of the court and sliding into the wall on his backside. He sat up and leant his head back against the wall gulping air furiously. Tomlinson hunched over, still holding his racket but resting his palms on his half-bent knees, also sucking in huge gasps as he tried to recover from his exertions.

"Good game, Mr Tomlinson," said the gym instructor, each word interspersed by an intake of breath. "You certainly weren't holding anything back this time."

Tomlinson straightened up and slowly paced back and forth, trying to regulate his breathing and heart rate. "Thanks," he half smiled. "I needed a release."

Back at the lowest level he showered and dressed again, dropping his kit into one of the labelled bags that he had retrieved from his locker and then into the basket in the corner of the changing room. Once they had been laundered, they would be folded neatly and replaced in his locker for him in anticipation of his next visit. He shuffled into his overcoat and then climbed the two flights of stairs to the gymnasium where he nodded a grateful goodbye to the instructor who had shared his game. Around the walls of the gym were several flat screen televisions, running streaming news, apart from one that had music videos from MTV or some other such station playing. As he walked across the room, passing the weights and cycling machines, he watched an image of a single figure leaving the unmistakeable front door of Number 10 Downing Street on one of the screens and realised it was him. Those news boys must just leave their cameras constantly rolling, he thought.

"Shit," he muttered as he pushed the door and walked past the lobby to the stairs up to reception. The ground floor entrance lobby to the high-rise office block was a large circular room with a semi-circular reception desk deliberately positioned in the centre of the floor with two large, comfortable looking sofas flanking it, facing each other across the huge space between the outer edges of the building. Above each sofa, fixed to the walls were flat screen televisions. They were positioned in that awkward manner that would make the person sitting opposite think that you were staring at them when in fact you were watching whatever program was being displayed on the screen above their head. In this case the program was a 24-hour news channel playing on both screens. Checking closer he could tell that they were actually different news channels, but they were both playing the same footage of Tomlinson leaving the front door of Number 10, a very visible scowl on his face as he marched out of shot. Beneath the footage ran the ticker tape headline informing the world of his dismissal.

"Tomlinson first to go in expected reshuffle" it repeated.

"Shit," he muttered again, crossing the lobby floor, and donning his cap before pushing through the revolving doors and out to the street. Opposite, was his usual next port of call after the club, a noisy and lively pub, where he would go for a burger and a pint on the basis that by whatever exertions he may have just put himself through, he had earned it. He crossed the road and looked through the glass on the entrance doors to the pub. It was just early enough in the day for it not to be too busy, but it would not be long before it would start to fill with those looking for a pre-commute drink and chat.

Having made his order at the bar and carried his pint of Fuller's over to the shelf underneath the window that over-looked the street, he pulled out a high stool from beneath it and sat down, looking out at the bustle beyond. He didn't remove his coat or his hat, preferring instead to retain some anonymity. His mobile phone buzzed and rang in his pocket. When he withdrew it, the photograph of his wife smiled up at him. He pressed answer.

"Hi," he said, glumly.

"Daniel," she replied. "What's happening? It says on the news that you've left Government. That there's going to be a reshuffle."

Tomlinson sighed.

"Daniel?" she asked again.

"Yes, it's true," he said. "I've been sacked."

"But why?" asked his wife. "I thought you were valued. Unsackable?"

This time Tomlinson snorted with not a little derision. "Apparently not."

They were both silent for a long time. One of the pub employees brought Tomlinson his food and placed it down in front of him on the shelf. He half nodded his thanks and looked down at the plate and the huge tower burger filling most of it. Next to the burger was a small wire basket in the shape of a deep fat fryer used for frying chips, which was full of skinny fries.

"Are you at home?" he asked eventually.

"No. I'm at school, waiting for the kids. It's just come on the radio that you were seen leaving Downing Street amidst a rumour, leaked from inside, that there is to be a reshuffle of various senior posts. I thought they only did that for the Cabinet?"

"Normally, yes," he sighed again. "Look, don't go home. It will be like a pack of wolves outside the house and they'll be shouting and pushing, trying to get you to say something and it won't be pleasant. And they're bound to scare the kids. Drive out to your mother's. She'll let you and the kids stay there for a few days, won't she?"

"Of course she will," replied his wife. "She'll love seeing the children. But what about you? What are you going to do?"

"I'll join you tomorrow, or the day after. I don't mind fighting through that lot outside the front door. I'll sort a few things out and then get a cab over to Essex."

"That'll cost a fortune," she said. "Why don't I come and collect you?"

"No, seriously. It'll be fine. When you get to your mother's, drop me a text to let me know you're ok and let me have a list of anything that you or the kids need me to bring over. Try not to worry," he said. "Everything will sort itself out. I love you."

"Love you, too," she replied, before hanging up.

Tomlinson stared out of the window for a while, lost in thought, before eventually turning his attention to the food in front of him. His appetite hadn't quite disappeared, but his sullen mood had certainly dented it. He ate slowly and only nursed his pint of beer. Outside, the darkness began to creep in, streetlights and headlights began to glimmer and inside, the pub became busier and busier and the hubbub became noisier and noisier, distracting him from his thoughts.

He pushed the plate with the half-eaten burger along the shelf away to his left, closer to the wall where it was less likely to be knocked onto the floor by the bodies jostling around him. Occasionally, somebody's back would knock against him or press against his side, as people vied for space in the small and increasingly busy hostelry. The front door would open every couple of minutes and more bodies would add to the throng, invariably amidst cheers and loud calls of recognition. Someone discarded an Evening Standard on the shelf to the right of Tomlinson as they entered the pub. He looked up and then reached out for the newspaper, unfolding it as he did, in order to see the front page. If he'd given it half a thought, he could probably have predicted the headline:

"Tomlinson Sacked" it read in large capitals. An old photograph of him sat beneath the headline. He refolded the newspaper with a tut and shoved it away from him, before downing the rest of his pint and then standing and pushing his way through the crowd to the door and out into the cold air. It was still early evening and he needed to kill time, rather than head straight back to the house and the pack of reporters that would be waiting to shout random, nonsensical, unanswerable questions at him as he tried to force his way through them. The later he left it before he headed home, his hope was that fewer, or can you even imagine, none of them, would still be there. An unlit house and a cold late November evening would hopefully be sufficient to drive them all away to no doubt return another day.

He crossed the busy road as the Pelican lights flashed a green man at him and he headed into the park on the other side. It was well lit and still quite full of people wrapped up warm against the cold, either wandering aimlessly, in couples, or individuals, or some walking more purposefully, head down and heading for whatever mode of transport would carry them back to the warmth of a home.

A brightly lit café occupied one corner of the park, opposite a fountain set in a large base, dry now in anticipation of frosts, and burst pipes. In front of the café had been erected a large Christmas tree, lit up and standing about twelve feet high. Tomlinson walked past with a Scrooge like shake of his head, silently bemoaning how Christmas decorations and preparations seemed to start earlier year on year.

It was a large park, and it took at least half an hour to cross at a slow pace to the other side where, once back out onto the pavements of the Capital, he continued to walk slowly, taking in the brightly lit shop windows and the noise of the traffic.

Eventually he decided that it was too cold to spend any longer dawdling around the streets, wishing the time away in the hope that he would not be harassed when he finally got home. A black cab came around the corner ahead of him, its amber 'For Hire' light beaming at him as he held up his left arm and flagged the driver down. Traffic was still busy enough to lengthen his journey home, but he could live with the increased taxi fare if it meant that the delay in getting back would mean that the reporters might have given up for the day.

They hadn't, of course.

When the cab finally turned into his street, he craned his neck to see the steps up to his front door and breathed a long sigh of relief when he saw that no one was there. He instructed the driver to pull over in front of his house and paid him before climbing out. Tomlinson could not tell where they had all been hiding, but before he closed the cab door, he heard shouts of "There he is!" and "Mr Tomlinson!" and "Daniel", as the pack emerged from all sides, surrounding him. He had to push quite aggressively in order to pass through them, amidst shouts and cries and the most ridiculous of questions.

"Did the Prime Minister get sick of you, Mr Tomlinson?"

"Any regrets, Daniel?"

"Was the job too much for you, Daniel?"

He climbed the stairs to his front door, not deigning to reply or even to afford a courtesy to any of them. They continued to shout their banal questions even after he had closed and locked the door behind him. He deposited his hat and coat on the coat stand and went into the lounge, a large whisky on his mind. When he flicked on the light switch, flashes of light from outside peppered the room as photographers pressed buttons on cameras. Tomlinson walked to the large bay window and almost flamboyantly pulled the curtains together, shutting out the annoyance and then returned to his thought of whisky. He had an unopened bottle of Dalwhinnie in the cabinet which he collected along with a crystal glass before switching on a standard lamp, turning off the main light switch and collapsing into his comfortable, wing backed chair.

One large glass turned into two, then three. By the time that he had poured the fourth and rested it on the coffee table, his eyes were getting heavy, his brain drowsy and his body relaxed. His head rested back in the corner of one of the wings and within moments he was fast asleep, his breathing slow and deep and regular.

CHAPTER SEVENTEEN

When McDermott had arrived at the train station in the seaside town where his cottage was situated, he had toyed with ordering a minicab to take him home but leaving the station at the top of the hill that overlooked the sea, and breathing in the cold, clean air and taking in the bright sunny day, he had elected to walk the couple of miles instead, slinging his bag over his shoulder as he set off.

The coastal path undulated as he walked along it, taking him close to the edge of the cliff top beneath the lighthouse and the sheer drop to the ocean below before it turned away from the edge and led him a short way inland and then downhill until it eventually joined the pavement that ran down towards the pier. A couple of times he paused and looked out across the crystal blue water drinking in the view. Retirement was most definitely the right choice.

He could see a few people walking around on the pier, enjoying the beauty of the Victorian structure. The end of the pier was empty, much too early for the night-time fisherman. He had considered a night's fishing later, but it would have to wait for another time, a time after he had completed his plans for his retirement and carried out whatever needed to be carried out. His pace had slowed as he enjoyed the unspoilt view before him. This small seaside town had held a special place in his heart for a long time. It was unlike so many contemporary seaside towns that were full of pleasure rides and arcades and late-night clubs for the younger tourists. This place had none of those attractions. It was instead a step back in time to peace and quiet and the beauty of the ocean. It generally attracted an older market of tourist because of that, and that suited McDermott down to the ground.

Walking past the entrance to the pier he had turned down the path that led towards his cottage. He felt relaxed and unguarded, which was probably why he had not spotted the Battenburg livery of the police car parked on the tarmac road that ran to the side of the sand dunes. McDermott walked across the sand covered pathway to the gate at the front of his cottage and then up to the front door of his home.

It was ajar.

He stopped dead in his tracks, lowering the bag he was carrying from over his shoulder to his side. He quickly looked around him to see if anyone was near, or if there was anything else out of the ordinary. All was quiet, so he cautiously reached out with his right hand and pushed the front door inwards. It made no sound. No squeaks, or creaks. He was fastidious in his maintenance of his property and the hinges on the door were regularly oiled.

When it was opened to its fullest extent he paused and listened. He didn't hold his breath. He simply stopped breathing, so that no noise was made by any inhalation of air. No sound came from within. Then, breathing shallowly, he stepped over the threshold and into the small hallway, pausing again to listen intently. Still no noise.

Slowly, quietly, he stepped into the front room, a flashback of his visit to the house on the Isle of Wight momentarily jogging a memory. The front room was empty, so he wheeled slowly around and stepped quietly back into the hallway and moved down to the kitchen. That too was empty, so he quickly moved to the back door of the property to look through the glass into the small courtyard at the rear.

Nothing.

Quietly, he moved back into the hallway, checking again with a swift glance that the front room remained empty, and round to the foot of the stairs. He leant with his back against the wall and craned his neck to look upwards as best he could. Then, slowly and stealthily, he began to climb the stairs. He did so in a sideways movement, his back pressed against the wall so that he could see as much of the upper landing as possible as he ascended towards it. There were three rooms in the upstairs part of his cottage. A tiny bathroom sat at the top of the stairs; its door closed firmly to him. The other two rooms were bedrooms. The master bedroom was to his left at the front of the house and at the end of the short landing, and the much smaller, guest bedroom was at the back, behind the master and to the side of the bathroom. Both of those doors were open.

He couldn't remember in what position he had left any of the doors on the last occasion that he had been upstairs.

McDermott reached the top of the stairs and looked over to his left into the master bedroom, watching intently for any movement, or sudden shift of a shadow, or slash of a beam of sunlight. At the same time, he listened carefully for any sound. He was well skilled in a cat and mouse game and knew what signs and sounds to listen for when searching for an opponent. The faintest of movement, given away by cloth moving against cloth, sometimes a scratch of skin, where someone had been standing for too long in the same place and dust, or an insect or a mite had rested momentarily on an exposed spot of flesh, prompting an instinctive scrape with a fingernail. And sometimes, just the faintest sound of breathing.

But he heard nothing.

Deciding quickly on his approach, he stepped silently over the landing and into the guest room. It wasn't big enough for anyone to hide in, the three-quarter size bed almost filling it, so he knew immediately that the room was empty. He stepped back out onto the landing, after first focussing on the doorknob to the bathroom, ensuring that it wasn't moving, being turned slowly, carefully, by someone ready to pounce the moment his back was turned. He kept his back to the wall and looked right, through the open door of the master bedroom. Through the front window he could see the froth of the waves out beyond the sand dunes. Slowly and carefully, he inched his way along the landing, eyes on the front bedroom, with intermittent swift glances at the bathroom door, anticipating that at any moment it would fly open and an assailant would bear down on him. All the while, his senses heightened, he listened, waiting for the slightest sound that would give away the intruder.

After what felt like an age, he reached the entrance to the master bedroom and carefully looked through the gap between the hinges on the open door. That revealed nothing. He listened intently. Still nothing. With a quick snap of his neck left and right he again checked that the bathroom door had remained closed before switching around as silently as he could, his back now against the balustrade, the bathroom to his right and his own bedroom to his left. Slowly, cautiously, arms raised, and elbows bent, fists half clenched and ready to engage, he slid sideways into the room.

Nothing. It was empty.

Quickly he turned and faced the closed bathroom door. Should he charge it? Or continue with the stealth approach. He decided on the latter, moving slowly down the landing, checking over his right side over the balustrade and down the stairs to ensure there was no threat from below. When he arrived at the bathroom door, he stepped left and into the spare room before leaning and reaching out with his right hand and taking hold of the doorknob.

A quick intake of breath, a swift turn of his right hand, followed by a thrust inward and he jumped into the bathroom, turning slightly to his right as he did, his left arm extending, fist clenched, anticipating contact.

But, again, the room was empty. He stood still, confused and beginning to wonder whether he had just been absent minded and failed to close his front door when he had left. But he could not accept that. He didn't make those kinds of mistakes.

"Hello," came a voice from downstairs. McDermott froze and half crouched, left leg forward, arms moving to a fighting stance instinctively.

"Hello," came the voice again. "Mr McDermott? Is that you?"

No-one knew his real name. He was certain of that, so how could this person below be calling it? Sure, the locals called him Scotch, but that was a nickname that he had acquired because of the slight Scottish lilt in his voice. He had never told any of them his name and they had been content to stick with the one that they had given him, not the least because he responded to it.

So who was this? This person that knew his name and not any of his pseudonyms. There was no threat in the tone of voice that had shouted his name. It was only questioning. McDermott stood up straight and moved to the top of the stairs, looking down. At the foot, looking up, a smile on his face, was a policeman. He was holding the bag that McDermott had dropped silently at the front door.

"Mr McDermott?" he said again. "Is that you, sir?"

McDermott slowly descended the stairs, staring intently at the police officer all the while. As he reached the bottom few steps, the officer stepped back a few paces in order to give him room.

"Mr McDermott," said the policeman again, taking the lack of objection or denial to be a confirmation that this was indeed McDermott. "My name is PC Bergman. I hope you don't mind my just coming in, but I've been waiting for you and the front door was open. Is this your bag?" He held it out to McDermott, who took it and placed it on the floor at the foot of the stairs.

McDermott studied him for a long, uncomfortable moment. "Why?" he said, eventually. "Why have you been waiting for me?"

A hint of confusion passed over the police officer's face. He turned and looked at the front door and then back at McDermott.

"The break-in, sir."

McDermott thought for a moment. "I haven't reported a break-in," he said.

The confusion on the policeman's face deepened. "Really?" he questioned.

"Really," said McDermott, flatly. "So, thank you for coming, but you can be on your way, now."

More confusion appeared on the officer's face. "Er, I'm supposed to bring you to the station with me, sir," he said.

McDermott had already stepped off the bottom step and turned towards the kitchen, his back to the policeman in a dismissive gesture. He stopped and turned back towards him.

"Why?" he asked.

"To be honest, sir, I don't know," replied the officer. "My orders were to wait for you and bring you back with me. I presume to take your statement about the break-in." He half looked around as if trying to identify the evidence of a burglary, but as there wasn't any, he just shrugged and continued to look confused.

"But as I've already said," replied McDermott. "I haven't reported a break-in, so there is no need for me to go anywhere. Look, PC Bergman, I'm afraid that you've had a wasted visit. Now, if you'll excuse me, I have things that I need to do."

"Of course, sir," replied PC Bergman. "I'm sorry to have disturbed you." He nodded politely, then turned and walked out of the front door, leaving it open as he went. As he walked down the short path to the gate, McDermott could hear him speaking into his radio as he stepped forward and pushed the front door to close it.

Before it reached the doorframe, he felt it being pushed back towards him and, looking down, he saw a large boot obstructing the door. He let it open fully again and frowned at the police officer who had returned.

"I'm sorry, Mr McDermott," said PC Bergman. "I've just been on the radio to my superior and he has insisted that I bring you with me back the station. So, if you wouldn't mind coming with me, I'm sure it won't take long."

"Why?" asked McDermott.

"I'm sorry?" replied PC Bergman, again looking confused.

"Why?" repeated McDermott. "Why has your superior insisted that I go with you to the police station?"

"Er," the officer looked confused and embarrassed. "To be honest, sir, I don't know. He just said that I have to."

"Ask him," said McDermott, pointing to the radio clipped to the front of PC Bergman's high viz jacket.

The officer thought for a moment. "Ok," he said slowly, raising his left hand and pressing a button on the top of his radio.

"7891 to control," he said. McDermott didn't hear a response because PC Bergman had an earpiece fitted to his left ear with a cable running directly to the radio. "Yes, I'm here with the owner at the seafront cottage. He says that he didn't report any break-in and he doesn't want to come with me back to the station. He is asking why we are insisting, over."

McDermott watched the officer's face intently as an unheard response made him frown.

"Received," said PC Bergman into his radio. He looked up at McDermott. "Sir, I have instructions to bring you with me to the station." He paused. "If you refuse, sir, I have instructions to place you under arrest."

McDermott was unperturbed. "Arrested on what grounds, exactly?" he asked.

PC Bergman looked uncomfortable. "Obstruction of justice," he almost coughed.

McDermott studied the police officer intently for, to PC Bergman, what felt like an excruciatingly long moment. Then he turned away and walked into the kitchen. After a moment, the policeman followed.

"With respect, PC Bergman," said McDermott. "I can tell that you have been put on the spot here and you know, as well as I do, that you have no authority to arrest me, so humour me. Who has given the instruction to bring me in?"

"Sir," replied PC Bergman. "Chain of command for me starts with my Sergeant. I can't say where he has got his orders from."

Again, McDermott studied the officer's face for a long time. "Who gave you my name?" he asked.

PC Bergman thought for a moment. "I think it just came with the job, sir. I was radioed to attend this property following a report of a break-in. I would have been given your name then. I think the call said that you had reported it,"

"And therein lies my confusion," said McDermott. "I didn't report a break-in. I didn't report anything."

"Sir," replied PC Bergman. "When I arrived here, the front door was open and no one was present, and a report had been made of a break-in, if not by you, by someone. Now please, Mr McDermott, come with me." His hand moved to his hip where his handcuffs were clipped to his belt.

McDermott shrugged. "Ok," he said. "Let's go." He gestured with his hand towards the front door. PC Bergman smiled and relaxed a little, his hand moving away from his belt as he turned towards the front door. McDermott immediately lashed out with a snap kick to the back of the policeman's leg, causing him to fall forward awkwardly to one knee, shouting in pain. As soon as McDermott's foot made contact with the floor again, he stepped forward with his left, the knee connecting with the back of the police officer's head, stunning him, and sending him reeling to the ground face first. McDermott dropped onto PC Bergman's back, pressing his knee into the spine, and pinning the stunned officer to the floor, at the same time snapping free the handcuffs from his belt. He quickly pulled one of PC Bergman's hands behind him and clicked one of the bracelets over his wrist, then reached for the other hand and secured that next to the first. PC Bergman was too stunned to fight or resist.

McDermott stood up.

"Sorry," he said to the policeman lying face down on his hallway floor, his wrists cuffed behind his back. "Nothing personal and I know you are just following orders, but I'm being set up here and that just isn't going to happen."

Moving quickly and determinedly, he went into the kitchen and opened one of the cupboards above the sink. He removed a small, zip up fabric bag from the cupboard, about the size of an electric shaver case. Next, he ran upstairs, two at a time, and went to the master bedroom. In a hollow bottom of a drawer in the base of the wardrobe was a small wooden box. He opened it to check on its contents. Various passports and several rolls of cash in different currencies and denominations were in there. He carried it and the zip up bag back downstairs and put them both inside the overnight bag that he had brough back from Norwich.

PC Bergman had managed to shift himself around so that he was sitting up, his hands still cuffed behind him, leaning against the front door. He could not conceal his anger when McDermott came downstairs.

"You need to uncuff me, now!" he said. McDermott ignored him, instead checking through his bag, carrying out his mental inventory.

"I'm serious, Mr McDermott," continued PC Bergman. "You are just making things worse for yourself. Assaulting a police officer is a serious offence." McDermott still ignored him.

"Look," said PC Bergman. "Uncuff me. I won't say anything about the assault. I'll take you in just on my instructions and I'm sure you'll be out and about in no time. No-one needs to know about what happened here. I can tell you just overreacted, and that is fine. Come on, now. Please, Mr McDermott. Uncuff me."

Once he was satisfied that he had everything that he needed, McDermott zipped closed his bag. He then stepped forward, straddling the police officer, and bent over, placing a hand under each of his armpits. Half lifting and half dragging, McDermott moved him away from the front door. He then patted the man's thighs at pocket level and then dipped his hand into one, withdrawing a bunch of keys. He checked them to be sure and then put them in his own pocket.

"It's nothing personal, Bergman," he repeated. "But if I let you take me in, I can assure you that I wouldn't be leaving anywhere again on my own two feet."

"Oh, come on, Mr McDermott," said the policeman. "Don't be ridiculous. They just want to ask you some questions."

McDermott gently tapped him twice on his cheek with the palm of his hand.

"I know that's what you believe, Bergman. And that's the only reason I'm not going to snap your neck. Trust me, if I thought you were part of this, you wouldn't still be breathing."

PC Bergman frowned. "Part of what?"

"Never mind," said McDermott standing up and picking up his bag. He quickly did a mental inventory and, satisfied that he had what he required, opened the front door, and stepped outside, pulling it closed firmly behind him. Closing the gate at the end of the path, he walked back towards the main road and for the first time saw the police car. The keys that he had taken from PC Bergman had a button fob on the ring and he pressed the one to unlock. He heard the thud of the doors unlocking and saw the indicator lights flash. A moment later he was in the driver's seat, his bag on the passenger seat and he drove away from his beloved seaside cottage in the knowledge that he would never see it again.

His journey took him down the Suffolk coast and then west, around the northern part of Chelmsford and then dropping south, heading towards London on the M11. As he passed through Woodford, he turned the police car in a westerly direction and after two and a half hours of driving, he arrived at his destination, Alexandra Palace. He parked the car in the car park near the huge transmitter mast that points into the sky from the top of the building at the east end, then, leaving the keys in the ignition and taking his bag, he walked down the hill towards the train station at the bottom.

He took the train from Alexandria Palace to Moorgate and then the tube to his intended destination, South Kensington.

And then he waited.

Once it was good and dark, and late, and the Press pack had decided to call it a day, McDermott had silently moved around to the rear of a property and had deftly used a flat blade to shimmy open the lock of a sash window and then quietly climb inside.

And that was how he came to be in the front room of Daniel Tomlinson's home, probably about an hour or so after Tomlinson had fallen asleep in his wing backed chair. McDermott had known for some time where Tomlinson lived. It was generally easy enough to locate personal homes of famous or senior people simply by observing the media and their apparently complete disregard for the privacy of individuals, but McDermott had undertaken his own investigations immediately after Tomlinson's initial contact. The very fact that Tomlinson had not followed the usual protocols had put him on his guard and he had therefore made it a personal priority to find out as much detail as he possibly could about Daniel Tomlinson.

Silently, he checked the rest of the house to satisfy himself that they were alone. Once he had completed a sweep of the large Victorian end terrace and was satisfied that they would not be disturbed, he entered the room where Tomlinson slept in his chair and took one of the other crystal whisky glasses from the sideboard. Lifting the bottle from the coffee table, he poured himself a healthy measure of the malt whisky. Tomlinson's glass was still on the coffee table and McDermott placed his own down on the side opposite to Tomlinson. Opening his bag and removing the small shaver bag that he had brought from his kitchen at his cottage, he removed a vial, opened it, and poured half of the contents into Tomlinson's glass. He replaced the vial and then topped up the glass with more of the whisky, before sitting down in the chair opposite and taking a sip of warmth from his own.

He studied the man opposite for a while. His head was back, cradled by the corner of the wing backed chair, mouth open, breathing deeply with a faint hint of a snore emanating from it. It might have been McDermott's intense stare, but something caused Tomlinson to stir and one eye opened. As it slowly and hazily began to focus, the other eye joined it and he awoke with a start, a short cry of fear escaping his mouth. His legs scrabbled around, his feet kicking at the floor as he tried to push himself backwards into the chair and then tried to stand.

"Sit down," commanded McDermott. Tomlinson kept moving and didn't look like he would comply. "Now!" shouted McDermott. Fear turned into terror and Tomlinson dropped into the chair, whimpering.

"Who are you?" he asked, his mind already working out the answer for him, but a faint hope remaining that this was not who he thought it was and maybe this man was just a burglar, or something equally awful, but significantly less terrifying than the alternative.

"I'm confident you know who I am, Mr Tomlinson," replied the man. Another whimper came from his still open mouth. "We need to have a talk."

Tomlinson was visibly shaking, so McDermott took another drink from his glass and nodded towards Tomlinson's. "Slainte," he said. "Cheers."

Tomlinson stared wide eyed at McDermott, his heart beating rapidly. Eventually, he reached out and lifted the glass, but his hand shook so violently, he had to put it down again. He tried with two hands and this time managed to lift the glass, still shaking, to his lips and take a good glug, drawing some comfort from the smooth warmth of the liquid as it slid down his throat.

McDermott smiled.

"Now," he said. "Mr Tomlinson. You know, I've been doing what I do for an awfully long time, and even though I say so myself, I'm particularly good at it."

Tomlinson watched him with growing terror and took another swig of the whisky.

"What's more, in all the years that I've been doing what I do, I can't think of a single occasion when things went wrong, horribly wrong. Drink up," he said, smiling and sipping from his own glass whilst nodding again at Tomlinson, who obediently took another gulp.

"And then," continued McDermott. "You make contact with me. Not in the manner which I expect, but directly. Now, of itself, that might be forgivable as an oversight, or a mistake, by someone who just isn't used to dealing with people like me, and when I looked into your background and who you are, it seemed as if that assessment might be correct. But then, things began to happen. Very unusual things. Things out of the ordinary that made me begin to question your motives, Mr Tomlinson." Again, he nodded at the glass and again Tomlinson took a swig.

"For example. You contacted me a second time and sent me back to the Isle of Wight. Why was that?"

Tomlinson stuttered. Fear gripped his throat, and his chest was tight, making breathing difficult. The whisky was making him woozy and his vision was drawing in, as if someone were squeezing his head with oversized blinkers, wiping out his peripheral vision and blurring what vision remained. The man opposite him was beginning to look fuzzy around the edges.

"It was to tidy up," stuttered Tomlinson. "The note. You had to get the note."

"Yes, the note," nodded McDermott. "But you had another surprise waiting for me, didn't you?"

Tomlinson frowned. A small dribble formed in the lower part of his lip, right in the middle, and it slowly slid forward until it fell from his mouth, hanging there and refusing to let go. He wiped it away with his hand.

"What surprise?" he asked. His words were slurred now so that it sounded like 'surpwithe'.

"Really?" said McDermott, sarcastically. "Are you denying it? You had someone waiting for me."

Tomlinson squirmed in his chair and shook his head, more dribble escaping his mouth. "No, no," he protested. "I didn't."

"Don't lie, Tomlinson. When you sent me to the house on the island, you had someone there waiting for me. What was the plan? To cover your own tracks left from hiring me?"

Tomlinson leant forward in his chair and a pang of nausea hit him, his hand flying to his mouth as he thought that he might be sick.

"I swear to you," he said, his tongue swollen and dry. "I don't know what you are talking about. I didn't send anyone else. Jesus, I wouldn't know who else to send. I only ever had your details."

McDermott thought about his answer for a moment. "What about in Norwich?" he asked.

Again, Tomlinson looked scared and confused. "Norwich?" he stuttered. "I don't ... understand. I don't think I've ever been to Norwich."

"Did you send me instructions for a job in Norwich?" asked McDermott.

"No!" squealed Tomlinson. "You know I didn't. The last time we spoke was when I sent you back to the Isle of Wight."

"Not spoke," replied McDermott. "The usual manner of instruction."

A frown rippled across Tomlinson's forehead. He was really struggling to focus on the man in front of him now and he couldn't make sense of the questions being asked.

"I phoned you," he said, eventually. "That's how I instructed you. What is the usual method?"

McDermott took another sip of the whisky, paused, and nodded at Tomlinson and the glass in his hand. Obediently, Tomlinson tipped the glass back, draining the contents into his mouth.

"Pour yourself another," commanded McDermott.

"No, thank you," said Tomlinson, shaking his head. "I don't feel very good."

"I said, pour yourself another," said McDermott, staring intently into Tomlinson's eyes.

With a sigh, a whimper, and the faintest sound of bile rising in his throat, gagging him slightly, Tomlinson leant forward and picked up the whisky bottle, pulled out the stopper and poured himself probably the smallest measure he had ever had. He looked up at the man opposite who almost imperceptibly shook his head and then pointedly nodded at the glass, the silent instruction to pour a larger measure quite clear. So he did. He poured a measure about halfway up the crystal glass, almost emptying the bottle, consoling himself that, just because he had poured it, he didn't have to actually drink it.

"Look," he slurred. "I don't know anything about Norwich and the Isle of Wight thing, that was just to recover the note. It's all the fault of that Carlson woman. Zoe Carlson, the reporter, the one I told you about on the phone. She's the one that had been to the house on the island and she was the one that had seen the note." Despite the wooziness he felt, and the rolling sensation in his head and upper body, almost like he was tumbling forward, Tomlinson leant forward, picking up his glass, arm wavering left to right and then took a swig.

"She came here, shouting and threatening, saying she was going to tell all. She was going to show the world the note .... and your photograph." He remembered the threat that he had used when he had called John Smith from the red telephone box inside the café south of the river.

"That's a bloody good point," his voice was becoming more

slurred. "She knew about the house and the note. Maybe she was waiting for you."

McDermott shook his head thoughtfully. "It was a man," he said.

"So what?" said Tomlinson, waving his arm, the one without the glass in it. "She probably sent him there. It's obvious when you think of it. It must have been Zoe Carlson who had somebody waiting for you. To stop you getting the note." He sank back into the wingback chair, a smug, satisfied expression on his face, drool pouring from the left side of his mouth until it touched his clothes.

Slowly and patiently, McDermott let Tomlinson's answers process through his brain. There was some logic to what he had said, but it left questions unanswered. What about Norwich? And what about his seaside cottage?

"Who told you my name?" he asked eventually. Tomlinson's eyes had begun to close, heavy with stupor, during the pause in questioning and now they snapped back open.

"Smith?" he replied. "Not very imaginative, I have to say." His voice was slurring even more and, worryingly, he could feel his heart rate increasing, pounding in his chest, which itself felt tighter and tighter and his breathing was becoming laboured.

"No," said McDermott, measuredly. "My real name."

Tomlinson struggled to focus on John Smith's face. "I don't understand," he said. "I presumed John Smith wasn't your real name, but ... what are you saying ... is it?"

"Are you saying that you don't know my real name?" asked McDermott, leaning forward, and staring intently at Tomlinson.

"Smith," he replied. "I've only ever known you as John

Smith."

"And how do you know that name?" asked McDermott.

"Langley."

"Who?" asked McDermott.

"Langley," repeated Tomlinson. "Of the Yard." McDermott's expression didn't change.

"Chief superintendent Bob Langley of Scotland Yard," slurred Tomlinson. "I thought you knew?"

McDermott was silent for a long time whilst he processed this new information, whilst Tomlinson's eyes became heavier and heavier and finally closed as he drifted into a disturbing, almost psychedelic sleep.

"Is Carlson working with Langley?" asked McDermott eventually, startling Tomlinson back awake with a kick to his shin.

Tomlinson was struggling to concentrate even more now. His vision was almost entirely blurred, wavey, coloured lines streamed downwards across his eyes reminding him of an occasion when he had suffered an ophthalmic migraine. His stomach felt leaden and his arms were pinned down by invisible forces. Everything seemed to be slowing down and occasional flashes of light filled his vision.

"What?" he managed to say.

"Carlson," repeated McDermott. "Is she working with Langley?"

It took an age before Tomlinson answered. "I don't know," he said, finally.

"Finish your drink," ordered McDermott, after he had worked through his thoughts.

Tomlinson shook his head wearily. "I don't feel well," he said. "I don't want any more."

McDermott stood up and took the glass out of Tomlinson's hand, which had involuntarily gripped it throughout. He held it to Tomlinson's lips.

"That will be the Psilocybin," he said. "Drink." He tilted the glass, pouring more of the whisky into Tomlinson's mouth.

Tomlinson swallowed and choked, coughing and spluttering. "What?" he managed to say, eventually.

"Magic Mushrooms to you," said McDermott, placing the glass back on the coffee table. "And the whisky."

Tomlinson looked terrified. He tried to stand but couldn't move his legs. The lights that flashed across his vision started to take on different colours and shapes. He had never been high and didn't understand what was happening to him. His chest tightened and his breathing became laboured.

"Are you killing me?" he asked, his voice shaking and fear in his eyes.

McDermott sat back down opposite him again. "Why not?" he replied. "You tried to kill me."

Tomlinson floundered around in his chair. "No!" he wailed in utter distress. "I didn't. It was nothing to do with me!" He stared at McDermott with eyes pleading, tears welling up in the corners. "Please don't kill me," he whimpered.

McDermott sat quietly studying Tomlinson for what felt to Tomlinson like an absolute age, during which his heart pounded, and his breathing laboured, and his chest felt like an elephant was sitting on it. Eventually McDermott leaned forward and spoke.

"This is what you are going to do, Mr Tomlinson," he said, his tone measured and serious, but threatening. "You are going to speak to Langley, and you are going to give him one quite simple and clear message. You tell him that John Smith has retired. Do you understand me?"

"Yes," whimpered Tomlinson, his body shaking. "Please don't kill me. I'll tell him."

"Make it very clear," said McDermott. "Any records of me need to be cleared. If anyone else tries to come after me, there will be serious trouble. The kind of trouble that none of you want. Understand?"

"Y... yes," replied Tomlinson. "But what about me? Do I need an antidote for what you have given me? Please, the feelings I am having are so strange. And I can't see properly. I feel like I'm going to die! Am I? Am I going to die?"

McDermott stood up and moved to Tomlinson, slapping him gently on the shoulder. "So long as you do what I have told you to do," he said. "You'll be fine." He then picked up his bag and walked out of the room and down the hallway towards the back of the house, where he had entered, only this time, when leaving, he used the rear door, rather than the window.

Daniel Tomlinson remained seated in his wingback chair, palpitations in his chest and his breathing erratic. He was hallucinating now. He could see spiders, huge, black, hairy spiders crawling on the coffee table in front of him. Screeching, he pulled his legs up, pushing his feet underneath him on the seat, his hands and arms cradling his knees, his eyes bulging out of their sockets. He sat shaking and shivering like that for several hours before the effects of the drug, exacerbated by the alcohol, began to wear off. When the morning sun finally began to fight through the thickness of the front curtains, and when he was satisfied that the huge hairy spiders had disappeared, he braved leaving the safety of his chair so that he could find his phone and call Chief Superintendent Bob Langley.

CHAPTER EIGHTEEN

After taking delivery of her personal possessions and her phone, Zoe had been distraught to find that everything had been wiped from it. The clothes went straight into the bin. There was no way that she was ever going to wear those again, even if they were boil washed to get rid of the blood stains of Michael. When she thought about him and pictured him in her mind, she cried. She had known him for such a short space of time, but during that time he had proved to be so helpful and, well, just nice, that she couldn't hold back a feeling of deep sadness whenever she thought of him. Yes, he had insisted on a price for everything, to the extent of really pushing the barrier between negotiation and downright taking the piss, but there had been something about the way that he had negotiated and chanced his arm that had an endearing quality about it.

About him.

And now, he was dead, and it was her fault. She constantly and silently chastised herself for sending him to the island, berating herself for going to Tomlinson's house, pissed out of her brains, and disclosing everything relating to the case to him. She was certain that Tomlinson had arranged Michael Frazier's death. There was no other explanation. She couldn't imagine that he had carried out the deed himself, he would never have dirtied his own hands, but he must have sent someone to kill Michael. The obvious suspect was John Smith, but she had no way of proving that and certainly no way to prove that John Smith, if it had been him, had acted under the direction or instruction of Daniel Tomlinson.

She could be certain of that, because she had tried to run the idea past her editor, who, no matter how nuanced an argument she tried to present, had cut her dead every time. He iterated and reiterated to her that she had no proof, not even anything circumstantial, that supported any kind of case that Tomlinson had hired a hit man.

During the same period, she bought a new laptop and hoped beyond hope that, somehow, probably through a factory setting, her photographs had been saved to the Cloud.

But no.

She took her phone into the nearest franchise that sold that particular brand and asked them to use whatever wizardry they had in their power to undelete the former contents of her phone, but disappointingly, they confirmed that it had been wiped clean beyond any recovery.

She even went underground, using her contacts from years of journalistic 'pushing of luck' and sailing close to the wind, paying an exorbitant amount of money to a computer nerd to try and recover what had been held on the device, only to be told that it was all gone. What is more, it hadn't been wiped accidentally, but professionally, by someone, or some organisation that knew exactly and clinically how to permanently destroy everything on an electronic device, without simply destroying the device itself. And she knew that the nerd was telling the truth, because she had used the same nerd in times past to recover data from tech that had been trashed.

She had already tried the obvious route, contacting the Ferry company for the Isle of Wight crossing, and asking for copies of the CCTV footage from the date of Sir Julian's alleged suicide, but after first running up against GDPR and Data Protection grounds for refusal over a period of days of repeated requests, she was eventually told that all of those recordings had been overwritten because the equipment automatically deleted everything after a certain time period. The police might have copies from the original investigation, but she knew that there was absolutely no chance of getting hold of those.

As December came and the nights grew longer and darker, the fervency of her search to find the lost material began to subside and with that loss of energy, her mind, now no longer actively and constantly engaged in a heightened state of determination, succumbed to the post traumatic sadness and depression of the experience that she had suffered when she had discovered Michael Frazier's dead and bloody body in Sir Julian's kitchen.

Zoe began to disappear within herself, locked away in her apartment, ignoring all attempts at contact and wallowing in a deep depression and self-loathing arising from the guilt that she felt over Michael's death. She tried to work but couldn't. Each day became more and more of a struggle than the last and she would rarely venture out, instead hiding away inside, the curtains closed, spending most of her time in bed.

She came from money, her family wealthy, not the landed gentry type, but rather the commercially savvy. Her father had died when she was young, but her mother was still going strong and it was her that, having heard that her daughter had dropped off the grid, had begun visiting, trying to drag her out of her doldrums and back to the bright sunshine of life. But even that intervention was failing. Attempts to persuade her to engage in therapy, or counselling, had elicited tones of derision and impatience until, even Zoe's mother was permanently refused access to the apartment.

She missed the deadline for her piece with the paper, spending all her time instead focussing on the piece on Sir Julian, but failing to produce anything that was worthy of publication. For a time, her guilt led her down the path of confession. She believed that her only route to some form of absolution was to accept total responsibility for Michael's death, irrespective of a full knowledge of the facts. In her mind, it was always and inevitably, her fault.

She began to spend more time hiding under a duvet on her bed in a room with the curtains permanently closed than she even had when she had been just a lazy teenager. For most of her life, apart from the years immediately after her father's death, she had always been a happy and energetic soul. As a journalist, she had undoubtedly stepped over the mark on occasion and acted in ways that might raise a professional eyebrow, but she had always tried to avoid being associated with those journalists whom she considered to be the vultures within the profession. Now, wracked with guilt, she didn't even feel capable of stringing a legible sentence together.

So, she stayed in bed.

She would get up and use the bathroom when she needed to do, although not quite a complete ablution, and she would eat something, more often than not cheese on toast, and sometimes she would sit in her armchair in the living room and look out of the window, particularly now that the Christmas lights were erected and in bulb. But not for long. She would soon creep back to her bed and cover her head, crying a little, and trying to overcome her guilt.

And that is how Andrew McDermott found her when he silently broke into her apartment one night, only a few days before Christmas Eve. She was asleep in bed on one of the few occasions when, rather than just hiding away, she was genuinely tired and in need of some sleep.

He had done his usual thorough sweep of the residence to ensure that he wouldn't face any sudden surprises and then he gently and carefully sat down on the edge of the double bed in which she slept, towards the bottom end and watched her intently. She breathed deeply as she lay on her side, her mouth open, and she produced the occasional nasal snore that she would undoubtedly deny if she were in a relationship. He studied her sleeping face which, even though unanimated, yet still displayed hints of stress and unhappiness and a general sense of unease. He thought it was a pretty face. One which, unusual to his experiences, looked innocent.

She continued to breathe deeply, so he reached under the duvet until he found a foot and then began to gently tickle the sole. Completely involuntarily and still asleep, her leg recoiled, bending at the knee, and drawing the foot away. McDermott surprised himself when he smiled in response.

A few moments later, Zoe stirred and rolled off her side and onto her back, releasing a loud snore at the same time and straightening her legs out, the right foot prodding McDermott's thigh. He reached down with his hand again and tickled the sole. Again, the foot twitched and the leg drew it back sharply, but it was only a moment before she straightened her leg, and her foot was in reach of McDermott's fingers once more. He tickled a little harder this time and the foot was drawn away with force and Zoe's eyes sprang open. Immediately, they were filled with fear and she scrabbled backwards up the bed towards the headboard, drawing her knees up to her chest, her eyes wide open and her mouth trying to scream, but her throat constricting in terror and denying her the ability.

"Hello Zoe," said McDermott in an entirely normal, everyday manner, yet one which nevertheless filled her with dread.

She knew immediately who he was. The images from the CCTV on the ferry were burned into her brain and she had no difficulty recognising John Smith, the man who she was convinced was responsible for the deaths of Sir Julian Hebburn and Michael Frazier.

With an outward breath a scream finally managed to emerge from her throat, the fear constricting it limiting the sound. At the same time, she rolled away from Smith, scrabbling in terror with her hands to pull herself away from him and thrashing her legs in an attempt to propel her to safety. She was held back as Smith, coolly and calmly grabbed her right ankle, preventing her from pulling away. She thrashed around like an animal caught in a snare, but his grip tightened, the strength in his hand squeezing agonising pain through her leg.

"Stop!" he commanded. She didn't and instead continued to thrash, strange cries and pants of breath escaping her mouth. His powerful hand squeezed even tighter and Zoe yelped in pain.

"Stop!" he said again, a little quieter as her thrashing subsided. Eventually she stopped fighting, lying at an angle, trying to stretch as far away from him as possible, her right leg stretched to its extremity in an attempt to do so, his hand maintaining a vice like, painful grip on her ankle.

"I'm not going to hurt you," he said, quietly.

Zoe thrashed her right leg again, to no avail. "You are hurting me!" she protested.

He released the pressure slightly, whilst still maintaining a hold, and, predictably, she tried to pull her leg away, prompting him to immediately tighten his grip again.

"Ow!" she wailed.

"Stop fighting me," he said calmly. "I only want to ask you some questions. Then I will leave."

Her struggling waned a little, then subsided, then ceased altogether. She looked at his face intently, trying to determine whether or not she believed him. Eventually, she slid back to the right-hand side of the bed, propping up against the pillows, still watching him, and not even realising that he had released her ankle.

"Go on," she ventured.

"Who am I?" he began.

Zoe frowned, staring at his eyes, then feeling compelled to look away because of their intensity.

"I don't ... understand," she said eventually.

"What is my name?" he asked, trying an alternative tack.

"Well," said Zoe, almost smiling wryly, but not for long when she remembered her predicament. "I doubt that I know your real name at all, but the one I do know is John Smith."

He nodded. "That's a good start, Zoe. Now, tell me how and why you know my name."

She hesitated as fear gripped her again. Should she really confess anything to this man, this extremely dangerous man? Sensing her thoughts, he tapped her ankle, reassuringly, although she still didn't realise that he was no longer holding it.

"You can be honest with me, Zoe," he said. "Indeed, you must be honest with me. That way I can leave you alone and I won't have to return. So, how, and why, do you know my name?"

"We saw you on the ferry cameras," she said hesitantly. "And then Michael," a sudden, unexpected sob caught in her throat and she had to pause. "Michael," she began again. "Found your details from a van hire place in Portsmouth. We saw the number plate on the van that you had rented."

"Who is Michael?" he asked.

Again, there was a sob in her throat. "He was helping me," she said. "That's all. But now ..."

He studied her face carefully for what felt like a long time. "He's dead?" he asked eventually.

Zoe nodded, a tear slipping from her eye and rolling down her cheek. Then, looking back up at him, realisation dawned, and panic struck again, her body almost involuntarily twisting away again to the other side of the bed, before being prevented from escape by his hand swiftly and powerfully grabbing her ankle once more.

"Ok," he said, measuredly. "That's the how. Now, tell me the why. Why do you know my name?"

"I don't understand," she said, her voice trembling. "What do you mean, why?"

"Why were you trying to find me? On the ferry CCTV?" he said.

At first, she didn't understand his question, because in her mind it was perfectly logical that she would be looking for him and it made no sense to question that, but, after a moment of thought, she understood that she was considering the question only from her perspective and not from why he was asking.

"Sir Julian," she said. "I'm a journalist. I had the scoop of the century from one of the highest Civil Servants in Government. He was going to blow the whistle on Broughton Stretton. I knew this because he left me a message telling me as much. But then he disappeared overboard on that ferry from the Isle of Wight and ..." she looked at him, trying to be brave, but the fear quite apparent in her eyes. "And then, when I investigated what had happened to him, I saw you. I watched you follow him across the deck of the boat and only you returned. Sir Julian was gone."

As he had listened, he had loosened and then released his grip again, without her realising, but now he pulled his hand away and she saw that she was free and drew her knees up to her chin, cradling them with her arms. He was quiet for a long time, his head lowered slightly in contemplation. Eventually, he looked up, straight at her, his eyes piercing.

"So, are you saying that you were not sent to look for me?"

"What?" she said in surprise. "Who would send me to look for you? No! My story was Sir Julian. The reason I started looking into you was because I didn't believe he had committed suicide."

Again, silence filled the room, until eventually, Zoe braved the question.

"Did you kill Michael?"

He didn't answer immediately. He mulled over all of the information that he had acquired over the previous weeks up until now.

"In Sir Julian's cottage?" he asked, eventually.

Zoe nodded, drawing her knees up even closer to her chin.

"Who was he?" he asked.

"He worked on the ferry," said Zoe. "He was helping me. He

had been on the ferry on the night when Sir Julian disappeared and then he had discovered that there was a house on the island. He showed me where it was and then ... I asked him to go back and retrieve the note, the shopping list, that Sir Julian had left in the kitchen, I thought it could prove that it wasn't a suicide." She paused.

"But you found him, didn't you?" she said slowly.

John Smith didn't answer. Instead, he posed another question. "What is your involvement with Tomlinson?"

She frowned again. "Daniel Tomlinson?" she asked.

Smith nodded.

"I don't have any involvement with him," she said. "Other than perhaps to implicate him if I ever get the opportunity to write my story." She was becoming calmer and in turn braver as she spoke. The man on the edge of her bed was terribly frightening and intimidating, but oddly, not threatening. At least, now that her breathing had relaxed a little, he didn't appear so.

"Was it him?" she asked. "Who paid you to ... to kill Sir Julian?"

Again, he didn't answer.

"What about Langley?" he asked after what felt like an age.

Zoe thought for a moment and then shook her head. "I don't know who that is," she said.

Now he understood. He had made some errors in the conclusions that he had drawn. This woman was just looking for a story and had played no part in what had happened to him since he had carried out his original task. The man on the island had just been unlucky. Wrong place and wrong time. Tomlinson had some involvement, but only at the beginning and this woman's account of the reasons why he had come across the man in Sir Julian's house ruled out any thought that Tomlinson had been behind the attempt on his life in Norwich, or the attempt to bring him in from his seaside home.

It had to be Chief Superintendent Bob Langley who was behind those attempts. Him and, no doubt, the Service. He stood up swiftly, startling Zoe who recoiled a little and pressed herself back against the headboard.

"Goodbye, Zoe," he said and headed out of her bedroom and towards the front door of her apartment.

Zoe was confused and scared and intrigued all at the same time. Surprising herself, she jumped out of bed and chased after him. He was just opening the front door and half turned to look at her.

"Wait!" she called. He paused, the front door ajar. "Who is Langley?" she asked.

He thought about the question for a moment and studied her face. "Best you don't know," he said eventually, turning back to opening the door.

"No, wait!" she said again. "It was Tomlinson that paid you, wasn't it? I could write that. You could tell me your story and I could write it. It's obvious from the questions that you were asking me that you thought Michael was someone else. Talk to me. Let me tell your story."

He sighed and smiled at her. "Now, wouldn't that be nice. Goodbye Zoe." He opened the door and stepped through, pulling it firmly closed behind him.

Zoe stood in her living room staring at the closed front door to her apartment for an age. She was standing stock still, but in a strange way was the most animated that she had been for days. Her mind was racing, processing information, putting two and two together and sometimes getting twenty-two, but sometimes, just sometimes, perhaps getting four.

Where was her phone?

She ran into the bedroom to look for it, moving the quilt and the pillows when she saw it wasn't on the bedside table. It wasn't there, so she rushed back into the living room, checking the coffee table and the sofa. Finally, she found it on the island in the kitchen diner, next to the plate holding a half-eaten piece of toast. When she pressed the button to illuminate the screen, she was frustrated to see that the battery bar was a vivid red and showed only four per cent of charge. She hunted around in the kitchen and then in the living room for her charger, but couldn't remember where she had put it, so with the utterance of a word that would have made her mother pull a face, she dialled the number of her editor anyway. It seemed to ring for ever, until a groggy male voice finally said "hello?".

"Eric!" she said excitedly. She heard a rustling sound at the other end of the phone and then the word hello was repeated.

"Eric! He was here!"

"Who ... who is this?" said the voice.

"Eric!" she repeated, frustration and excitement in her voice. "It's Zoe. Zoe Carlson. Eric, he was here! In my flat!"

"Zoe?" came the sleepy reply. Then a pause. "Do you know what time it is?"

Zoe looked at her wrist, but her watch wasn't there. She looked around the room aimlessly searching for a clock, but she knew that she didn't have one.

"It's three in the morning," said Eric, helpfully.

"Is it?" she was genuinely surprised, having lost all sense of time over the preceding days. "Sorry, Eric. I hadn't realised. But I need to talk."

There was a loud sigh on the other end of the phone and more rustling, then a female voice asking who was calling at that time of the morning.

"Zoe, it's lovely to hear from you," said Eric's tired voice. "Particularly after all that has happened, but can't this wait until the morning?"

"I can't wait," she said, excitedly. "He was here. John Smith was here. In my apartment." There was more silence and then rustling at the other end of the line.

"What do you mean he was there?" said Eric. "Did you find him, or something?"

"No, he broke in," she said, a smile on her face.

"What?!" cried Eric. "Have you called the police?"

"No," said Zoe. "There's no need, he's gone. But Eric. It was him. It was John Smith. And he all but admitted that he killed Sir Julian Hebburn and Michael."

"He said that?" asked Eric, with some urgency in his voice. "He actually admitted to murdering Sir Julian?"

"Yes. Well, nearly. Look, he didn't deny it. The point is, he was asking me questions about Michael and how we knew who he is, and I told him about Sir Julian and how I had seen him follow Sir Julian on the ferry, and he didn't deny it."

"Look, Zoe. Not denying it, is not the same as admitting it," said Eric. "As you well know. And anyway, are you certain it was this Smith fella?"

"Yes! Of course!" she was indignant now. "I would never forget that face. Especially not after what happened to Michael."

"Ok, fair enough," said Eric. "But you still don't have a confession. And you let him go and didn't call the police. What are you supposing I ... we can do about what he told you?"

"He asked me about Daniel Tomlinson," said Zoe, all the

fear, anxiety and glum moods from the previous days now suddenly replaced with a kind of warped and almost vulgar, smug satisfaction. There was another long pause.

"What about Tomlinson?" asked Eric. Zoe could almost hear the Editor's brain switch into interested journalistic overdrive.

"He asked me if I was involved with Tomlinson. Right on the back of my asking about Sir Julian. I asked him if Tomlinson paid him to kill Hebburn. He didn't deny it, and I know you're going to say that's not the same as an admission of guilt, but why would he ask me about Tomlinson? I'm telling you Eric. I'm as sure as sure can be, that Tomlinson arranged the death of Sir Julian Hebburn and John Smith was the implement he used. He mentioned someone else as well. Langley? Any ideas who that is?"

There was a very long pause before Eric replied. "Bob Langley?" he said.

"I don't know," said Zoe. "Who is Bob Langley?"

"Chief Superintendent Bob Langley of Scotland Yard? Come on, Zoe. You must have heard of him?"

Her mouth dropped open. "Of course," she said. "I hadn't made the connection. It can't be, can it?"

She waited for a response, but none came. "Eric?" she said. "Do you think it is the same Langley?"

Still there was silence. Confused, she pulled the phone away from her ear and looked at the screen. It was dead. She pressed the button to try and generate some life into it, but that didn't work. She swore and dropped it onto the kitchen island, looking around for her charger, and then instead thinking of her laptop. She decided that she would write an email to Eric and then set about with the beginnings of the piece that she had hoped to write all along, now with a different twist. There was no point in going back to bed now. For the first time in a long time, she felt alive.

CHAPTER NINETEEN

"Daniel Tomlinson for you, sir," came the voice of the secretary of Chief Superintendent Bob Langley over the desktop intercom.

Langley looked away from the large computer screen on his desk at the telephone intercom. He leant forward and pressed a button. "Tell him I'm unavailable," he said, turning back to his screen. There was a short silence and then the voice returned.

"He says that he has called a number of times already this morning."

Langley frowned and looked at his watch, then pressed the button again. "It's only eight thirty. What is he? An insomniac?" He paused and tutted, reminding himself that his wife had frequently told him to stop being such a grumpy old sod. "I'm sorry," he said to his secretary. "Please just tell him that I'm in meetings and can't be reached."

Again, Langley turned back to his screen and the report that he was studying. He tried to push the thought of Tomlinson to the back of his mind so that he could concentrate on his work, but he was struggling to do so, given what the damned idiot had taken upon himself to do. But, in reality, Langley was particularly angry with himself for ever having agreed to provide Tomlinson with information about the existence of beneath the radar operations and worse, the actual contact details of an asset. It is wise to learn by one's mistakes, he had thought, but best not to make such damaging mistakes in the first place.

After discovering what Tomlinson had orchestrated, Langley had quickly taken the necessary steps to clean up what in naval terms was referred to as a clusterfuck. Mark Carter at The Service had not been best pleased to find out what had happened and, perhaps more importantly, that an asset had been misused and thereby compromised. The level of work and time and organisation that was absolutely necessary to ensure that an asset was indeed, first an asset, and then, an absolute, incorruptible asset, was almost immeasurable, so he had been entirely unimpressed that Langley had disclosed any information to someone who was not within that extremely small inner circle of individuals who were authorised to know about such things, and even more unimpressed to discover that the individual that had become privy to that information had then taken it upon himself to utilise the asset. To then discover that the asset had been compromised was the final straw, to the extent that Mark Carter had suggested that a possible distraction method that might misdirect those that may express an interest in the said clusterfuck, could be to have Daniel Tomlinson have a very unfortunate, and deadly, accident.

Fortunate for, and unbeknown to, Daniel Tomlinson, Chief Superintendent Langley had talked Mark Carter out of the idea, suggesting an alternative, potentially cleaner option to close the matter down.

Langley pushed the thoughts from his mind and resumed

reading the report on his screen. It was detailed and complicated, taking a long time to digest and understand. He took occasional breaks, either stepping out into the open plan office and engaging with the staff on that floor, or just standing at the windows of his office, looking out at the road and the pedestrian walkways beyond it and the river further beyond that.

He was deep in concentration, uninterrupted for almost two hours or so, when he heard a hubbub of activity outside his office, just before the door swung open and Daniel Tomlinson marched in, followed by Langley's extremely apologetic secretary.

"Sir," she announced. "I'm sorry, but I told him that you are otherwise engaged, yet he won't listen and simply barged past me." She paused in her stride and looked indignantly at Tomlinson. "Please tell me I am to have someone come upstairs and arrest him!"

"We need to talk," said Tomlinson to Langley, the urgency in his voice almost vibrating the room.

Once more, Langley heard his wife's chastisement in his mind just as he was about to stand and order Tomlinson to leave. In his brain, he could picture almost cartoon caricatures of him and his wife and Tomlinson, Langley having been chastised by his wife for being a grumpy old sod, yet pointing to the cartoon of Tomlinson and exclaiming 'I have to be!" by way of defence.

He settled back in his chair and gently shook his head towards his secretary. She, in turn, raised her eyebrows and shrugged her shoulders, throwing a look of disgust in the direction of Tomlinson and then left the office, pulling the door closed behind her.

"What is it, Tomlinson?" asked Langley.

Tomlinson hurried over to the chairs in front of Langley's desk and sat down in one of them, wringing his hands.

"John Smith came to my house last night," he said, once he had steadied his nerves. "He tried to kill me."

Langley studied Tomlinson carefully. "I doubt that very much," he said eventually.

Tomlinson threw his hands up above his head in despair. "Yes he did" he exclaimed. "He drugged me, and he told me that I have to pass a message to you."

"He drugged you?" asked Langley, the sarcasm heavy in his voice. "With what?"

Tomlinson stood up and began to pace back and forth, one hand rubbing his forehead just above his right eye.

"I don't know," he said as he paced. "He said it was magic mushrooms, or something. He said some scientific name. But that's not the point. He told me that I have to tell you that he is retiring, and you have to leave him alone."

"Really?" said Langley, in a tone that made it clear that the question was rhetorical and not a little sarcastic.

"Yes, really," said Tomlinson, returning to his seat and wringing his hands again in a manner that Langley found a little disturbing. "You must delete any record of his existence. He was quite adamant about that."

"Look, Tomlinson. Daniel," said Langley in the best deliberately patronising tone that he could muster. "Much as I would love to see you squirm and worry, the truth is, you don't need to. Whoever came to see you last night, if indeed anyone actually did, given your apparent penchant for controlled substances, is not the person that had previously caused us some ... difficulties. Rest assured, that individual is no longer of concern. He suffered a tragic accident, and his body was recovered from a river in Norwich. I can only think that your experience was, well, an hallucination."

Tomlinson's mouth fell open in disbelief. He shook his head vigorously.

"I know what I saw, Langley," he said. "It was not an hallucination. How dare you suggest that I am some kind of drug addict. John Smith came to my house, he asked about you and that Carlson woman and the Isle of Wight, and .... Wait. Did you say Norwich?"

"Yes," smiled Langley. "As I told you, it is taken care of."

"Well, there's your proof that I didn't imagine him," said Tomlinson. "He asked me about Norwich. I had no idea what he was talking about, but now you tell me that Smith was supposed to have suffered an accident in Norwich. That explains why he was asking me about the place. You say that a body was recovered?"

Langley was beginning to feel a little less smug. "Yes," he nodded. "Yesterday morning."

"Well, if I were you," said Tomlinson. "I would double check the identity of the body that you have, because I can assure you, it isn't John Smith. And more than that, you need to listen to what I've been telling you. He wants out and if he doesn't get out, I dread to think what he will do. To me, and to you."

Langley harrumphed. "Don't be ridiculous, Tomlinson," he said confidently. "Now, if you don't mind, I have work to do." He nodded towards the door.

"Don't you understand?" said Tomlinson. "He knows about you. He knows who you are. Which means that whatever happened in Norwich, he knows that you were behind it. You can't just ignore me on this, Langley. I don't intend to have another visit from him in the middle of the night, and I doubt very much that you want one, either."

"Goodbye, Mr Tomlinson," said Langley, his arm gesturing towards his office door.

Stunned at how dismissive Langley was being but realising that he was not going to be able to persuade the man to do as he asked, Tomlinson stood and marched to the door. He turned and looked angrily at Langley as he opened it.

"You're going to regret this, Langley," he said, before walking through and half slamming the door behind him. Tomlinson had no intention of heading back to his house. Instead, he would hail a cab and have it bring him to Essex where he would join his wife and children.

When Tomlinson had left, Langley opened his desk drawer and withdrew the same device that he had used previously when contacting Mark Carter at the Service. Once the lights were green, he dialled the number and a moment later was connected.

"Have you had confirmation of identity of the body taken from the river in Norwich?" he asked.

There was silence for a moment before Carter replied. "Why do you want to know?"

"I've just had Tomlinson here and he claims that he received a visit from Smith last night. He said that Smith was insisting on retirement and removal from records, but I didn't think we retired ... those people," said Langley.

"We don't," replied Carter. "They tend to have a natural expiry date that brings about their own retirement. That's the nature of the job. This Tomlinson, is he certain it was Smith?"

"He seemed pretty adamant to me," said Langley.

"How would he recognise him?"

"I don't know," said Langley. "I don't see how he could."

Whilst he was talking, Langley clicked through some files on his computer until he arrived at one marked 'Carlson'. He double clicked on it and then entered the password it required. A list of items appeared on screen and he opened one of them, the photograph of John Smith driving a van, taken from Zoe's phone, appeared on the screen.

"But, as I said, he was pretty adamant. He said that Smith asked him about Zoe Carlson and the Isle of Wight. He also said that he asked about Norwich. That's why I think you should check the identity of the body."

"Hmm," said Carter. "That is unfortunate."

"What is?" asked Langley. "What is unfortunate?"

"The body in Norwich wasn't Smith," said Carter. "Unfortunately, Mr Smith got the better of our ..." he paused. "Our other asset."

"And you didn't think to inform me?" asked Langley.

There was a long pause.

"Why would I do that?" asked Carter. "I don't report to you."

"Because I could potentially be in the middle of a shit storm!" said Langley, angrily.

"Indeed, you could," replied Carter, coolly. "One you brought upon yourself, you might recall. However, that was not what I meant by that's unfortunate."

"Well, what did you mean?" asked Langley.

"Once I had received news that the other asset was the body pulled from the river in Norwich, I took the liberty of arranging for your people to pick Smith up from his cottage on the coast. I decided that it would be best to have him brought in directly, rather than wasting more operatives trying to cover up your mess. He wouldn't have any inkling that the Service knows about his little hidey hole, so I thought a uniform picking him up and bringing him in would be nice and simple. Given what you have just told me, it would appear that I underestimated him."

"How dare you!" said Langley. "How dare you use the police for your dirty work."

"I could as easily ask how dare you, Chief Superintendent," said Carter, his voice remaining calm. "Might I remind you that it was you who broke protocol and divulged information to this Tomlinson person."

"Yes, alright, I know," said Langley, his voice a little contrite, but not much. "But what do we do now?"

"Sorry, Bob," said Carter. "This is your shit show. You should never have disclosed the details of an asset to Tomlinson. Now Smith is probably in the wind and I can't risk anything blowing back on the Service by getting any further involved. I've already done more than I should have by agreeing to your idea and seeking an elimination. I can't believe that I let you talk me into that. It would have been better if Tomlinson had been found floating in a river. An asset killed whilst on a mission to kill another asset, if that ever came out, is potentially a million times more damaging to this Agency. I suggest we simply do what he asks and treat him as retired."

"We can't do that," said Langley. "He knows too much that could be damaging. He knows who I am, for God's sake."

"I wouldn't worry too much about that, Bob," said Carter. "He won't be after blackmailing you or anyone. He just wants out of the job. Leave him alone and forget about him and that will be the end of it, I'm certain."

Langley was shaking his head, looking back and forth between the phone and the computer screen displaying John Smith's face.

"You must be kidding?" he said. "I can't have loose ends like that hanging around, waiting to come out of the woodwork at any moment with a threat of exposure or a demand for something that I can't give. He needs to be taken care of."

"Like I said, Bob," replied Carter. "I can't help you. Anyway, I've got to go. Good to speak with you Bob." The line went dead.

"Fuck," whispered Langley. He pressed the button on the device attached to the phone, waiting for the lights that had now gone out to change to green again. But they didn't. They got to orange and stuck. He unplugged and reinserted it and tried again, but still no green lights. It was obvious that Mark Carter had revoked his direct access immediately after the call.

Langley leaned back in his chair and stared at the image on the computer screen, wondering what his next decision should be. Every minute or so he would swear quietly to himself, before he eventually stood up and began pacing back and forth in his office, finally stopping at the floor to ceiling glass of the windows and staring out at the river, the sun reflecting off it and making the water appear clean, instead of the usual brown, muddy murkiness that he was used to from the Thames.

The embankment was busy, people rushing in opposite directions, heads down, headphones on, or pushed into ears, avoiding any eye contact. Other people, most likely tourists, standing around, pointing and smiling, taking photographs and selfies. This was Langley's escapism. Watching the world go by. It was how he refocused his mind in times when so many issues muddied his concentration. The distraction of simply watching ordinary people, ordinary, law abiding citizens, go about their daily routines, always helped him to centre his mind and bring his thought process back under control.

One person on the pavement opposite Scotland Yard wasn't moving. The individual appeared to be alone and was looking at the building itself. In fact, he appeared to be looking directly up at Langley's office.

At Langley himself.

Langley raised his right hand to shield his eyes from the sunlight as he focussed on the face of the man. It took a moment or two, but suddenly he recognised him. The face on Langley's computer screen was a little grainy, but it was clear enough for him to realise that the lone figure across the road from his office, staring directly up at him was John Smith.

"Karen," he half mouthed, continuing to stare at the man down on the pavement. "Karen," he said, a little louder this time, still staring. The man stood motionless, staring back at him. Even from this distance it appeared that he was making direct eye contact with Langley.

"Karen!" he shouted. "Karen!" he half turned and looked through the glass walls of his office to the outer room, then back out at the pavement. The man was still there. His secretary opened the door to his office and rushed in, a puzzled and concerned look on her face.

"Chief Superintendent?" she asked.

Langley didn't turn around. He maintained his gaze on John Smith down below, still looking up at him, unflinching, unmoving.

"Get me an armed response unit to meet me in the front lobby immediately!" ordered Langley.

"Yes, sir," replied Karen, heading back out of the office. She knew better than to question her boss or to ask him to repeat an instruction.

Langley stepped quickly over to the metal upright coat stand in the corner and removed his uniform jacket from the coat hanger that was holding it there, neatly. He stepped back to the window and pulled the jacket on as he continued to stare at the man down below. Slowly and deliberately, he fastened the silver buttons from the top down, running his hands down the side of his jacket after doing so, straightening it, and ensuring that it was neat and tidy. On each shoulder sat the epaulettes with a crown above a single silver diamond pip.

The man below remained where he was, head still raised slightly, eyes staring unflinchingly up at Langley. The uniform that Langley wore was completed when he took his cap from the same coat stand, the laurel wreath pattern on the pristine peak, and placed it squarely on his head. Then, giving one final look at Smith below, he turned on his heel and marched briskly out of his office and across to the stairs that led down to the ground floor.

In the lobby downstairs, beyond the internal security doors stood four burly police officers, baseball caps on their heads and body armour covering their torsos. Each had a utility belt with various items attached to it and a sidearm holstered over each hip. A strap hung over their left shoulders and attached to the end of it, held at the pistol grip by each officer's right hand was a matt black Glock 17 automatic machine gun. They came to attention as Langley approached them.

"On me," he commanded. "One suspect, across the road, about five ten, maybe taller, stocky, dark coat, bald head. He is considered armed and dangerous. If he makes any wrong move, you have my authority to take him down. Understood?"

A chorus of "yes sir" confirmed his orders as the four of them followed him to the glass front of the building. A glass carousel door dominated the centre of the front wall with large glass swing doors on either side of it. Langley moved to the left swing door and two armed officers followed him, the other two peeling off to the right and taking the other door. Once outside, the five of them ran down the pedestrian ramp to street level and Langley led the way, running out into traffic, one hand raised authoritatively bringing cars and buses to a halt, the four armed officers moving with him as they crossed Victoria Embankment and arrived at the pedestrianised walkway on the other side. Langley stopped and looked around, spinning on a heel.

"He's gone," he said angrily. The RAF monument dominated most of the pavement to his left and to the right of that stood a bench, which Langley ran towards and climbed upon, straining his eyes, and trying to catch a glimpse of his prey.

"There!" he suddenly shouted, pointing towards a group of people walking in the direction of the statue of Boudicca.

"He's heading for the tube station at Westminster." Langley jumped off the bench and began to run, the armed officers joining him at speed, each occasionally shouting 'Police' warning people to get out of their way.

Andrew McDermott watched them from the relatively inconspicuous safety of a red London telephone box on the embankment. He regarded with interest Langley's decision to bring armed officers with him when coming to look for John Smith. That had been an unpleasant confirmation in his mind that he wasn't going to be released from his arrangement very easily.

He opened the door to the telephone box and crossed the

road, walking deliberately up the side of the building at Scotland Yard, towards the Cenotaph and beyond, thinking carefully about the few options that were now left open to him.

CHAPTER TWENTY

Zoe had tidied her flat and opened all of the curtains to allow as much natural light in as possible. She had cleaned everywhere and made the place look like it was lived in once more, before showering and making herself feel human again. Then she had set up her new laptop on the kitchen counter, a cup of strong black coffee on one side of it and her new mobile phone on the other.

As terrifying as it had been, the visit from John Smith had reinvigorated her and given her a new sense of purpose. The trauma of the previous weeks, the death of Michael Frazier, her subsequent arrest and all of the mixed-up emotions that she had suffered were not gone and forgotten. They were still very much there in her mind and occasionally she would find herself drifting off and staring into space, before she pulled herself out of that dark place and back into the now, but she had a new purpose since the invasion of her home by the man that she had all but given up on finding. Now she had proof that he existed. Now, she knew that she had her article, her story, and, more to the point, now, people would listen.

First, she had spoken again with her editor, Eric, ensuring that he was on side for her to write the piece. He had been understandably cautious and at the same time concerned for her safety and general welfare.

"Are you certain that you have enough for a story?" he had asked. "I mean, Zoe, are you sure that this chap that broke in was in fact John Smith? And if it was, are you certain that you can link him to the death of Hebburn? And can you implicate Tomlinson? And the Government? You need proof, Zoe, not supposition and speculation. I'm not having the Paper sued over some unsubstantiated hunch."

She had reassured Eric as best as she could. "The story is there," she had said. "Think about it, Eric. Everything, up until the other night when he broke in and sat on the end of my bed, had been my supposition and hypothesis. I was putting the pieces together and seeing a link, but there was always a doubt that the evidence was circumstantial. Until he turned up at my flat in the middle of the night and started questioning me on everything that had happened. Come on Eric, think about that. That is more than circumstantial. Random, suspected killers don't turn up in the middle of the night for no apparent reason."

She had surprised herself, and Eric, when she had laughed at her comment. But only a moment later she had again taken on a serious demeanour.

"I have to write this, Eric," she had said, seriousness and a sombreness returning to her mood. "Sir Julian Hebburn was a good man. And Michael Frazier. Well, he was just someone trying to help me. He was innocent. Hell! They both were."

Eric had given her his blessing, but with conditions, mainly related to his concern about her wellbeing. She must keep him in the loop and not take any unnecessary risks. Her next call was a difficult one, for which she had to prepare herself and consider what she was going to say carefully before picking up the phone. It was to Eloise Sharp, the widow of Benjamin Sharp, who had died because of some apparent bacterial leak at Broughton Stretton. Eloise was still, quite naturally upset and her distress was compounded by the fact that her husband's body had still not been returned to her post-autopsy. Zoe was surprised by this and questioned where the body was. To her amazement, she was told that the body had not been returned yet from Broughton Stretton. She made arrangements to meet with Eloise in the New Year at the Sharp's home.

Next, Zoe began to write.

The story poured out of her onto the laptop screen, starting with the information that Eloise had provided for her and developing further as she wrote about Sir Julian Hebburn, detailing the history of his work and his successes and then setting out the story up to the point when Sir Julian had left her the voicemail message and then his sudden, unexpected demise. Hours passed without her realising as she typed away, until she was interrupted by her phone ringing. It was Eric.

"Have you seen the news?" he asked.

"No," said Zoe. "Why, what's happened?"

"Put it on," he replied.

Zoe opened a new web browser on her laptop and logged into a twenty-four-hour scrolling news program. Immediately, her screen was filled with a still and slightly grainy photograph, before it was minimised to the top right-hand corner and the news broadcaster dominated the remainder of the screen.

"Scotland Yard has released this photograph of an individual wanted for questioning in relation to the death of a ferry worker from Portsmouth. Michael Frazier was found stabbed to death by police officers on the Isle of Wight and a short time ago, Chief Superintendent Langley of the Metropolitan Police made the following statement."

The screen changed again, and this time was filled with a live recording of Bob Langley, outside Scotland Yard, speaking into the furry microphones of various Press agencies.

"We are today asking the public for any help in apprehending this individual. He is regarded as highly dangerous and the public must avoid approaching him or engaging with him, but if there is any information as to his whereabouts, please contact the number that will appear on your screens. He is wanted for questioning in relation to an horrific murder and we believe that he is armed and dangerous."

"Son of a bitch!" said Zoe into the phone. "That's my photograph! That's the photo that I took of John Smith from the CCTV off the ferry."

The slightly grainy photograph had been the image of John Smith driving the hired van up the ramp onto the ferry to the Isle of Wight.

"I had a feeling that it might be," said Eric. "What's going on, Zoe? I thought you didn't have the photo anymore."

"I don't," she almost shouted. "When I got my phone back from the police it was wiped. They must have downloaded what was on there." She let her thoughts run their natural course for a moment.

"It must be Langley," she said eventually. "He must have copied the phone and then had everything deleted."

"Why would he do that, Zoe?" asked Eric.

Again, she thought through her ideas. "He has to be involved," she said. "That must be why Smith was asking me about Langley when he came to my flat."

This time it was Eric that was silent for a long time as he processed that thought. Eventually he responded.

"So, if Langley is involved, why would he now be putting out a Press release to put Smith on everybody's radar as most wanted? If Smith works for Langley, which I think is what you are trying to say, Zoe, why now is he having him hunted?"

"He's cleaning up!" said Zoe in reply. "It's obvious, now I think of it. He's getting rid of the evidence. I'm going to have to think this through, but the way I see it, Langley must be involved, perhaps he is the kingpin, the one who commissions people like Smith to do the type of jobs that Smith does, but this time, things haven't gone to plan. That must be it," she said after pausing again to think for a moment. "He needs to get rid of Smith to clear up loose ends."

"I can understand your thought process to an extent, Zoe," said Eric. "But, if you are correct, the last thing that Langley would want to do is have Smith arrested and brought into custody where he could blab freely to his lawyer and anyone else who will listen about Langley's involvement. That bit doesn't make sense. Why would Langley take that risk?"

"You're right," she said. "That's what I'm struggling with. Smith questioned me about things that had apparently happened in Norwich which I don't know anything about. But it was obvious that he didn't know what was going on, either. What if Langley, or whoever, was already trying to clean things up and was trying to have Smith taken out of the picture? Let's say that didn't work and now, Smith is still at large, and Langley is getting more and more worried. He's just told the world that Smith is armed and dangerous. Langley has armed police at his disposal. What if he intends to have Smith killed as part of a police exercise?"

Eric blew air from his mouth and if Zoe could have seen him, she would have watched him lean right back in his chair with one hand sliding up his face from his chin to his forehead and over the top of his hair in a silent expression of "Oh fuck!"

"Eric, can you reach out to anyone in Norwich? Can you find out if anything has happened there recently? Anything unusual?"

"Absolutely," said Eric. "I've got an old school mate that works on the local television news. Give me half an hour." He hung up without saying goodbye.

Zoe continued to watch the news reel on her computer as the presenter repeated the same story every fifteen minutes and a scrolling ticker tape message ran across the bottom with the headline, a request for information and a telephone number.

It was over an hour before Eric called back. Not that Zoe had noticed. She had been too absorbed in the running commentary and the repeated recording of Chief Superintendent Bob Langley. When her phone did eventually burst into life it made her jump.

"Hi Eric," she said as she pressed the green telephone symbol on the screen. "Did you find anything?"

"Two weeks ago, a male body was pulled from the river Wensum. Local news understands that he was in his forties, with no identification on him and died of what appeared to be a heart attack. The odd thing about him not having any ID is that local police don't think that he was homeless. His clothes were casual, but modern and expensive. He was wearing expensive casual shoes. No alcohol in his body and no one knows where he was from, or why he was there, or how he managed to fall over a sold metal railing, four and half feet high into the river after having an apparent heart attack."

Zoe was excited.

"Just around the time when John Smith came to my flat,"

she said. "That explains why he was asking me about Norwich. They're trying to clean up, Eric. They're trying to clean Smith up. But he was obviously better than they thought he was."

Eric was also excited, but cautious at the same time. "Let's not leap into the dark, Zoe," he said. "I've asked my mate to get me more details about the guy in the river and, whilst I can see your thought process and I agree, it looks like there could be a link, let's not just yet start pointing fingers at a senior officer in the Met, eh?"

"Come on, Eric," she replied. "Join all of the dots! Anyway, for now I intend to find out why Langley wiped my phone."

"Zoe," said Eric, the nervous caution in his voice very apparent. "Let's not go crazy."

She laughed. "Already there," she said.

After hanging up the phone to Eric, Zoe called the scrolling number on the screen in front of her. It was answered promptly by someone asking whether she had any relevant information about the suspect that the police had released details about.

"I do," she said, a little bit too gleefully. "But I am only willing to disclose those details to Chief Superintendent Langley."

"I'm sorry, madam," came the reply. "We don't have the facility to transfer you to the Chief Superintendent, but I can take all of the details that you would like to provide to us, along with your name, and I will then pass that information on to the team investigating."

"No, I need to speak directly to Chief Superintendent Langley," she insisted.

"As I have explained, madam," said the voice. "I don't have that facility available to me. If you could provide me with the information that you have that relates to our public request, I can assure you that it will be passed on to the relevant police officers who will look into it. We are assuring all of the general public that all information will be taken seriously and investigated appropriately."

Zoe sighed.

"Try this," she said. "Tell the Chief Superintendent that it is Zoe Carlson calling..."

"I'm sorry to repeat myself, madam," interrupted the person on the line. "But..."

"And John Smith came to my home," Zoe interrupted in return.

There was a pause before the voice spoke again. "When was this, madam?"

"It's Zoe Carlson, not 'madam'," she replied. "And I will provide that information to Chief Superintendent Langley. Personally".

Again, there was a pause. "It may take me some time to locate him, ma.... Miss Carlson," said the voice.

"That's fine," smiled Zoe. "I can wait."

There was no hold music to listen to when the other end of the line went quiet and after waiting for rather a long time, Zoe began to wonder whether she had in fact been cut off, but eventually there was an unusual and loud click, before she heard the baritone of Chief Superintendent Bob Langley.

"Miss Carlson," he said. "I understand that you have some information relevant to my investigation?"

"Is that Chief Superintendent Langley?" she asked.

"It is indeed," he said. "So, what do you have for me, Miss Carlson?"

Zoe smiled with excitement and her heart began to race a little.

"Well, first," she said. "I have a question."

"Oh?" said Langley.

"Did you delete everything off my phone?" she asked.

He was silent for a moment. "I don't see how that could be, Miss Carlson," he said after some thought. "I don't believe that we have ever met."

She smiled again. "I know!" she said excitedly. "That's why I was confused as to how you managed to be running a television campaign for information using a photograph that I took with my mobile phone. One that I hadn't shared with anyone."

"Miss Carlson," said Langley. "I can't reveal the source that provided me with that photograph, but I can assure you that it was independently acquired and taken from footage disclosed to the police."

"Bollocks!" said Zoe, with half a laugh.

"Now, really, Miss Carlson," objected Langley. "I don't think that there is any need for that."

"I know it's the photograph that I took," said Zoe. "And you know it, too. I might not have suspected that you were responsible for wiping my phone. I might even have believed you about the photo being 'independently sourced', if John Smith hadn't come to my flat in the middle of the night and questioned me about you." She emphasised the word 'you'.

"Why would he be so interested in you, Chief Superintendent?" she asked.

"Miss Carlson." His tone was patronising. "I'm investigating a murder that I believe he was responsible for. It is perfectly understandable that he might be interested in me."

Her excitement was suddenly dampened. Her conspiracy theory was suddenly and unexpectedly undermined.

"But why would he come to me? To my flat?"

"Really?" asked Langley. "It was your friend that he killed. Michael Frazier. Did you forget?"

It was Zoe's turn to be silent.

"So, Miss Carlson," continued Langley. "Tell me about John Smith's visit. All of the details, please."

After a further moment's hesitation, the wind taken out of her sails somewhat, Zoe recounted the details of the visit to her apartment in the dead of night by John Smith. She told Langley about the questioning relating to Daniel Tomlinson and about how Smith had been so interested in Norwich, but she didn't tell him anything about Eric's findings in relation to the dead body in the river.

"That's all very helpful, Miss Carlson," said Langley. "Now, one more thing. It is extremely important that, should John Smith make any contact with you again, you must contact us immediately. In fact, you can contact me directly. Is that understood?"

Deflated, she agreed.

"Good," said Langley, his voice had a slight air of triumphalism. "Let me give you my mobile number."

Zoe wrote it down and then hung up. She decided that she had to retake stock of all of the information that she had and make a distinction between what was fact and what was supposition. She remained confident about the links between John Smith, Langley, and Tomlinson, but she recognised that she had to be capable of demonstrating with certainty how the dots were joined.

CHAPTER TWENTY-ONE

Zoe awoke suddenly in the middle of the night, her mind buzzing with excitement.

"How did you know that?" she asked the darkness of her bedroom. Sitting up, she swung her legs out of bed.

"How did you know that Michael was my friend?" She reran in her mind the telephone conversation between her and Langley. What had he said to her?

"It was your friend that he killed."

Zoe gave a triumphant "Hah!" and a huge grin spread across her face. "Oh, Chief Superintendent," she said to the room. "How would you know that Michael Frazier was my friend? You wouldn't have had any link between me and Michael if it hadn't been you that had cleaned my phone. You would never have known about me. You would have only had Michael's murder, nothing about me."

She stood and began pacing back and forth in the room, her mind racing. That slip up by Langley confirmed to her that he was involved with everything that had been going on. In her mind she had to work through the link between him and Sir Julian. That could only be John Smith. The only people who had known Smith's identity were Zoe and Michael and the photograph that had been released by Scotland Yard was, without any doubt the one that she had taken with her phone. For Langley to release that photo in a manhunt for the murderer of Michael, and for him to also release the name of Smith could only mean that by looking at the photograph, Langley knew who he was looking at.

It also must mean that her phone had been sent to Langley from the police station on the Isle of Wight, after her release. From that could she conclude that it was Langley who had arranged her release from custody?

Did that mean that Langley knew what had happened to Sir Julian? What really happened? If he did, why wasn't he also adding that allegation to his 'wanted for murder' statement? Why continue to perpetuate the suicide lie? Albeit indirectly.

She checked her watch which confirmed that it was too early to call Eric and speak to him without incurring the wrath, if not of him, at least of his wife. But her mind was buzzing. She wouldn't be able to go back to sleep now. She walked purposefully into the kitchen and sat at the breakfast bar, opening her laptop. The screen came to life, illuminating her face in the darkness. Various applications were already opened, never to be shut down unless the battery died, but not the application which contained her notes and the draft of her story. That was secured in the cloud by password known only to her. That way, if this laptop went the same way as her previous one, she could still access everything that she had written.

Opening the secured file, Zoe began to write, documenting her thoughts prior to the phone call to Langley, the detail and her opinion of the conversation that had taken place between them, and his slip up, the error he had made, no doubt arising from overconfidence, that had confirmed to her that there was a conspiracy to cover up anything that may have happened at Broughton Stretton, the real reason behind Benjamin Sharp's death, Sir Julian and Michael Frazier, and that conspiracy stretched farther than she had originally ever considered. This could potentially be the type of scandal that could topple Governments.

A popup appeared in one corner of her screen, informing her that she had new email. She clicked on the popup and a new window opened on her screen, opening the email at the same time. The message looked strange and she panicked for a moment in fear that she might have opened a virus or other such damaging program that might harm her computer. She checked the bottom right-hand corner of her screen in order to ensure that the logo for the antivirus software that she used was still there; and running.

It was.

Her email address could easily be found. She freely displayed it on her social media sites, professional as well as personal, and various News outlet sites that had published her work. She was a reporter, after all, and wanted to be easy to find by anyone who might have a story, or information worthy of interest and, perhaps publication.

But this email was unusual. There was no information in the 'From' field and there was no message or text in the body of the email itself. The only content was an eleven-digit number in the 'Subject' field. She stared at the number for a long time, trying to figure out what it might mean. It took quite a while for the thought to arise that it might be a phone number. It began with a zero, which was a good indicator, but she then had to count out the digits of her own mobile phone number to confirm that there were eleven, before concluding that the number in the 'Subject' field was indeed a phone number.

But who did it belong to? And why send it in an email communication with no other information attached?

Her heart rate was elevated with a mixture of feelings, ranging from excitement to fear. Twice, she picked up her phone and began to tap the digits, before cancelling them and replacing the phone on the breakfast bar. Still nervous about dialling the number, she decided to make some coffee and let her emotions calm down before deciding what to do. She sat on the window ledge in the kitchen and looked out at the cold, clear night sky and sipped her hot coffee. Eventually, she plucked up the courage and returned to her phone on the breakfast bar, tapped in the eleven digits and then pressed the green telephone symbol to initiate the call.

It rang for a long time. So long, in fact, that Zoe began to have second thoughts about whether the number in the email was in fact intended to be considered a phone number or whether it was actually intended for some other use, and that by pure chance, it happened to also mirror a mobile telephone number. It occurred to her that she might be about to wake some random stranger who, no doubt, would not be best pleased at the unexpected intrusion.

"Hello," a voice answered.

She hesitated for a moment before replying.

"Oh, hello," she said. "I'm terribly sorry to bother you at this hour, but I received an email with this phone number and I....".

"Zoe," interrupted the vaguely familiar voice. "It's me, Smith. I sent you the number."

Her excitement peaked again. "H... hello," she stuttered. A sudden fear gripped her, and she looked around irrationally expecting him to be in the apartment again. She went to the window and looked out at the deserted street.

"Where are you?" she asked.

"I need your help, Zoe," said Smith.

She was silent for a long time before she replied. "How? How could I help you?" Her tone held an air of incredulity. "Why?"

"You said that you wanted to write my story, did you not?" The faint Scottish accent was just a little more noticeable in his tone.

"Yes," she said, excited. "Are you going to let me?"

"Perhaps," he replied. "If you do as I say. I need you to meet me."

"Why the change of heart?" asked Zoe.

"You've seen the news broadcasts?" asked Smith. "The request for information leading to my arrest?"

"Yes, of course," replied Zoe.

"What do you think will happen to me, Zoe, if the police find me?"

"You'll be arrested?" she ventured.

She could hear the smile, if not the sarcasm in his voice when he replied. "That's unlikely, Zoe. I've been described as armed and dangerous. The instructions will be, no doubt, to shoot on sight."

Zoe was horrified at the thought. "No," she objected. "We don't do that. Not in this country."

"That's wonderfully naïve of you, Zoe," said Smith. "I'm hardly going to submit quietly to an arrest and, let's face it, the powers that be, wouldn't really want me spilling my guts in Court. So, someone with an overly enthusiastic, slightly itchy trigger finger, will undoubtedly ensure that I never get that far. That's why I need to ensure that you have the true story, not the spin that will come out afterwards, but the facts."

"That's all I want," said Zoe, determination and excitement in her voice. "You can tell me now. Over the phone. I can be writing everything in a matter of hours."

"No, Zoe. I need you to meet with me."

She was more hesitant now. "Why? Why can't we just talk over the phone?"

"Don't worry, Zoe," said Smith. "I'm not going to hurt you. And I'm willing to tell you everything. Absolutely everything. But it must be in person."

She had a strange sensation in the pit of her stomach. In one sense, she was fairly confident that he was being honest with her. If he had wanted to hurt her, he could have done so on the night that he broke into her flat. But in another sense, he terrified her. He was a killer, after all. A skilled assassin paid to murder people. And now he was asking to meet with her.

Alone.

He knew that she had information about him and what he had done. Was this an attempt to tie up loose ends and get rid of Zoe?

But no. That didn't make sense. He would not need to send her some almost unintelligible message with the intention of luring her into a death-trap. He could simply have snuck in to her flat again one night, unheard and unseen, and slit her throat, or smothered her with a pillow whilst she slept. So, maybe, she wasn't at risk in meeting with him.

"Why does it have to be in person?" she asked.

"I have the note," he said.

Zoe's mind processed what he had said. "I don't.... what? .... The note?"

"The note that Hebburn left for his cleaner. The shopping

list," he said.

She sucked in her breath. Never mind the deleted and then undeleted photographs. That small piece of paper, written in his own hand and, no doubt with traces of his own fingerprints, or even DNA on it, in Zoe's opinion was an absolute confirmation that Sir Julian Hebburn did not commit suicide. Taken with a statement from the man whom she was convinced had killed Sir Julian, it really did not matter to her story that the photos she had taken of John Smith had been deleted.

"So where do you want to meet?" she asked.

"On the Isle of Wight," said Smith. "At Hebburn's house. I need you to drive there. I don't want you taking a passenger only ferry."

"Why?" she asked. "I don't have a car."

"Hire one," said Smith. "You can drive, can't you?"

"Well, yes," she replied. "I've got a licence, but I haven't driven for ages. I don't need to. I live in London."

"Hire one and make sure it is parked outside your flat today. I want to see it. I need to be certain that you are following my instructions."

"Can't I simply hire one from Portsmouth and get the train down there?" she asked.

"No," replied Smith.

The conversation continued with Smith giving full instructions of what he wanted Zoe to do, including booking the ferry slot and once disembarked, driving to the island home that had belonged to Sir Julian Hebburn.

When he finally hung up, Zoe sat staring at her phone and laptop for some considerable time, thinking carefully about her next steps and whether or not she should play along with John Smith. As the sun finally began to rise, she called Eric and told him that Smith had been in contact and wanted her to meet with him on the Isle of Wight. Eric was not keen on the idea, making the point that he considered it to be too dangerous and that she should instead contact the police.

"That was going to be my next call, Eric," said Zoe. Then, without unnecessary drama or exaggeration, but in a serious and sincere tone she gave Eric instructions about how to access her files in the cloud should something happen to her.

"Oh, come on, Zoe," said Eric. "This is ridiculous. If you think that you might be in danger, you simply cannot do this. You must go to the police instead."

"I know, Eric," she replied. "But I have thought this through, and it seems entirely illogical that Smith would ask me to travel down to the Isle of Wight when he could just as easily kill me in my bed if that was his intention. I'm going to call Langley next and tell him what I'm going to do."

"Good," said Eric. Then he questioned himself. "Actually," he said. "If you think that Langley is part of this whole conspiracy theory of yours, isn't telling him what you intend to do a little risky?"

"Very probably," said Zoe. "That's why I'm telling you how to access my files. Anyway, I must go now, I've got things to arrange. Goodbye, Eric. I hope I'll see you soon."

Her next call was to Scotland Yard, not on the number splashed over the television screens, but instead on the one for the front desk. She expected, and was right to do so, that there would be no problem being put directly through to Langley.

"Good morning, Miss Carlson," said Langley. "Do you have some relevant information for me?"

Zoe bristled a little at the undisguised patronising tone of Langley.

"He wants to meet me," she said, hoping that her news would knock at least some of the smugness from the Chief Superintendent.

"When?" he replied. There was no patronising tone now, just an earnest insistence on the detail.

"Tonight," said Zoe. "I have to take the ferry to the Isle of Wight and meet him at Sir Julian's house there at eight o'clock tonight."

"Why does he want to meet you?" there was a mixture of excitement and distrust in Langley's voice.

Zoe took a deep breath.

"He has something for me," she said. "The note that Sir Julian left on his kitchen table. Apparently, he took it when he ..." she paused, a sudden catch of breath and a lump in her throat preventing her from speaking for a moment. "When he killed Michael," she eventually managed to finish.

"Right," said Langley, authoritatively. "I will send some officers over to you. We will take it from here. You should stay at home and I will arrange for a team to be waiting for him on the island. Thank you for your assistance, Miss Carlson."

"That won't work," she interrupted. Langley was in the middle of protesting as she continued. "He has told me that he is watching me. If he doesn't see me leave and board the ferry, he will simply disappear."

"Well, that creates a problem for us, Miss Carlson," said Langley after a moment. "I can't risk putting you in danger by letting you go alone."

"You can't send someone with me," she said. "If he sees me with someone in the car that will be game over."

"Yes," said Langley. "You're probably correct. What time is the ferry? I'll arrange to have some men on board and at the house."

"I'm going to book the one at seven pm," she said.

"Fine," said Langley. "I will make the arrangements."

"It won't work," insisted Zoe. "If he sees lots of police around, he'll simply leave."

"Don't worry, Miss Carlson," said Langley, trying to reassure her. "There won't be any uniforms in sight. My officers will all be plain clothed. Now, make your arrangements, and if he makes contact again before you set off, contact me immediately. Call me on my mobile number. You still have it, don't you?"

She had forgotten that he had given it to her, but now remembering, Zoe confirmed that she had the number. After the call, she used her laptop to go online and book a hire car and a ferry ticket.

The car hire company agreed to drop the vehicle outside her apartment and post the keys in an envelope through the front door. When she had confirmed the registration number with them, she could then book the ferry ticket. She chose a single journey for now, unsure what time she might be returning to the mainland. Then, looking around her apartment and then the breakfast bar, she wondered what she needed to take with her, deciding in the end that her wallet, phone, and a good warm coat were all that she needed.

She stood up and went to the en-suite to shower and prepare for the day.

CHAPTER TWENTY-TWO

It had been a long time since Zoe had driven a car. She had taken and passed her test some years previous, but never felt the need to buy her own vehicle. Living in London meant that there was no need. She was nervous about driving, particularly such a long way, and had to spend time downloading a satellite navigation app to her phone, only to then find that there was already one fitted within the dashboard of the car as standard. When she had figured out how to use it, which had involved some delving into the glovebox and finding and then studying the manual that came with that model, it informed her that the journey to Portsmouth would take two hours and four minutes.

The ferry confirmation, informing her that she was booked on a seven o'clock crossing, was now stored on her mobile phone, but she was not confident enough in her driving ability to wait until the mid, or late afternoon before setting off, determined instead to make the journey whilst it was still daylight, allowing her plenty of time to travel at her own pace and arrive early and without the additional stress and anxiety of risking being caught in traffic. The purpose of her journey was stressful enough, without risking adding other complications to it.

She stopped along the way at a service station for a comfort break and a coffee, before setting off again, sitting safely in the nearside lane of the motorway, never exceeding fifty miles per hour, and arriving at Portsmouth in good time, with still a couple of hours to spare before she would have to enter the waiting area for vehicles preparing to board the ferry.

As she approached the ferry terminal for the Isle of Wight, the road markings indicated that she should enter the middle, right turn only lane. The words 'IOW Ferry' were painted in large letters on the tarmac. Immediately to the left, however, was a public car park, and Zoe turned the vehicle into it, pulling into a bay and applying the handbrake, before turning off the engine. The winter sun was setting now, and traffic was passing back and forth in front of her with headlights on. It was almost New Year's Eve and the afternoon sunset was taking place gradually later each day, but only by a minute or so.

She got out of the car to stretch her legs and walked up to the pavement. Opposite her, on the other side of the road, was the exit from the ferry port, large letters painted on the tarmac forbidding entry to vehicles by that route. To her left, illuminated by the streetlights, she could see the entrance to the Terminal framed between two high brick walls. In the near distance, straight ahead, stood the Spinnaker Tower, its skeletal bulbous stomach lit up in the dark, the colours changing from blue to magenta.

Her breath steamed as it left her mouth and she rubbed her hands together trying to fight off the cold, grateful for the warmth from the coat that she had worn but ruing the fact that she had not considered bringing gloves. She checked her watch. The booking confirmation had indicated that she would not be able to drive into the waiting area until an hour before sailing, so she went back to the car and sat in the driver's seat waiting patiently until that time.

Eventually it came, and she started the engine, turned on the lights and drove out of the car park, turning left and travelling the hundred or so yards in the middle lane until she reached the entrance to the ferry port and turned right, staying in the right-hand lane, and following the painted white signs on the road confirming that she was heading for the vehicle check-in point. The road led to a waiting area that looked like a huge car park, with numbered bays painted on the ground and for a moment she felt panicked, not knowing what to do. But fortunately, the Ferry staff were there, in their large blue coats, to assist and direct her to the appropriate spot. She felt a pang of sadness as she recognised the warm coats and remembered how Michael Frazier had worn one and found one for her to wear, ridiculously oversized, but warm and comfortable.

Whilst she waited in line, she tried to watch her surroundings in the artificial light created by the various lampposts around the waiting area, wondering if she would be able to spot any of the police officers that Langley had told her would be there. She couldn't of course and hadn't really expected to be able to do so. The artificial lighting and the headlights from the vehicles created a weird effect that, whilst not reducing visibility to nothing, nevertheless made recognising faces, particularly at a distance, almost impossible. Many people in Hi-Viz coats milled around the area near where the Ferry itself would dock, and plenty of vehicles of varying shapes and sizes began to fill the other marked spaces behind and to the right of Zoe, but it was impossible to identify any particular individual.

With about half an hour to go before the scheduled leaving time, even though the vessel had not yet docked, the Terminal staff worked their way up the lines of vehicles, checking printed travel passes and the electronic ones on various devices. Zoe held her mobile phone out of the driver's window, a bar code filling the display, which was scanned by the device held by the man working his way up her line.

A quarter of an hour later she could see the lights of the ferry as it approached the mainland. She looked around once more, but still couldn't identify anyone that might be an undercover police officer. But then, how would she?

The huge boat moved towards those waiting onshore and was skilfully manoeuvred into position against the dock, lowering its tail ramp moments later. Vehicles began to exit the vessel, driving down the ramp and onto the tarmac before heading away toward the lanes leading to the exit. It did not take long before the ferry was empty and the staff in the Hi-Viz coats began to wave vehicles onto the ramp, line by line. When Zoe's turn came, she cautiously, and a little too slowly for those waving her forward, and those behind her, drove onto the ramp and onto the ferry, following the vehicle in front. As soon as she drove onto the ferry, one of the Hi-Viz staff directed her to the right-hand side of the boat where another ramp led up to the second level. Leaning forward as far as she could whilst still able to reach the pedals, to see over the steering wheel as the car began to head upwards, she inched it forwards. A set of headlights filled her rear-view mirror, and her anxiety began to increase as she continued upwards cautiously with the impatient, no doubt, experienced ferry-goer, driving close enough behind as to almost be able to push her up the ramp.

Finally, she reached the top and eased the vehicle around to the left, where another Hi-Viz employee directed her towards the back of the boat. Yet another stood at the stern and directed her to halt within a white marked bay, before he moved to the rear of her vehicle and directed the tailgater who had followed her up the ramp to park behind her within another white lined bay.

After turning off the engine, she continued to sit in the driver's seat for a while, watching the other vehicles pull up alongside and behind her and their occupants getting out and stretching backs and legs. The impatient 'sod' behind her got out and marched off purposefully and deliberately to the doors in the side walls. Eventually, taking his lead, Zoe got out of the car, closed the door without locking it, and followed him. The doors in the walls led to a staircase running down to the level below or up to the seating deck, which was the direction that Zoe took. At the top of the stairs, automatic sliding doors parted, allowing her to enter the warmth of the deck. Already, more seasoned travellers had found their preferred seats around the floor and Zoe looked for somewhere that was vacant, opting for a bench in the middle of the floor, a second bench backing onto it.

She sat down and waited.

She felt a 'push' as a couple sat down and lent back on the bench behind her. The sensation made her sit up straight, which in turn prompted her to start surveying the deck and the many people sitting, standing, talking, or just peering out of the windows into the darkness. There was no sign of John Smith, or of Chief Superintendent Langley. She continued to watch, looking in all directions, not very subtly, and then she felt the boat move.

As it pulled away from the mainland and changed its course in the direction of the island, the windows of the vessel were filled by the lights on either side of the dockside, creating the optical illusion that the land was moving away from the boat, rather than the other way around. The crossing was smooth, the water quite calm for the time of year. Half an hour of the journey passed and still, Zoe did not recognise anyone. She began to wonder if she had boarded the wrong ferry, checking her watch to confirm to herself that she hadn't. Surely it wouldn't be long now before there would be an announcement instructing everyone to return to their vehicle.

More time passed, yet none of Langley's men, if they were indeed aboard, made themselves known to her.

She felt him arrive, rather than saw him. She just kind of knew he was there, stood to her left, at the other end of the bench, although when Zoe turned her head and looked at John Smith, she was surprised at how he looked. He was wearing a bright orange, huge puffer jacket, distorting the size of his upper body, and hanging low over his thighs, the arms so large that his hands were held away from his body in an unnatural manner. Zoe was so surprised at his appearance that, at first, she couldn't speak. Smith sat down on the far end of the bench, looking forward and not at her.

"Hello, Zoe," he said.

She looked at him, her mouth open, then quickly looked around the large room, checking whether anyone was watching them or if she recognised anyone else on the deck.

"I.... I thought you were meeting me on the island?" she said.

"Well, I'm here now, Zoe. Are you alone?"

Again, she looked around, her head turning quickly from left to right.

"I did as you asked," she said, her throat tightening with nervous tension. "I hired a car and drove here alone."

Smith continued to look forward. Zoe was still surprised at how ridiculous he looked wearing the huge, bright orange coat.

"So, what now?" she asked.

"One moment," said Smith.

"I don't mean to be rude," said Zoe. "But you are hardly inconspicuous wearing that coat."

Finally, he turned and faced her. "That's the point, Zoe," he said.

As his head turned towards her, Zoe noticed in her peripheral vision sudden movement from seats over Smith's left shoulder. Two men stood simultaneously and began moving towards them. Her eyes widened in a mixture of surprise and fear.

And Andrew McDermott, Zoe's John Smith, noticed.

His head shot up, looking over Zoe's shoulders, quickly assessing the surroundings behind her. Then he stood, quickly and fluidly, moving directly in front of her.

"Stand up," he commanded.

At the same time, an announcement over tannoy speakers requested that all passengers make their way to their vehicles as the ferry would be arriving at Fishbourne shortly. Some people, no doubt the regular ferry commuters, had already begun standing and moving towards the doors before the announcement had been made, but now, large groups of people began standing and picking up and donning coats, moving slowly and erratically towards different doorways positioned at the sides of the deck and leading down to the car areas.

Zoe did as she was told and stood, looking in the direction of the two men that her peripheral vision had picked out. They looked directly back at her, making eye contact whilst trying to push through what was quickly becoming a throng of people between them and Zoe and Smith. She turned her head and looked in the other direction and immediately identified two other men, also staring at her and Smith and pushing their way through the traffic of people towards them. They must be Langley's men. The clear determination on the faces of all of them indicated that they were not simply ordinary passengers.

Smith grabbed her wrist and then he turned towards the exit doors and set off, shoulders hunched forward, moving swiftly, barging other passengers out of his way, pulling Zoe along behind him. Shouts of objection and consternation followed them as he pulled her towards the door. Helplessly, she snatched a quick look over her shoulder and saw one of the men about six feet away, determinedly forcing his body through the crowd of people, pushing some out of the way. For a fleeting moment, she wondered why he didn't do as in the movies and shout "Police!" in order to command a way through.

But then Smith pulled her through the door and onto the stairs leading down towards the second deck, where her car was parked. She resisted against his grip, her arm at its fullest extent, the hold he used painful. There were many people around them, not one appearing interested in the fact that she was being pulled along.

Down the stairs they went to the second deck and Zoe immediately saw two other men, similar to the others on the passenger deck, tall, athletic, short hair, with determined expressions, standing on either side of the doorway. Passengers milled through the entrance in no particular hurry, creating an unintentional barrier between the two men and Smith and Zoe, but rather than retreat, or move towards the stairs to the lower deck, Smith continued to drag her towards the door that led to the second deck.

It crossed Zoe's mind that perhaps Smith had not seen the two men. She looked back over her shoulder as she was dragged along, up the stairs through the mass of bodies descending and she could just make out one of the other men from the upper deck, she presumed a police officer, trying to push his way through, but being obstructed by irate passengers not prepared to permit such rudeness. She turned her head back forwards and saw the two men at the door move forward and close together, forming a bifurcation in the flow of people heading towards the second deck.

As they neared the two men, Smith suddenly pulled Zoe forward forcefully in front of him, eliciting a short, shocked scream from her, before suddenly and violently thrusting her in front of him and directly into the oncoming men. One of them raised his arm in surprise and Zoe involuntarily banged her head against his elbow, causing her to howl in pain and stumble further, knocking the man backwards, her arms flailing to grab onto something that might help her to stay upright, but only managing to grab the coat of a man behind her, causing him in turn to stumble, falling in the other direction, catching the second man with his shoulder, and knocking him backwards.

There followed an almost comedic domino effect as person toppled over person, blocking the entrance to the second deck, and causing the descent from the passenger deck above to come to a halt with various shouts and profanities from some of those caught unawares.

It took a few moments for everyone to realise that the hold up was caused by a mass collapse of people, after which those still standing began to assist those who had fallen to regain their feet, good humour filling the air as it became apparent that there were no serious injuries. A bustling of voices and polite laughter continued until everyone was finally standing and people began to move again towards the door to the second deck where their vehicles were waiting.

Zoe looked around for Smith.

He was gone.

She winced with pain as a strong grip took hold of her elbow and she turned to see one of the men who had been waiting at the door.

"Where did he go?" the man asked.

Zoe tried to free her arm, but his hold would not loosen.

"I don't know," she said. "I fell over!"

She spun her head in different directions but could not see Smith. The police officer from above finally managed to join them in the stairwell and asked the same question. One of the men pushed through the now diminishing group of people making their way through the door to the second deck and reappeared a moment later confirming that Smith was not there.

"Downstairs!" shouted the one who had questioned Zoe, moving his grip to her wrist, and dragging her behind him as he headed towards and down the metal stairway. As Zoe was pulled along, she saw that where his black, bomber jacket flapped open, a gun was holstered by straps under his armpit. She was horrified and tried to pull back, but too late. The other three men were behind her and were ushering her forward to the lower deck.

There were fewer people on the stairs and lower gangway than there had been above, already having made their way to the lower deck and their vehicles whilst those above had tumbled over each other in the collapse caused by Smith. The police officer dragged Zoe to the entrance to the lower deck and stopped, pulling her close to him whilst two of his colleagues stepped through the doorway and onto the deck, heads turning swiftly left and right and hands reaching beneath bomber jackets and grasping no doubt, she thought, the pistol grips of the weapons that were harnessed in concealment there.

The tannoy speaker again announced that the ferry would be shortly arriving at Fishbourne and encouraged everyone to be ready within their vehicles in preparation for disembarking.

The man holding Zoe's wrist released her and then turned and pushed her back against the wall on the stairwell.

"Wait here and don't move!" he commanded. His tone was more than just professional, or military. It was threatening. Zoe nodded silently and the man stepped through the doorway, his hand reaching up under his armpit to hold the grip of his gun at the ready.

Zoe leaned back against the wall, her heart racing, terrified that the next thing that she would hear would be gunfire. But it did not come. She heard some intermittent shouting, but no loud bangs or cracks of weapons being discharged. Under her feet she felt a shift as the ferry slowed and turned about, ready to reverse into the Terminal at Fishbourne on the Isle of Wight. Then came a fresh announcement over the tannoy. This one was not a pre-recorded announcement. The slight hesitation and apologetic tone in the voice confirmed that it was a live announcement.

"Ladies and Gentlemen," said the voice. "Please remain in your vehicles. Due to a security issue, all vehicles will be directed to exit the ferry individually and only on instruction. We have been informed by the police that, owing to a potentially serious security issue, vehicles may need to be searched on disembarkation from the Ferry. We are grateful for your understanding and we apologise for any inconvenience caused."

Zoe felt the vessel shudder as it came to a halt at the dock at Fishbourne. She didn't move. The man who had given her instructions not to was frightening enough to ensure that. Eventually, she heard a few questioning voices, replied to by shouts of 'stay in your vehicles' before she heard another voice, a familiar, but not friendly voice.

"Where is she?"

"Just through here, sir," was the reply.

Chief Superintendent Bob Langley, dressed in the finery of his uniform, stepped through the doorway, and turned to face Zoe.

"Where is he?" he demanded. In his hand, he held the bright orange puffer jacket that Smith had been wearing on the passenger deck.

Zoe looked confused. "What?" she asked. "I don't know. Your officer has had me stood waiting here whilst he chased him. How would I know where he is?"

Langley's face contorted in undisguised fury. He leant forward, his nose almost touching Zoe's.

"We had a deal," he snarled.

"Hang on!" Zoe half shouted. "I told you that Smith wanted to meet me, and I told you where. That was my being a good citizen! You didn't bother to tell me that you intended to ambush him on the ferry! Ambush him by men with guns for God's sake! I mean, what the fuck? You were only going to watch him and then pick him up at the house!"

"I had to be certain that the two of you weren't in cahoots," said Langley. "Anyway, the opportunity to intercept arose onboard and so we took it. For your safety, of course," he added as an undisguised afterthought.

Zoe looked at the orange puffer jacket. "What does that mean?" she asked.

"I don't know," said Langley. "It was at the stern, by the railings. He's either jumped overboard and tried to swim to shore, or he's dropped this tyring to mislead us and is still on the boat."

"So, what are you going to do?" asked Zoe.

Langley handed the jacket over to one of the other men. "We're going to find him, Miss Carlson. That's what we're going to do. We have uniformed officers on the shore searching the vehicles as they disembark. There is nowhere for him to go."

"Do you really think that he might have jumped overboard," said Zoe, looking pointedly at the orange jacket held by Langley's man.

"It's possible," said Langley after a moment of thought. "The ferry was close to shore when he disappeared."

He suddenly looked directly into her eyes, obvious excitement in his own. "Do you think he would go to the house?"

Zoe shrugged. "I don't know. Maybe. That's where we were supposed to meet. But how? You don't really believe that someone could jump overboard from a ferry in the middle of winter and survive, do you?"

"Miss Carlson," said Langley. "I have no illusions as to the abilities of this particular man." He turned to the four men now stood around them. "Search the boat," he ordered. "Top to bottom."

They moved without any further instruction, in pairs, two heading back out onto the lower car deck and the other two towards and up the stairs.

"Come with me, Miss Carlson," commanded Langley.

She followed him through the doorway and onto the car deck where a small group of ferry workers waited. They all walked over to where the ramp on the rear of the boat was, waiting to be lowered to allow the vehicles onboard to leave. As they reached the railings, Zoe could see blue flashing lights down below on the ferry terminal. Various uniformed officers in Hi-Viz yellow police coats stood waiting next to their vehicles. Langley took a police radio from some pocket in his outer unform coat and spoke into it, looking over the side at the police officers below.

"I want each vehicle searched as they exit the boat," he said. "Check the drivers and the passengers against the photograph that you all have. If you see him, hold him there and contact me immediately. He is armed and dangerous, so let the armed response guys deal."

There was a crackle of static over the radio, followed by "Understood, sir."

Langley nodded to the ferry staff and two of them moved in unison to open and lower the ramp. Once it was touching the concrete of the Terminal, they stood either side and waved the first vehicle onwards, the driver looking confused and a little frightened as his eyes moved from the ferry employees to the Chief Superintendent and back. Slowly he drove across the ramp to the island and was immediately directed by a police officer into a coned off area to the left. Three more vehicles followed before the ones following were stopped and told to wait. Zoe watched the police officers down below shine torches into the vehicles, studying faces against an image that they held on clipboards, before waving them on and allowing them to drive up the road towards Fishbourne.

Slowly and methodically, all of the vehicles on the ferry were directed to shore, one at a time, and then into the coned areas where the police checked the occupants. When the lorries drove onto the concrete, they were directed to a separate coned area and police officers climbed into the cabs to check that no one was hiding there.

Eventually, the four plain clothed officers that were Langley's men returned and informed the Chief Superintendent that they had searched the boat, but there was no sign of Smith. Langley looked at Zoe.

"Where is your car, Miss Carlson?" he asked.

She pointed upwards. "Second deck."

Langley turned to one of his men. "Go with Miss Carlson to retrieve her car and bring it here to me."

The man led Zoe back to the stairwell and the two of them made their way up to the second deck. It was clear now, save for Zoe's hire car parked at one end of the boat. When they got to the car the man climbed into the passenger seat and Zoe nervously started the engine and steered the vehicle towards the ramp that led to the lower deck. As she drove down the ramp, she repeatedly pressed the brake pedal when the vehicle picked up even a small amount of speed. Her passenger looked at her quizzically.

"I don't normally drive," she said by way of explanation. "And I've never driven up and down ramps on a ferry before."

The bottom of the ramp led straight to the stern of the boat and where Langley was stood waiting with the other three of his men along with the remaining ferry employees. He walked around to the passenger door and the man next to Zoe opened it and climbed out of the car.

"I want the four of you to fan out in both directions on the shore," said Langley to his men. "If he jumped overboard and swam for shore he won't have got far. In this temperature he might just wash up as a corpse." The four men trotted across the ramp to land, whilst Langley got into the passenger side of Zoe's car. "If we're lucky," he said to Zoe.

She looked at him a little bewildered.

"Well go on," said Langley in his authoritative tone.

"What? Where?" asked Zoe.

"The house," said Langley. "Where you were going to meet him."

"Oh," she said, a little surprise in her voice. "Ok then."

"You do know where it is?" asked Langley.

"Er, I think so," said Zoe. "I got a taxi last time. I think we turn left at the exit up there."

Langley sighed. "Just drive off the boat for now and pull into that coned area on the left," he said.

She did as she had been instructed and, once she had reapplied the handbrake, now safely on shore, she winced as bright torch light was shone into the car. The light moved from her and fell onto the face and then uniform of Langley who cursed and impatiently waved it away. The uniformed officer holding the torch moved to the driver's side window and bent down. Zoe immediately recognised him as the police officer who had arrested her at Sir Julian's house. She remembered that he had been kind to her.

"Wind your window down, would you," said Langley.

Zoe pressed the button on the interior handle and the driver's side window descended silently.

"Hello again, Miss Carlson," said the police officer.

"What's your name, officer?" said Langley.

"PC Lock, sir," said the uniformed officer, his body almost

involuntarily straightening to stand to attention before his mind realising the futility of such an action in this situation.

"Do you know where this house is, Lock?" asked Langley. "The Hebburn house?"

Zoe looked at Lock. "Where you first found me," she said.

"Oh, yes sir," replied Lock.

"Good man," said Langley. "Jump in and give Miss Carlson directions."

Lock did as instructed and opened the rear door climbing into the seat behind Zoe and immediately launching into navigator mode.

When they arrived at Sir Julian's house, two liveried police vehicles were parked outside, four uniformed officers congregated around the front gate in conversation. Zoe turned off the engine and waited in the car whilst Langley and Lock got out and went to speak with the other officers. Moments later, two of the police officers went through the gate and around to the back of the house, whilst the other two returned to their respective vehicles, started the engines, and drove them away. Langley and Lock returned to Zoe's car and got back in.

"What now?" asked Zoe.

"We wait," said Langley.

CHAPTER TWENTY-THREE

They waited all night.

And it was cold. So cold that on a couple of occasions, much to Langley's frustration, Zoe restarted the car's engine, waiting for the temperature gauge to move to a point where she thought some warm air would blow onto them when she turned on the car's heater.

She nodded off a couple of times, then woke with a start, with that sudden feeling of falling which often wakes the snoozer. The two policemen in her vehicle did not seem to need sleep, or if they had slipped off into a doze at any point, Zoe hadn't noticed.

And the sum total of absolutely nothing happened all night. The two police officers that Langley had sent around to the back of the house were waiting inside it, ready to pounce at any moment that Smith might present himself and the other two had moved their liveried vehicles to a distance and a position where anyone approaching the house, whether it be on foot or by car, wouldn't notice them.

But nothing happened. Smith did not appear. Neither did anyone else for that matter. By around seven thirty in the morning a glow appeared on the horizon and by eight o'clock the sun rose lighting up the frost on the ground. Slowly it pushed away the blackness of night, changing it to a mauve and then golden orange and finally a clear blue sky that heralded a bright, but cold day.

Langley shifted in his seat, then looked over his shoulder at Lock, who was looking out of the window at the house. Eventually, without a word, he opened the passenger door and climbed out of the car, stretching his tall frame, his body making cracking noises as he did so. Lock, understanding his position in the hierarchy of things, immediately opened his door and joined the Chief Superintendent on the pavement.

Zoe watched Langley make a call on his mobile phone and then he and Lock crossed the road and entered the house through the front door. The two liveried police vehicles reappeared and parked outside the front gate. They were inside for a long time and Zoe wondered what they could be doing. Eventually, the front door of the house opened and one by one the police officers filed out. Lock and Langley returned to Zoe's car, whilst the others re-joined their colleagues waiting for them in the other vehicles.

"Follow those two when they set off," commanded Langley to Zoe.

She complied, and after around ten minutes of driving, just as she was about to ask where they were heading, the lead car, followed by the second, turned into the car park of the police station at Ryde. Zoe's heart sank when she recognised the place, remembering her last experience there. She must have hesitated, because Langley pointed with his right arm, extending it across her field of vision.

"Just in there, please Miss Carlson."

She parked behind one of the police cars and Lock got out from behind her. Langley was halfway out of his seat when he looked back at Zoe, who had not made any attempt at movement.

"Come on," he said. "Let's get some coffee."

Zoe did not want to go back into that building, but reluctantly, she opened the driver's door and climbed out, following the Chief Superintendent through the security doors at the rear of the Station. The Duty Sergeant did not bat an eyelid as she and Langley walked through the custody suite, led by PC Lock. The other officers stayed behind and were chatting amongst themselves.

Zoe and Langley were led upstairs and eventually to a small conference room where a uniformed Inspector was waiting for them. He introduced himself with the necessary level of deference to Langley and the appropriate politeness to Zoe. Cups and brushed steel thermos dispensers stood on a cupboard in the corner and the Inspector poured cups of coffee for all of them. When they sat, Langley looked pointedly at the Inspector.

"Any news?"

"I'm afraid not, sir," replied the Inspector. "At first light we got the boat out checking east and west of Fishbourne, but nothing yet. We also have various units joined with your men on the shoreline searching, but so far nothing has been found and there is no evidence of anyone coming to shore."

He hesitated for a moment. "I have to say, sir. If he went into the water and tried to swim to shore, at this time of year, in these temperatures, his chances of survival are somewhere between very slim and non-existent. If he did go overboard, that may well have been a risk not worth taking."

Zoe watched Langley as he pondered over this information, his hands together, in an almost prayer like situation, the fingertips resting on his chin.

"Keep looking," he said. "We'll wait."

"Oh, absolutely sir," said the Inspector. "The boat is still out there as we speak, and the men are still combing the shoreline."

The door opened and a woman in civilian clothes entered without salutation. She was carrying a tray with several items wrapped in tinfoil upon it. The Inspector bristled.

"Joyce," he growled. "Knock. Please."

She stopped dead in her tracks, straightened to her full height and looked at the Inspector in a manner suggesting that he was being a naughty schoolboy and she was the one in charge.

"Bacon sandwiches," she said, curtly, then placed the tray on the conference room table with just enough force to make a slight, but petulant bang. Zoe turned away, hiding the smile that involuntarily appeared on her face. Langley did not seem to notice, but the Inspector blushed as if he had just been chastised by his mother. Joyce turned on her heel and marched out of the room, swinging the door shut behind her, again with such a practiced action so as not to slam it, but sufficient to mirror the bang that she had made with the sandwich tray.

And so they waited, munching on bacon sandwiches, and drinking coffee, with nothing to talk about. As the morning passed, Zoe began to feel more and more weary from the lack of sleep on the previous night and she dozed in her chair.

Eventually the door opened again, this time admitting a uniformed sergeant. The Inspector looked up hopefully.

"Sir," said the sergeant to the Inspector. "The patrol boat has reported no sightings, despite good visibility. The men on the ground," he turned to look at Langley. "Including yours, sir, report that they have found nothing. I took the liberty of sending a patrol back to the house to carry out another check, but there is nothing to suggest that anyone has been there. If he went overboard with the hope of making it to shore, I think he overestimated his chances, sir."

"So, you're saying that he has drowned?" asked Langley.

"At this time of year, sir," said the sergeant. "If the current got hold of him, he's likely to have been dragged out into the Channel. Sea temperature as it is now would shock him when he hit the water. The effect of that can be to cause him to stop breathing, or even a heart attack. So, yes sir. I'd say he's drowned. It's a terrible thing, but he will likely be washed up in a week or so, at Brighton or Eastbourne. That's what normally happens."

"Thank you, sergeant," said Langley. "Would you make contact with my men and have them meet me back here, please?"

"Certainly, sir," said the sergeant, before leaving and closing the door behind him.

Langley looked at Zoe who appeared to be deep in thought. "Well, Miss Carlson," he said. "It would appear that you and I have had a wasted journey. You are free to head back to London now, if you wish."

Zoe stood up, not requiring a second prompt. "Yes, I will, thank you," she said.

She made her own way, unaccompanied, down to the custody suite and then out through the doors at the rear of the building to her car on the carpark. She drove out of the police station car park with no real idea which direction to take, but after a few attempts down various roads she finally saw a signpost pointing her to the ferry terminal. Once there, she parked up and went inside to purchase a ticket back to the mainland.

During the crossing she snoozed on a chair with her back to the wall. The crossing was uneventful and when the vessel arrived at Portsmouth, she drove the hire car over the ramp, already more confident about doing so, and headed back up to the main road. She was feeling exhausted by now, so she pulled into the carpark opposite the ferry terminal, where she had waited on the previous day, prior to boarding for the island, and parked up, turning off the engine. She shifted around in the seat to make herself as comfortable as possible and then leant back and fell asleep.

When she awoke it was dark again. Annoyed with herself for sleeping for so long, but feeling much more refreshed, Zoe started the engine and headed out of the carpark for her long journey back home to London. As she drove, she thought through all that had happened leading up to the point when Langley had told her she could leave. What now, she wondered, would become of her story?

CHAPTER TWENTY-FOUR

Llanfairpwllgwyngyllgogerychwyrndrobwllllantysilio gogogoch, or Llanfairpwll for short, is a train station on the Isle of Anglesey in North Wales, on the Menai Strait, next to the Britannia Bridge, over which cars and trains cross the Strait to the breadbasket of Wales.

It was July and the sun was shining brightly and gloriously hot in a clear blue sky. Zoe Carlson leant against the bonnet of a different hire car, one she had rented from a garage local to the station that specialised in hiring vehicles for holidaymakers who wanted to tour the Isle of Anglesey, having travelled there by train.

She looked up admiringly at the pretty little red brick train station, with its impossibly long name sign stretching from one end to the other. She heard a tannoy announcement and moments later the sounds of an approaching train, and then the screeching of its brakes and the pungent smell of its diesel engines.

Eventually, a man appeared at the door of the station and came outside, squinting in the bright sunlight, a bag in one hand, his other raising to shield his eyes. When he saw Zoe, he smiled.

"Hello, Eric," she smiled back. "Long time." She stood up

from the bonnet of the car as he approached, then hugged him and kissed him on the cheek.

Eric looked around, smiling. "I love the station name," he said.

Zoe chuckled.

"But Zoe. Is this really necessary? Couldn't we have done this over the phone?"

"Don't be silly, Eric," she said, still smiling. "Look around. It's a beautiful day, this is a beautiful part of the world and talking through everything over the phone would have been soooo tedious! Come on," she said, walking around to the driver's side and opening the door. "Get in."

Zoe drove for about half an hour along a road that skirted the coast, whilst Eric enjoyed the rush of the summer wind through his open window and marvelled at the unpronounceable place names that flashed by. For a newspaper editor he was remarkably poorly travelled, and this was his first time on Anglesey, indeed, his first time in Wales. If he spent any time giving any serious thought to the point, he could not remember a time when he had headed north of Watford before. He and his wife would happily jump on the Eurostar to France but would never consider heading north within their own country.

It had taken some considerable persuasion, almost nagging, on the part of Zoe to persuade him to travel out of London all the way up to the Isle of Anglesey. Even with the undisguised robust persuasion, he probably would not have agreed to make the journey for anyone else. But he had a soft spot for Zoe and was conscious that the memories of the previous year were still quite raw for her. So, he had eventually accepted her offer to book him a room at a hotel on the island and pick him up from the train station.

They soon arrived at the brow of a hill and as the car moved over its summit and began to descend, Eric could see a pretty little village with verdant green fields on three sides and the glistening blue of the Irish Sea on the fourth. The sign at the entrance to the village welcomed them to Amlwch.

Zoe turned the car into a carpark at the front of a small, two storey hotel and parked up.

"Let's get you checked in," she said. "And then we can go down to the Port."

Eric smiled at her. "When are you going to tell me what this is all about, Zoe?" he asked.

"Soon," she smiled back, looking at her watch. "Come on, you need to check in."

He did as he was instructed and having signed in and been given a key, he was directed to the second floor and a comfortable, though quaintly old-fashioned room, with a single bed and a window that looked out onto the carpark. He dropped his bag onto the bed and looked out of the window. Zoe was back at the car, having first accompanied him to reception, and was again leaning against the bonnet, occasionally looking at the watch on her wrist. Eric left the hotel and joined her outside. Moments later they were in the car again, heading towards the sea.

It was only a short drive and the sign that greeted them when they arrived said Amlwch Port. Zoe pulled into the tiny little carpark and the two of them got out. Zoe led him across the road and onto a narrow concrete path that ran down the side of the road, eventually turning away from it, delving into a shallow, grassy valley that twisted and turned and finally opened out into a clearing and the tiny fishing port directly in front of them.

The road that they had left continued along the side of the port and was busy with people carrying boxes of fish off the various fishing vessels moored to the harbour wall to vans waiting on the quayside. A schooner, with two immensely tall wooden masts, was tied up at the farthest end of the wall and in front of it, towards land, were several small day-fishing boats. The sight held a quaintness, a moment in time, paused, or slowed sufficiently to allow the rest of the world to hurry by without noticing it.

The path that Zoe had taken them down led to a small café right on the edge of the quay and overlooking the Port, the boats, and the busy fishermen. Zoe beckoned Eric to follow and they entered the café and moved to a table away from the windows and in the corner. She sat down facing the entrance and patted the seat next to her when Eric moved to occupy the one opposite. A confused smile crossed his face, but nevertheless, he changed direction and slid onto the seat next to Zoe. A portly woman wearing a brilliant white apron over her clothes approached the table, note pad in one hand and stubby pencil in the other.

"Prynhawn Da," she said, then realising that they were English, probably by their confused expressions, she translated. "Good Afternoon. What can I get you?"

"Two teas, please," said Zoe. The woman scribbled on the pad and then walked away.

"Ok, Zoe," smiled Eric. "I'm bighting. What's going on? Why are we here? And couldn't we at least sit by the window? That Port looks beautiful."

"No," said Zoe. "Not by the window. And be patient. All will be revealed; shortly."

Eric shrugged and waited. The portly woman brought two

mugs of tea, the teabags still floating in them. She pointed to a jug of milk already on the table.

"If you need anything else, just let me know," she said with a friendly smile.

With a practised action, Zoe picked up a teaspoon and squeezed the teabag in Eric's mug against the side and then dipped it out, dropping it onto a circular metal dish in the middle of the table. She repeated the action with her own and then picked up the milk jug and poured milk into both, satisfied at the deep tan colour of the tea.

"Do you want sugar?" she asked, using the same teaspoon, and heaving a spoonful from the metal sugar bowl on the table into her own mug.

Eric frowned. "Er, no, thanks," he said, lifting the mug and taking a sip. His features immediately screwed up in response to the tart strength of the tea. "Actually, maybe a little," he said, holding out the mug. Zoe chuckled and spooned some sugar into it.

"You get used to the strong tea after a while," she said. "But it always needs a little sugar, just to take the edge off the tannin."

The door of the café opened, and a man entered. He was tall and stocky, with a full beard, wearing the waterproofs of a sea fisherman, a flat cap on his head. He closed the door in a manner that assured him that it was closed, firmly, and then turned to look around the café, taking in each of the customers dotted around and his eyes eventually came to rest on Zoe. The very faintest of a smile curled a corner of his mouth as he stepped forwards towards her and Eric, his hand reaching up and removing the flat cap to reveal a bald and slightly sunburned head. Eric looked up at him and thought he looked vaguely familiar, not realising that he was approaching their table until it was too late.

The man dropped his hat on the table and pulled out a chair, sitting down and looking at one and then the other of them, making direct eye contact.

"Hello, Zoe," he said.

She was grinning from ear to ear. Eric looked at her, confused, then back at the man sat opposite.

"Tea, Scotty?" shouted the portly woman, from somewhere behind Eric.

"Aye, love," said the man. "That'll be grand."

Again, Eric looked at one, then the other and eventually back at Zoe.

"Zoe, what is happening here?" he asked.

"Eric," beamed Zoe. "Let me introduce to you Mr Andrew McDermott. Also known as John Smith. Our whistle blower."

Eric's mouth dropped open, the recognition finally dawning on him. His heart rate increased rapidly and his mouth became dry.

"I ... I don't understand," he said, looking at Zoe and then back at McDermott. "You ... you're dead," he whispered. He began to panic a little and instinctively pushed his chair backwards, the metal legs scraping on the floor as he half rose to a standing position.

Zoe's hand went to his and gently gripped it, just as the portly woman arrived and put a mug of tea in front of McDermott, then gently patted him on the arm, smiled and walked back to the serving counter.

"It's ok, Eric," said Zoe. "He's..." she hesitated, then turned and looked at McDermott, the smile creeping back onto her face. "He's a friend."

Eric looked at her in disbelief, then back at McDermott, and then eventually slipped back down into his seat.

"But ... you're dead," he whispered again.

"Yes, I am," said McDermott, reaching out with his hand and taking hold of one of Zoe's. "Thanks to this lovely wee girl."

Eric frowned and shook his head in confusion. "I don't understand," he said.

"I would have been dead for real if Zoe hadn't come to my rescue," said McDermott.

"But all the news reports said that you drowned," said Eric. "Trying to escape the police on the Isle of Wight ferry. There was a Coroner's report. Death by misadventure."

"Ha!" laughed McDermott. "Yes, that amused me when I read it."

Zoe looked meaningfully at Eric and squeezed his hand. "I helped him, Eric," she said.

"But why?" asked Eric. "He's a ... a murderer. He killed your friend."

"I make no excuses for what I did, Eric," said McDermott. "To me, I was simply doing a job. I understand how crass it sounds when I say that what I did, those people that I killed, it was nothing personal. I was doing a job."

Zoe squeezed Eric's hand again. "He was a weapon of a State, Eric. Or at least something like that. I'm not saying that I forgive him." She looked at McDermott for a long time, neither of them breaking their stare. "He knows that I don't. I can't. Not for that. But what he did is not the whole picture, Eric. The real question. The important one. The most important one, is why he did it."

"Go on," said Eric.

"I have spent the last few months putting the story together," said Zoe. "It started with Benjamin and Eloise Sharp and an innocent short break holiday near Broughton Stretton. Whatever was leaked from Broughton Stretton, and I still don't know what that was, but whatever it was, it killed Benjamin Sharp. Sir Julian Hebburn knew what it was, and he was going to blow the whistle, until senior figures within our Government, I'm sure that you can guess who, took it upon themselves to secretly and without authority, utilise a security asset to ensure that Sir Julian never told his story. Andrew here was that security asset."

She looked at McDermott who gave an almost imperceptible nod to continue, his hand still grasping Zoe's.

"But the rot goes further than members of Government taking matters into their own hands and committing illegal acts," she continued. "Senior police officials were involved. They too were acting without authority and when that was going to come out, they decided to hide the evidence, by terminating their asset. By terminating Andrew."

Eric pulled his hand away from Zoe's, breaking the link between the three of them, although Zoe and McDermott still held hands.

"I'm not sure that I'm comfortable with this, Zoe," he said, the nerves in his voice audible. "With him."

Zoe reached out and took his hand again. "It's ok, Eric," she said. "You're safe. I'm safe. Hell, we're all safe. Andrew isn't going to hurt us. He's dead, remember? The man you see here is someone entirely different. He's a fisherman. He's not called John Smith, or even Andrew McDermott for that matter, but he has the story that I want to write in your newspaper that is going to blow the establishment apart. But, I figured, even though we've known each other for a long time, the only way that you would be fully persuaded, is if you hear it from the horse's mouth, so to speak."

Eric stared at McDermott for a long time, trying to see beyond the cold, icy blue eyes into the man's mind. He turned and stared at Zoe, feeling her hand squeeze his, then looking down and seeing the gentle way that McDermott held her other hand.

"Ok," he said. "I'm willing to listen. But first, you must tell me how. How is a dead man sitting in a café with us on Anglesey?"

Zoe laughed, released both of their hands, leaned back in her chair at a forty-five-degree angle between the two of them, and with merriment in her voice, narrated the story of John Smith's instruction to meet her on the Isle of Wight and the determination by the police that he had died in the Solent.

After McDermott, or Smith as he was then known to her, had contacted her, she had called Chief Superintendent Langley. Not because she had wanted to set a trap, but because that was what Smith had instructed her to do.

She had then hired the car and when it was delivered to her flat and the keys posted through her letterbox in an envelope, she had gone outside and pressed the button to unlock it, before returning to her apartment. Again, as Smith had instructed her to do.

She didn't know at what point Smith would open the boot of the car and hide inside, but it would have been either at the point when she had unlocked the car, or on one of the occasions when she had stopped on the way to Portsmouth, perhaps the service station, or more probably, the car park opposite the ferry terminal.

"Well, which was it?" interrupted Eric.

Zoe just shrugged. "It doesn't matter," she said.

The incident on the ferry on its approach to Fishbourne had all been carefully orchestrated by Smith. The ridiculous bright orange puffer jacket was intended to ensure that Langley's men could make him out and keep him in sight when mixing within the melee of passengers. It would also be something obvious and outstanding to recognise when left on the deck of the boat next to the bulwark and not something that anyone would jump into the sea wearing, for the obvious reasons that the bulkiness and weight would drag them under and drown them.

Smith had earlier moved around the decks of the ferry, prior to donning the puffer jacket, and carefully and covertly studied the passengers, easily identifying the plain clothed police officers who looked so unnatural in the setting. He had then returned to Zoe's hire car and retrieved the puffer jacket from the boot in time to be ready to present himself for exposure to the police just before the tannoy announcement would instruct all passengers to return to their vehicles.

His timing had been impeccable, appearing in front of Zoe and dragging her through the crowd towards the stairs. Then the complete distraction, caused by pushing her into the two plain clothed officers on the second deck and causing a small avalanche of people to topple over her, affording him the opportunity to run down to the lower deck unimpeded, had worked to perfection.

"Yes. Thanks for that!" chastised Zoe with a smile at McDermott.

He shrugged and smiled. "If I'd told you that was what I was going to do, it wouldn't have worked. It had to be instinctive;

natural."

Once on the lower deck, Smith had removed the puffer jacket and dropped it next to a bulwark before heading to the port side of the boat and returning to the second deck by the stairway on the opposite side. Once he was certain that all the commotion was taking place on the starboard side, he had made his way back over to Zoe's car, opened the boot and climbed back in. Crucial to the plan from the very beginning was that Zoe was never to lock the car.

Then he just had to wait until Langley had decided that he had jumped overboard.

"Hang on," interrupted Eric. "How could you know that they wouldn't search the boot?"

"I didn't," replied McDermott. "I was relying to a large extent on their arrogance. Well, Langley's arrogance, if truth be told. I figured that he would be arrogant enough to believe that he had frightened me and surprised me enough to take my chances jumping overboard and swimming to shore. That's why I waited until the ferry was close to Fishbourne. I figured that he would be so quick and keen to declare that I had tried to escape over the side that any search of vehicles would be cursory. As it was, I hadn't gambled on him making Zoe stay with him and then actually getting in her car with her to go to the house on the island. That was ... unexpected."

"Did you know?" asked Eric, looking at Zoe.

"No," she laughed. "I genuinely believed that he had gone swimming. I thought the whole time spent sat outside Sir Julian's house all night was a complete waste of time."

"Bloody cold, though," said McDermott. "Lying in the boot all night in sub-zero temperatures had never been my plan. But I warmed up later with a kip at the police station car park whilst they searched for me."

"And then you just travelled back to the mainland in the boot?" asked Eric.

"Yes," said McDermott. "Zoe followed all of her instructions perfectly. She told Langley I might be on the boat and that gave me the opportunity to die, so far as he was concerned. And she stopped at all the places that I told her to stop. I didn't, and I still don't, want her to know when and where I entered and exited her vehicle, for her sake. All she needed to do was to take the breaks that I asked and not to lock the car."

Eric leaned back. "That is quite the story," he said. "But I presume from all of this that, if we go ahead and publish the story that Zoe wants to write, you can't be referenced as a source? You have to remain ... well, dead?"

"Yes," said Zoe. "He does." She reached into her bag and pulled out a piece of paper, encased in a clear plastic wallet, laying it on the table in front of Eric. "But this is Sir Julian's note that he left just before he died. Before he allegedly committed suicide. I've also spent many days speaking with Eloise Sharp, and I have been pushing and pushing Broughton Stretton to release Ben's body. Eloise's solicitors are this close to making it happen." She drew her thumb and forefinger close together with the most miniscule of gaps between them, figuratively to illustrate her meaning.

Eric sat quietly for a long time and Zoe and McDermott occasionally sipped their tea. Eventually, he looked up.

"So, the story," he said. "the implied evidence that Ben Sharp's death, and that of Sir Julian's was all part of a conspiracy, a cover up for something that happened at, or as a consequence of something from Broughton Stretton, is your existence? Your purpose? Your role? A role created and developed by the security services, but misused and aberrated by those in various positions of power?"

Zoe smiled and gripped Eric's hand tightly.

"Exactly!" she said.

CHAPTER TWENTY-FIVE

The autocue lined up on its track in front of the television news presenter and the Producer's voice in his ear informed him that they were live in five, four, three, cue Bob, one and, we're on air.

"Good evening," he said looking into the camera with the appropriate expression of seriousness. "Having spent the last few months denying the allegations made by a freelance reporter about a cover up at the notorious Broughton Stretton secret Government facility, the Prime Minister has just announced his intention to seek an immediate audience with Her Majesty the Queen to tender his resignation, pending a General Election.

We also understand that a senior Officer of the Metropolitan Police has been detained in order to be questioned on alleged terrorist offences. The Secret Service have indicated that they are unavailable for comment.

Sources also reveal that a former senior member of the Prime Minister's staff has apparently been found dead in his home. Initial indications suggest suicide, although nothing yet has been confirmed by Authorities."

About the Author

You can connect with me on:

- http://www.markthompsonoconnor.co.uk
- https://fb.me/MarkThompsonOConnor
- http://amazon.com/author/markthompsonoconnor
- https://www.instagram.com/mark_toc_author

Subscribe to my newsletter:

- https://subscribepage.io/Mark

Also by Mark Thompson-O'Connor

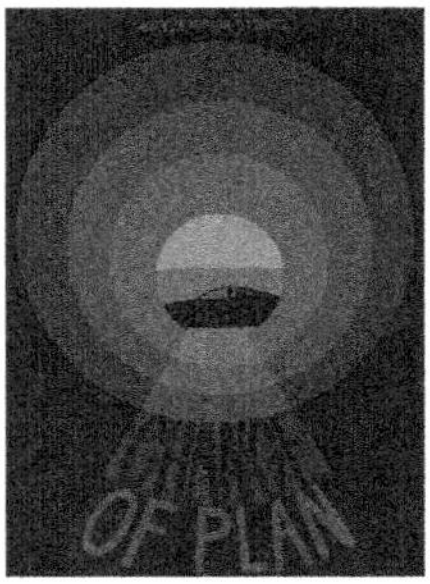

Change of Plan

What would you do if someone threatened to hurt the ones you love?

Liam Roberts is an everyday guy, living an ordinary family life in a quiet part of England when his life is thrown into turmoil.

Just an ordinary, unexciting man who unwittingly becomes the victim of organised crime.

When Liam's worst fears are realised, he will stop at nothing to protect what is most important to him. Even if that means challenging the most terrifying people he has ever met.

He must succeed, against the odds and against the kind of people who wouldn't think twice about making him and his family disappear; permanently!

Follow Liam through a dark and dangerous world, by going to your Amazon page and searching for Change of Plan or use ASIN: B08M8DBNXB

Printed in Great Britain
by Amazon

33426999R00169